I0691928

EMT
TRYST

First Edition

Published by The Nazca Plains Corporation
Las Vegas, Nevada
2009

ISBN: 978-1-935509-11-0

Published by
The Nazca Plains Corporation ®
4640 Paradise Rd, Suite 141
Las Vegas NV 89109-8000

PUBLISHER'S NOTE
EMT Tryst is a work of fiction created wholly by *Greg Reese*'s imagination. All characters are fictional and any resemblance to any persons living or deceased is purely by accident. No portion of this book reflects any real person or events.

Male Cover Photo, Vladislav Gansovsky
Art Director, Blake Stephens

DEDICATION

This book is dedicated to my life partner, who's love, patience and support are absolutely amazing.

EMT
TRYST

First Edition

Greg Reese

CONTENTS

NOTE

....

This story is a work of fiction. The characters in this story are over the age of 18. The characters in this story live in a disease free world, the use of condoms is not portrayed. The real world is very different, practice safe sex, use a condom.

CHAPTER 1

My name is Craig McFadden, I'm 43 years old, live in the suburbs of Phoenix and am an EMT with Ladder Company 49. I have a standing date with one of our fire fighters every Thursday night at eight. Tim Johnson and I met when I first started working at the fire station, about eight years ago, and we hit it off immediately. Tim would be any person's perfect catch, as he is the epitome of what every gay man and straight woman dream of when they think of their ideal man. Problem is, Tim hasn't quite accepted the fact that he's gay so we sneak around like two married people, secretly meeting one another at various places throughout the metropolitan area.

It's rather fun actually and since I'm certainly not wanting to "tie the knot" I enjoy having a steady fuck buddy.

It was on this particular night that I would meet my new neighbor. You see, it all started as I was backing out of my driveway on my way to meet Tim. I had double and triple checked to make sure the street was clear and was extremely surprised, to say the least, when I heard the dull thud followed by the loud howl of pain. I threw the car into park and got out to see what, or who, I had hit. Laying on the opposite side of the car, in the gravel, was a bicyclist, his bike, front tire smashed in, was laying in the street.

"Oh my God!" I shouted. "Are you OK?" as I bent down to check on the bicyclist.

"Yeah, I think so, help me up." he replied, handing me his arm so I could help get him to stand up.

"What happened? You weren't there a second ago when I looked!" I shrieked. "It's my fault, I came barreling out of my own driveway, had my head down adjusting my gears and when I looked up, there was the rear of your car." he said.

"Oh your bleeding, look at your right thigh. C'mon, I'm an EMT, we'll get you inside and I'll get you cleaned up and bandaged." I said, completely forgetting about my date.

"Bill, the name's Bill West." He said.

"Craig McFadden, nice to meet you." I replied as I threw his arm around my shoulder and helped him into the house, leading him to the kitchen. "Here, have a seat at the table. I need to move the car and then grab my first aid gear." I said.

When I reentered the house, he was examining the damage on his right thigh. He had been wearing the lycra riding shorts and the right side had all but shredded completely up to the waist band, exposing a very nice and muscular thigh along with his package. I squatted down to take a closer look and to also hide the erection that was beginning to spring up in my pants.

"Doesn't look too bad, looks like you just scraped yourself up good. Your shorts are shredded though. Why don't you slip those off, I have a pair that I think will fit you, plus it'll help me get you cleaned up" I said.

I turned as he stood to remove his shorts and headed to my bedroom. Coming back with a pair of my shorts, bottle of rubbing alcohol and peroxide, I saw him standing there and thought I was going to cum in my pants right there. He was completely nude from the waist down, I would have thought he would have been wearing at least a jock strap.

His legs were perfectly sculpted and completely shaved, as the lack of hair cuts down on the wind resistance, or so we're led to believe anyway. His cock hung over two beautifully shaped balls and I noticed he kept his pubic hair trimmed very short as well. I handed him the shorts and squatted down again to re-examine his leg, and get a much closer look at his cock.

"You've got some pretty good scrapes in here, but nothing that requires stitches." I said.

"That's good, I just started a new job and my insurance hasn't kicked in yet." Bill replied.

"This is going to sting as I wash out the cuts, you might want to brace yourself." I offered as I began to irrigate the area with a bottle of water.

"Hiiissss." Bill drew in his breath as the water hit the raw skin and jerking a little, the head of his cock brushed up against my cheek.

"Oh God!" I thought as my cock tried to rip out the zipper in my slacks.

"I'm going to put some peroxide on it, it'll help flush out whatever the water didn't get. It's..." I said but then was cut off.

"...going to sting, yeah, I know the line." Bill chuckled. "Son of a bitch!" Bill shouted as I poured the peroxide over the scraped and cut skin.

"Sorry." I said, looking up and noticing for the first time that he had sparkling blue eyes, like small pools of water surrounded by the thickest and longest eye lashes I've ever seen on a man.

"It's OK, sorry for the swearing." Bill said, looking down at me, a slight smile spreading across his lips.

I looked back down and could swear his cock had plumped up a little, as well as lengthened.

"OK, I need to pat this dry then I'll put some Neosporin on it, bandage you up and you should be good as new." I said. It took me a few more minutes but I soon had him bandaged and couldn't help notice that his cock was now half hard.

"OK, Bill, I think you can get dressed now." I said just as the door bell rang. I walked to the door and opened it to see my other neighbor holding Bill's bike.

"Is this yours?" he asked. "No, it's the new neighbor's we had an accident. He's OK though. Thanks for bringing it up." I said as I took the bike and without thinking, closed the door in my neighbor's face.

Halfway back to the kitchen I realized what I'd done and made a mental note to go and apologize to him later. "Hey, I think you're bike is trashed." I said.

Bill had now entered the living room where I was holding his bike, the front wheel completely caved in, handle bars bent and twisted.

"How much do I owe you for the bike?" I asked.

"Nothing, it was my fault, I told you that." Bill said as he studied his bike. "Yeah, it's trashed, well, there's a couple thousand dollars down the drain." He quietly said.

"A couple thousand dollars?" I shrieked.

"Yeah, it's a touring bike, I'm getting ready to enter the Tucson 500." Bill said.

"Oh man, now I really feel bad. Listen, at least let me file an insurance report. That should either pay for a new bike or maybe half of it." I said.

"Seriously, you don't need to do that. It's fine, I'll take care of it." Bill said. As he reached for the bike, he swooned and fell backwards, landing, thankfully, on my overstuff couch.

"WHOA! What the hell?" Bill said, shaking his head.

"Did you hit your head on anything?" I asked.

"Not that I can remember." Bill said.

"Maybe it's just the shock of the accident, but you really need to be watched tonight. Why don't you stay here, you can crash in the spare room. I'll come in and check on you." I offered, secretly hoping that I might be able to check on something else.

"Yeah, maybe you're right, I suddenly don't feel so good. Where's your bathroom, I think I'm going to be sick!" Bill shouted as he tried to stand.

I ran over, helped him up and guided him down the hall to the bathroom. We didn't quite make it there before he started throwing up. Luckily though I had installed tiled flooring a few years ago, all I would need to do was mop up the mess once he was done. I also suddenly remembered my date with Tim.

"Bill, you going to be OK? I need to go make a quick phone call." I asked. He nodded yes as he continued to get sick.

I quickly explained everything to Tim, who completely understood, and went back to my patient. Bill was now lying on the floor, the cool tile making him feel better. I reached over, flushed the toilet and told him I'd help him into the bedroom. We carefully stepped around the mess on the floor in the hallway and I helped him lay down on the bed. I then quickly cleaned up the mess and brought him a glass of water and a couple of tylenol.

"Here, sip this and let's see if you can keep a couple tylenol down." I said, handing him the glass. Bill took the tylenol and continued to sip the water. His color started to restore after a few minutes of lying down so I was pretty sure he was just having a reaction to the accident and wasn't suffering from a concussion.

"Oh man, that was weird." Bill said.

"Feeling better?" I asked.

"Yeah, thanks, what the hell happened?" He asked, looking at me.

"Mild shock, people react differently to it. I just want to make sure you don't have a concussion. You sure you didn't hit your head?" I asked again.

"Yeah, pretty sure." Bill replied.

I keep my EMT equipment in the spare bedroom, so I fished out my penlight and told him I wanted to check his pupils. Flashing the light in both eyes, his pupils responded normally, another good indication he didn't have a concussion. I then told him I was going to check him for potential fractures and began with his jaw.

"What a gorgeous square jaw, oh and he's unshaven too. Mmm mmm mmm, but I do like an unshaven man." I thought to myself. I then moved down his neck and to his chest.

"Oh my, such firm pecs and his nipples are hard. Umm..." I thought as my hands moved down to his stomach.

"Mind if I lift up your shirt? It'll help me be able to feel if you've ruptured anything." I asked.

"Sure, no problem!" Bill replied.

It really wouldn't help me do anything more than check out his abs, of which they were ripped and firm with a nice happy trail of fur leading into the waist band of the shorts. I moved on to his thighs, being very careful to avoid the bandaged area. I noticed the lump in his shorts was getting larger, "Oh good, this is having the desired effect." I thought. My hands were trembling as I rubbed and massaged his thighs, moving down to the calves of his legs.

"Umm...that feels good." Bill purred. I glanced up, his eyes were closed and he had his hands behind the back of his head.

"OK buddy, roll over, need to check out the back." I said patting his good thigh. Bill did as he was instructed only this time, he removed his shirt completely. His back was just as delicious as his front, his shoulders were wide and massive and he had another pleasure trail of fur that led from the small of his back down into the waist band of his shorts. I began to massage his back for him, moans and sighs escaped his lips as I worked his tense muscles.

"Hang on, if we're going to do this, let's do it right." Bill said as he lifted up and pulled his shorts down, kicking them off with his feet.

"OH MY GOD!" I screamed in my head. Before me lay the perfect ass. Tight, compact, firm, a very light dusting of golden blonde hair that started in the crack of his ass and fanned it's way out. He didn't trim his ass hair, course I guess there wouldn't be any need to do that and it was magnificent. It took all the control I had to keep from spreading his cheeks apart and diving in. But I did control myself as my hands gently worked the beautiful firm mounds of his ass. I moved lower so now I was working the bottom of his ass cheeks while working the top of his thighs as well. Bill spread his legs for me, offering me the perfect view of his ass and balls, the tip of his cock peeking out from under his balls.

"Oh fuck! Is that a drop of pre-cum on his cock?" I panted to myself as I continued to work his legs. Bill continued to sigh and moan his appreciation, occasionally he would lift up, as though he was adjusting his cock. I soon reached his feet and once I was done with those, gently slapped his beautiful ass and told him that the massage was over. Bill rolled over on his back and his rock hard cock slapped against his stomach. His cock was beautiful, cut, it had to be at least eight inches long and slender with a big mushroom head on it. I stared at it, licking my lips.

"Sorry, I get rock hard whenever I get a massage." Bill said as he reached for the blanket to cover himself up.

"DAMN! So close..." I screamed inside my head. Instead I stuttered out, "It's, WOW! OK, man, I mean, shit happens...yup...shit happens..."

I knew I was blushing, I could feel the heat rise from my toes and spread throughout my body. "Listen, if you don't mind, I'm gonna close my eyes and take a little snooze." Bill said, his hand cupping his still hard cock.

"Uh no...no...uh...I don't mind, don't mind at all. Holler if you need anything, seriously, if you need ANYTHING, just holler." I said as I stood and headed for the door.

"Hey Craig! Thanks!" Bill said as I closed the door behind me.

I ran to the bathroom, shucked my pants down to my ankles and jacked my cock furiously. I know he had to have heard me groan as my cum shot out the end of my cock and spattered the bathroom sink. I quickly cleaned up my mess, throwing the toilet paper I'd used into the toilet and flushing. As I entered the hallway, I heard a slight moan come from his room. I quickly walked down there and stopped when I heard the tell tale rustling sound of a hand jacking a cock against material. I peeked through the cracked door just in time to see his cock shoot, ropes of cum splashing over his stomach. My cock immediately sprang to life as I watched him slowly stroke the rest of the cum out of his spent cock.

6

I heard him whisper, "Fuck, I need to get my cock in his ass." as he wiped the cum off his stomach and licked it from his hand. I bit down hard as another orgasm hit and I felt the front of my underwear become soaked in another load.

"And you shall have my ass Bill, you shall have it." I chuckled to myself as I turned and headed to my bedroom to get cleaned up.

CHAPTER 2

Bill woke up a few hours later feeling much better. I checked his wounded leg, cleaned it again and put new bandages on it. His cock was semi-hard by the time I had him cleaned up and it took all the control I had to keep from wrapping my lips around his cock and sucking him off. His sex charged words of, "I need to get my cock in his ass." kept echoing in my head yet, for whatever reason, I didn't act on that and instead, watched with a raging hard on as he pulled the borrowed pair of shorts back up.

"I'll wash these and bring them back. Thanks again for everything you did, we'll work out the details of the bike later." Bill said.

"Too late, while you were sleeping I went ahead and filed a report through my insurance company. All I need from you is an estimate of what the bike is worth and you should get a check within 6-8 weeks." I said, keeping my eyes firmly glued to the still half hard cock in his shorts.

"You know, if you like what you see so much, why not dive in?" Bill asked, staring right at my now blushing face. My mouth drooled as he lowered his shorts again, offering me his now rock hard cock. I reached out, grabbed his hard cock and slid to my knees. With my face at crotch level, I slowly started stroking his cock, watching as my hand moved up and down and his balls began to tighten in their sack.

"Suck it, c'mon, suck it." Bill moaned. I stuck the tip of my tongue in his piss slit and tasted the first drop of his cock drool. Bill moaned again as I continued dipping my tongue in and out of his piss slit, my other hand wrapping around his balls and gently tugging them.

"Oh fuck yeah! Squeeze my balls, fucking squeeze my balls." Bill growled, grinding his hips causing his dick to fuck itself in my hand.

I quickly wrapped my lips around the head of his cock and slowly slid my mouth down to the base of his cock. It fit perfectly in my throat, deep throating him would be no problem. I heard him draw a sharp intake of breath and let out a long moan as I bottomed out on his hard cock.

"Oh fuck yeah, oh fuck it's been so long since I've had my cock sucked." Bill moaned again. I let go of his balls as I slowly began sucking his cock and grabbed both cheeks of his beautiful ass.

"Take your cock out, I want to see you stroke you're cock while you're sucking me off." Bill begged.

I complied and soon pulled my cock out from the side of my underwear clad shorts and was slowly stroking my cock while I continued to suck his cock.

"Oh yeah, you got a beautiful cock, yeah great fucking cock man. Oh shit, suck me off while you stroke that cock of yours." Bill continued.

I love dirty talk and Bill's verbal expression of his satisfaction was pushing me further and further to the edge. "Oh fuck yeah, c'mon, suck that cock, suck my cock!" Bill shouted at me.

I pulled off, stroking his cock I looked up at him and asked, "Wouldn't you rather fuck my ass?"

"Awe shit man, fuck yeah I would. I've been checking your ass out ever since I came in!" Bill squealed.

"Yeah? Well let me show you my ass." I said. I stood up, kicked my shorts and underwear off, pulled my T-shirt over my head and threw it on the floor, turned around and bent over right in front of him.

"You like this ass? You wanna fuck it?" I said as I wiggled my ass at him.

"Oh yeah, fucking nice ass, yeah I wanna fuck it, I wanna fuck it bad." Bill said, stroking his cock.

"C'mon, fucking get it." I growled back. Bill squatted down, pulled my ass cheeks apart and started eating my ass. I reached between my legs and managed to grab hold of his cock, sighing as I felt his tongue darting and licking my hole.

"Oh fuck yeah buddy, fuckin A. Yeah, lick that ass, c'mon, fucking get my ass good and wet." I groaned, bucking my ass on his tongue. Bill then started darting his tongue in and out of my ass, my moans and groans echoing through the living room, letting him know that he was doing an expert job and rimming my ass. His cock continued to leak out cock honey, coating my hand. I let go of his cock and brought my hand up to my mouth and started licking the pre-cum from my fingers. "Umm, you taste good." I groaned.

Bill removed his tongue from my ass and I soon felt the head of his cock knocking at my back door, begging for entrance. I gasped as I felt the head of his cock part my ass lips and slowly slide past the ring. "If only Tim were this gentle." I thought.

"Oh fuck, your ass is so tight." Bill whispered. "Yeah, so fucking tight around my hard cock." He said as he continued slowly sliding his cock until I felt his short pubes against my ass cheeks.

"Yeah Bill, oh fuck your cock feels good up my ass. Stay like this for a minute, it feels so fucking good." I said as I began to slowly grind my ass around his cock, causing Bill to moan.

His hands soon found my nipples and he began to tug and twist them, causing them to harden immediately and me to shout out with the pleasure he was giving me. His cock up my ass, his fingers toying with my nipples, was causing my cock to produce streams of cock honey. I looked between my legs and watched as the ropes of clear white juice leaked out of the tip of my cock and hung in long strands to the tiled floor in the living room. I knew the way Bills cock was angled in my ass that I wouldn't even need to jack my cock, I'd be able to cum with just him fucking me. That was one thing I had learned early in my gay adult life, that I could cum, hands free, while I was getting fucked. It all depended on how the person's cock was angled inside me, and how horned up I was. Usually it was the latter of the two that determined my hands free cum.

Bill began to slowly withdraw his cock and then slide it back inside me. Each time he'd pull out just to the point where he was going to completely pull out of my ass then slowly and deliberately slide back in. His dirty talk continued as he began fucking me harder and faster.

"God DAMN your ass feels so fucking good! Oh FUCK yeah! I'm gonna fucking pound your ass so hard you'll be tasting my cock for a week!" Bill shouted as he power fucked my ass. I was so caught up in his cock pounding in and out and of my ass that the only thing I could do was moan and shout and beg for him to fuck me.

"Fuck my ass please, oh GOD your fucking cock feels so good. Yeah, c'mon, fucking pound my ass, fucking pound it hard bitch!" I shouted.

"I wanna see your face when I blow my load." Bill said as he yanked his cock out of my ass, flipped me over on my back and slammed back into my upturned ass. I howled in pleasure as he shoved his cock back in my ass and started fucking me again.

"You like my cock up your ass? Yeah? You like me fucking you don't you slut!" Bill shouted.

"Uh Huh!" I panted back, reaching between the two us and grabbing his balls.

"OH FUCK yeah! That's it, squeeze my fucking balls, yeah, squeeze the cum out of them. Shit! I'm getting close, getting close." Bill shouted.

"Oh fuck yeah, I'm getting close too Bill. You're gonna make me cum!" I shouted as my balls withdrew, leaving only the tight skin of my sack. "Oh shit, fuck yeah, oh

GOD I'm gonna cum, gonna blow my load." I screamed, arching my back to get more of his cock inside me.

"FFFUUUCCCKKK!!" I shouted as the first rope of cum shot out of my hard cock and landed on my chin.

"Oh shit, you're cumming hands free, fucking hot man, fucking hot. Yeah, oh yeah, gonna cum, gonna..." Bill shoved one last time in me, tensed and howled as his cock let loose a torrent of cum inside my ass.

My own cock continued to shoot, cum landing on my face, chest, tits, finally dribbling out the tip and pooling on my belly. I felt each burst of cum shoot out of Bill's cock and knew his load was massive, hell as massive as it was I was sure I'd be shitting his load out for a week!

Bill collapsed on top of me, panting, his back and ass covered in sweat.

His withering cock soon slid out of my ass as he kissed me. We covered each other's faces in kissed as we came down off our orgasmic high. Bill licked my cum from my face and fed it back to me, causing my cock to flex and jerk, more cum dribbling out of the tip. Bill's breathing had finally returned to normal when he rolled off me and lay on his back.

"Shit, that was fucking hot man." He said.

"Yeah, you are a great fuck Bill!" I panted.

"Think we can make this a regular occurrence?" Bill asked.

"Works for me." I replied back, "do you take as good as you give?" I continued.

"I don't get fucked." Bill quickly said.

"Ever been fucked?" I asked.

"I don't get fucked." Bill said again as he stood and started getting dressed.

"You like to be rimmed though don't you?" I asked.

"Look, my ass is off limits, period." Bill said, slapping my ass as I stood up.

"Yeah well, we'll see about that." I said, slapping his now cloth covered ass back.

"Yeah, uh, I don't think so, but you just go ahead and try buddy." Bill smirked. There was something in his tone that made me think, given the right amount of persistence, I'd be able to at least eat his gorgeous ass.

His voice said "Off limits" but his body language said, "well maybe."

Bill was soon dressed and left, thanking me profusely for everything, including the great fuck. "Phew!" I groaned as I cleaned up the mess I'd made on the tile floor. "Haven't had my ass fucked like that in a long time." I said out loud.

My phone started ringing, "Hello?" I said. "Hey, buddy! How's it going?" the voice on the other end said.

"Great Tim, what's up with you?" I asked.

"Well, was thinking about your accident. I know you're OK but thought I might come over and check on you anyway." Tim said, a hint of sexual excitement in his voice.

"You wanna come over here? I thought you didn't want to be seen walking into another man's house. Thought you thought people might talk." I said, teasing Tim on purpose.

"Yeah, yeah, yeah, whatever, so you want me to come over or not?" Tim said.

"Sure, c'mon over!" I said, my ass twitching at the thought of getting fucked twice in one day.

Now, let me tell you about Tim. As I said, Tim and I met when I was first stationed at the fire department I'm at now. What I didn't tell you was that Tim is drop dead gorgeous, and I mean drop dead gorgeous. Tim's family is a mix of Latin American and Swedish, although his last name, Johnson, would not indicate that he's from either area.

He has the perfect mixture of both, dark skin and jet black hair from the Latin American side and the blue eyes and gentle demeanor of the Swedish side. He stands six foot six, is a solid 280 pounds of muscle, smooth skin, dark brown nipples that are permanently hard, wash board stomach, narrow tapered waist that flows into the perfect skaters ass massive tree trunk thighs with perfectly sculpted calve muscles and size 14 feet. He has very little body hair except for his bush, which he keeps neatly trimmed. His lips are thick and full and I love sucking on them while we kiss. His cock averages seven inches when hard but is at least two and a half inches thick with a long slender, tapered head. His balls are as big as Triple Grade A extra large eggs and pump out more cum than I've ever seen.

Tim is quick to cum on the first go around, usually, when he arrives I immediately sink to my knees, fish out his cock, give it couple of sucks and try to swallow as fast as I can while he pours his cum down the back of my throat. From that point on though, he can throw you a fuck like you've never had, delaying his cum for as long as he wishes. There have been nights that by the time he got done with me, I was nothing more than a massive puddle of cum, incapable of moving at all.

It isn't too long before the door bell rings and Tim enters. I sink to my knees and start to fish out his cock when he stops me, "Not so fast buddy. I need to talk." he says, zipping the fly of his jeans back.

"Sure Tim, what's going on?" I ask. Tim moves over to the couch, sits down and asks me, "You happy with the things between us the way they are?"

I sit next to him, look at him for a few moments and answer, "Sure, why?"

"I don't know, just thinking that's all." Tim shrugged. "Was he a good fuck?" Tim asked.

"What?" I responded.

"Your neighbor that you hit, was he a good fuck?" Tim asked again.

"What are you talking about?" I said, blushing lightly.

"C'mon Craig, your living room smells like fresh fucked ass." Tim giggled.

"Oh, yeah he was." I sighed. "You jealous or something?" I asked, poking him in the ribs causing him to jerk away and giggle.

"Naw, fuckin turns me on knowing you got a fresh load in your ass." Tim said, looking at me, his eyes filling with lust. Tim leaned over and started kissing me. There was something tender in his kiss tonight, it wasn't the usual, "let's get busy and fuck" roughness. I moaned as our tongues gently caressed each other, Tim grabbed my hand and placed it in his crotch, he was rock hard.

"God you taste good tonight." Tim moaned.

I pulled away, "Tim, are you OK?" I asked.

"Uh huh." he said as he placed his mouth over mine and began kissing me again. My hand rubbed his hard cock through his jeans.

"Baby, you're going to make me cum." He whispered.

"Go ahead, I'll clean your cock off." I whispered back. Tim soon grunted and buck his hips as he shot his load in his underwear. I pulled off his mouth, ripped open his jeans and with him pushing up off the couch, soon had them down around his knees and was cleaning his cum soaked cock with my tongue. I love the taste of Tim's cum, it's a tangy sweet with just a light saltiness to it.

While I cleaned his cum covered cock off, he removed his shirt, kicked his sneakers off and managed to pull his jeans off followed by his underwear. I nursed and sucked and licked on his cock, a few more shots of his cum shooting to the back of my throat. Before too long he was hard as a rock again and ready to go.

Tim pulled me off his cock, kissed me again, moaning at the taste of his cum on my tongue and, pulling away, said, "I wanna try something different tonight."

"Yeah? What?" I asked as I continued to nibble on his lips and chin.

"I wanna try some ass play with you." he said, excitement ringing in his voice.

"Don't we always?" I responded as I continued kissing, licking and nibbling, moving down his neck and searching out his left nipple.

"Oh fuck!" Tim whispered as I sucked his hard nipple into my mouth and wrapped my hand around his hard cock.

"No, I mean I want you to try some ass play on me." Tim groaned.

I stopped what I was doing, looked up and said, "Wait. You want me to do some ass play on you? Your ass is off limits, what did you have in mind?"

I asked, excitement quickly crawling into the back of my head at the prospect of getting to play with his gorgeous ass.

"You know, I want you to..." Tim trailed off.

"To what?" I teased as I nipped his right nipple with my teeth.

"I want you to eat my ass and maybe fuck me." Tim said.

"Seriously?" I squealed, my cock jerking in my shorts.

"Just go easy, I watch how you enjoy it and I've been playing around with my ass and it does feel good, so I thought, why not with you?" Tim said, a pleading look replacing the sexual charged up look that was in his eyes.

"Um yeah, sure, you bet." I said. "C'mon, let's take this to the bedroom." I said, standing, grabbing his hand and trying to pull him to his feet. I quickly undressed once we were in my bedroom. Tim was already laying on his stomach on the bed, his ass arched up in the air. My cock was leaking like crazy, never in my wildest erotic fantasies did I think I'd ever get to play with his ass. Now I was staring down at his beautiful skater's ass, thrust in the air, a hint of pink peaking out between his cheeks. His cock was rock hard and as my eyes took in the feast before me, I watched as a long silver string of his cock juice hung from the tip of his cock and slowly extended downward, eventually soaking into the comforter on my bed.

"Fuck, that thing can be dry cleaned, but this, this is fucking Christmas come early!" I thought as my hands spread the cheeks of his ass. Tim jerked at my touch, jerked and also moaned.

"Go easy baby, easy." he panted as I leaned forward and inhaled the muskiness of his virgin ass. It was like a sweet aphrodisiac for me and my cock jerked, a rope of cum shooting out of the tip, landing on the comforter to soak in with his sweet cock honey.

I dove in on his upturned ass, my tongue lapping and running over the folds of his pink rosebud. Tim moaned and panted as I licked his tender hole and up and down the crack of his ass.

"Fuck, oh fuck, oh this feels so fucking good." Tim moaned. "Oh yeah, yeah Craig, eat my ass." he sighed.

I continued lapping at this hole and licking the entire length of his ass, Tim moaning and bucking as I took him to a new plane of ecstasy. I felt his hole twitching around my tongue, reached between his legs and realized he was cumming again. I soon scooped up his load and smeared on his already wet hole and started feasting on his ass again. Tim panted and moaned. I reached up and started to finger his hole, rubbing the lips of his hole, gently inserting my finger. Tim bucked as my finger slid in to the first knuckle.

"Awe fuck, shit dude. If I'd known it was going to feel half this good, I'd have let you do this a long time ago." Tim cried out. I said nothing, I wasn't done yet. Once I was sure he was used to one finger in his ass, I quickly added a second, amazed at how tightly his ass gripped my fingers, I slowly entered him. Tim bucked more and yelped, begging me to fuck him, begging for my hard cock up his ass. I wasn't ready to enter him yet, much to my cock's disappointed.

Pre-cum was flowing out of both of our cocks by now as I continued my slow and deliberate ministrations on his virgin hole. He had adjust to two fingers quicker than I thought he would and so I soon added a third finger, figuring that would best estimate the thickness of my own cock. I had all three fingers half way in his ass when he reared up, howled and started shooting another load.

"Geez Tim! FUCK! I can't believe you've had two huge orgasms already and I haven't even started fucking you yet." I said as I stroked his cock, helping him finish his cum.

"I can't take anymore Craig, fuck me please, oh GOD fuck me. I want your cock inside my ass so bad. Please baby, please, please fuck me." Tim begged and whined.

"Roll over and pull your legs up to your chest." I instructed, easing my fingers out of his ass. Tim did as he was instructed and I soon had his legs over my shoulders and the tip of my cock pointed at his sweet virgin hole.

"Just relax Tim, push out as I push in and you'll be OK." I said, leaning forward and kissing him. Tim shoved his tongue in my mouth, kissing me with a hunger I've never experienced with him before. He grabbed the back of my neck and was pushing my head down so hard that his teeth busted my upper lip.

I started to gently push my cock into his ass. He didn't need any coaxing at all, his ass just started sucking my cock in, deeper and deeper I slid into him. I pulled off his mouth and watched the expression on his face as my cock slid into him. His eyes widened and rolled in the back of his head, his mouth agape as though he was going to scream but no sound came out. He shuddered as my cock soon bottomed out in his ass. He was panting so hard I was afraid he might start to hyperventilate so I started talking to him, telling him to slow his breathing down. Tim's eyes were screwed shut and his head was rolling from side to side as I slowly began to fuck his ass.

Tim must have thought I was moving too slow as before I knew it, he'd rolled us over so he was on top of me and was slamming his ass up and down on my cock. His rock hard cock bounced and slapped my stomach. Tim panted and moaned and bucked his hips on my ass while he twisted and played with his nipples. He was speechless and, for the most part, I was too. Here was this six foot, macho, powerful man, riding my cock as though he'd been doing this his entire life. You'd never have known that this was his first lay, his first time of feeling the exquisite pleasure of a hard cock sawing in and out of your ass, pushing and pulling you ever higher as you soar to another level of pleasure.

"Fuck Tim, fuck your ass is so tight around my cock. Baby, I'm gonna cum soon!" I shouted as I felt the rapid approach of my orgasm.

"Yeah, oh fuck yeah, fucking fill me with your hot cum!" Tim shouted for the first time, collapsing on me, his ass still riding my cock as he started fucking my mouth with his tongue. I grabbed his ass and started helping him, pushing him up and pulling him down on my cock as my orgasm began to race through my cock. Tim sat up, shouted and slammed down on my ass. His cock started shooting again, his cum dribbling out and pooling on my stomach.

This triggered my own orgasm and I thrust up and screamed as the cum fired out of my cock and into his ass. Each time my cock were jerk Tim would moan as he felt my hot cum shoot deep into his ass. We were a mass of sweating skin, panting as we fell into each others arms, Tim rolling to the side, taking me with him, my cock still buried in his ass. Tim showered me with kisses and continued to somehow, grind his ass on my cock.

My cock was not going soft, it was as if it wanted to go again. Tim's own cock was still rock hard and I reached between the two of us and started stroking his cock. We stayed like this for a few more minutes, him grinding on my still hard cock, me stroking his.

"Tim, oh fuck, Tim, I'm gonna cum again, get ready!" I shouted as I slammed into him one last time. I felt him stiffen and his cock spasmed in my hand as he too came again. It was a dry cum though, he'd already spent the load that his balls had produced. We fell asleep still entwined with one another.

My cock softening and falling out of his ass, his cock softening in my hand.

Just as sleep was beginning to take me, I heard Tim whisper, "Fuck, that was...fuck..." this was soon followed by his light snoring indicating that he was now in that blissful sleep state that sex induces. I smiled, my cock twitched again and I too was soon drifting off.

CHAPTER 3

I had at least had the foresight to turn my alarm clock on at some point and at six the next morning it was telling me, quite loudly, that it was time to get up and get ready to go on shift. I rolled over to snuggle up next to Tim and discovered that he had left at some point during the night.

I replayed yesterday's events in my mind and my cock soon let me know that it really enjoyed the adventure, unfortunately my bladder was letting me know that it needed to be emptied.

I got out of bed and managed to will my cock down enough to start pissing. Tim had written a short note and had taped it to the mirror, thanking me for the wild fuck and hoping I'd enjoyed taking his virginity as much as he enjoyed having it taken. My cock hardened as the last drops of piss dribbled out. I sat on the toilet and proceeded to stroke my hard cock, crying out as my cum shot out and pooled at the base of my cock. I love the taste of my own cum and was soon wiping the pool with my hand and cleaning my cum off my hand with my tongue.

"Fuck Tim, you were fucking hot last night." I whispered to the quiet air and proceeded to get ready for work.

The firefighters at my station work a schedule of four days on and four days off while the EMTs work five days on with five days off. Today was the start of my normal five day schedule, I would spend the next five days sleeping at the fire station. The door bell rang while I was packing my clothes, I looked at the clock, seven in the morning, and went to answer the door. Bill was standing at the door, steadying a new bike in one hand and holding out the clean shorts for me in the other.

"Hey Bill, you're up early." I said as I reached for the shorts, "thanks, you didn't need to get these back to me this soon though." I continued.

"No problem, I'm usually up this early as I like to get a couple hours in of riding before work. Don't think I'll go that far today though, am still sore. So, you busy tonight? I thought I might come over and see if we couldn't get ourselves into some more trouble." He said, winking at me.

"Can't tonight Bill, I'm on shift." I replied.

"Oh what time do you get off?" Bill asked.

"Umm, seven at night on Friday." I said, "I work five on and five off, I'll be staying at the station." I continued to explain as I saw the look of confusion wash over Bill's face.

"Oh, well, I guess I'll see you on Friday then." Bill said and started to turn around to leave.

"Yeah, I'll come over and see you when I get home." I said.

"Sounds good." Bill said waving as he hopped on his bike and rode out of the driveway.

"Fuck I gotta taste his ass, and I will, I will have some of that if it's the last thing I do."

I thought, patting my hardening cock and silently telling it to settle down. I locked the door behind me, threw my gear in my car and headed to work.

I arrived at the fire station a few minutes later and headed for the locker room to put my stuff away. Matt Billings was just coming out of the shower as I walked in. Nude, dripping wet, I had just enough time to check out his body and cock before he wrapped a towel around his waist.

"Hey Craig!" He shouted.

"S'up Matt? Quiet night?" I asked.

"Yeah, had a car fire at three this morning but other than that, nothing." He said as he removed the towel and began to towel dry his hair.

Matt Billings always reminded me of a young version of Joey Lawerence. Same sleepy, dopey good looks that Joey had, his body was a spitting image of Joey's and his cock was truly a beautiful masterpiece.

He was cut and, soft, he didn't appear to have much in length (not that that matters to me, I've always made it work!) but was thick, very thick and his piss slit was on the underside of his cock head versus in the center. I never inquired as to why or what had happened, no need to really, but knew he was unable to use a urinal because of it so all of his business was done in the toilet.

Matt also had two dimples above the start of his ass that matched the two dimples in his cheeks when he smiled. You didn't know which you wanted to do more, hug him because he's so damn cute or just fuck the shit out of him because he's so damn hot. I always sensed a mystery with Matt, he rarely talked much about girls, in fact he rarely talked much about his life outside of work. There are private people in this world and I greatly respect that but I couldn't help but wonder and fantasize that maybe by day Matt was a pure wholesome clean cut lad but by night maybe he turned into a leather pig or a cum slut.

What I felt pretty sure about was that I'd never be able to taste his cock or tap into that ass of his, I just didn't pick up a vibe that he and I shared the same tastes, if we even shared anything at all, regarding men. I left Matt to finish drying off and headed to check in with the Captain.

James Rockwell was the Captain of our fire department. Most of the men called him "Cappy", which I think is a pretty standard nickname for the men in those positions, I just called him Big Jim. Cappy isn't a big man, height wise he stands around five foot seven. Body wise though the man is built and built very well. Big Jim was an amateur body builder in his day and the trophies he has lined on a shelf behind his desk, attest to the success he had when he was competing.

Big Jim is also the perfect "Daddy", he's in his fifties, a thick head of salt and pepper hair, closely cropped on the sides, thick mustache that outlines his thick, full lips and a beautiful tuft of salt and pepper hair that sticks out of the collar on his shirt. My mouth always waters and my cock always twitches whenever I'm around the Captain. Big Jim speaks softly but has a loud booming laugh when something strikes him as funny and an even louder and booming voice when he's chewing one of us out for something stupid that we may have done.

I've often fantasized about him turning me over his knee, yanking my pants down and spanking my ass until it's a bright red and then gently caressing my ass, trying to take away the stinging, his gentle voice telling me he's sorry but I must behave and he'll make me feel better if I want him to.

Eventually his fingers find their way to my hole and his voice takes on a huskiness as he asks me if I'd like for him to make me feel good. In my fantasy I begin to pant as he wets his finger and begins to slowly slide it inside my ass, I groan and I imagine I can feel his hard cock poking my stomach as I lay, spread eagled over his lap.

I fantasize him asking me if that feels good and I groan and nod my head yes. I fast forward in my fantasy and now I'm naked, standing in front him, he's nude as well and sitting in his chair, his hand is wrapped around my cock and he's gently stroking me while he strokes his own cock. I look down to take in the thick head of his cock, it's an angry purple and the lips of his piss slit are swollen and wet with his pre-cum.

"You want your Big Jim to make you feel better?" he asks me.

"Uh huh!" I nod and pant and watch as he leans forward, his mustached lips purse and he kisses the tip of my wet cock and then slowly slides his mouth over the head of my hard cock and down to the base. He's looking up at me, his browns eyes asking me if this feels good. I throw my head back and sigh, answering him that it does feel good and please keep going. I groan again as I feel a finger enter me again, followed by another and then another. I place my hands on top of his head and guide him up and down the length of my hard cock while he adds another finger, I'm now bucking my hips, my cock thrusting down his throat while I fuck my ass on four of his fingers. The fingers soon leave my ass, his mouth comes off my cock and, in my fantasy, he stands, pulls me too him, the hair on his chest scratching and scraping the flesh on my chest, my nipples hardening, he kisses me.

He grabs our cocks and begins to stroke both of us while his tongue tenderly searches out my own. My fantasy continues to play out in my mind as I imagine him pulling off of me and asking me if I want his daddy captain to fuck me. I groan and nod my head yes as he spins me around, bends me over his desk and impales me with his thick cock. There's no pain as he thrusts into me, his cock bottoming out, his thick bush tickling my ass. I arch my back and I groan as he begins to fuck me hard, his hands slapping my ass. My cock twitches and throbs as the first orgasm hits me and I rear up, my cock shooting cum over the top of his desk.

I hear his voice shouting at me, "Yeah, that's it pup, shoot that fucking cum all over my desk, soak the top of daddies desk." while he continues to pound my ass.

I whimper and whine and thrust back, the hands that were slapping my ass are now pinching and twisting and pulling on my nipples. His fantasy voice tells me how much he likes fucking my bitch ass. He asks me if I like riding his daddy cock and I scream out yes. He tells me my bitch ass is making his daddy cock feel good and he asks me if I want his daddy cum and I scream out yes. He continues his dirty talk to me, telling me what a dirty bitch I am and how hot my dirty bitch ass feels around his cock. His fucking me is steady and I think he's never going to cum. He shoves his fingers in my mouth and I eagerly suck and nurse on them, as a pup nurses on his mother's teat.

I scream out and cum again, he swipes his hand through the puddle of cum I've left and feeds it to me. He asks if I want to taste his daddy cum and I shout yes as he yanks his cock out of my well fucked and abused ass, spins me around and forces me to my knees. I open my mouth, waiting for his cum as though I'm taking communion, he slaps my face and tells me to close my bitch mouth, he wants to cum on my face. My cock fires again, my cum splashing his leg. He strokes his cock in front of me telling me he's going to paint my face with his daddy cum and to get ready.

I close my eyes as he howls and I feel the first spray of his cum hit my forehead and begin to run down the bridge of my nose, my cock fires another load. I don't think he's every going to quit cumming as I feel spray after spray hit my face. It lands on my chin and drips onto my stomach, my cheeks, my hair, my ears. He finally lets out one long growl and tells me to open my mouth. I comply and I feel the cum covered head of his cock push past my lips, instinctively I begin to nurse his cock, my tongue cleaning the remains of his orgasm off his cock.

He grunts and another stream of cum shoots out past my tongue, landing in the back of my throat. He pulls his cock out of my mouth and I soon feel his tongue cleaning his cum off my face. He gets a mouthful of his cum and then feeds it back to me, our tongues dueling over how much each of us are going to get. He does this until my face is clean, my cock fires another load and I'm amazed that I can still cum. He orders me to get on my knees and clean up my mess and I begin to lick at the pools of my own cum that I've left on the floor of his office.

He's stroking a hard cock again while he watches me lapping and licking at the floor, I see the mess I've made on his leg and I start with his foot, licking the top of his toes and foot and work my way up his leg. Before long I'm sucking and licking his balls, my tongue darting back and tasting the musk of his hole. I reach out for his cock and he gives me just the head of his dick, stiffens, and shoots another load down my throat.

"Any questions Craig?" Big Jim's voice brings me back from my fantasy.

"Huh?" I ask, a dazed look in my eyes and I can feel the wetness in my underwear from my leaking cock and hope that I haven't soaked through the front of my uniform slacks.

"I asked you if you had any questions?" Big Jim says again, a tone of irritation entering his voice.

I glance down, relieved that I haven't soaked through the front of my pants, "No sir, no questions." I say, totally oblivious to anything he'd been telling me, I was too busy playing out the fantasy in my head to hear anything he was telling me.

He stands and I take a quick glance at his crotch, "Oh my GOD! He's half hard!" I scream in my head as I notice the obvious tenting in his slacks.

"Well if you have no questions, go check your equipment, make sure the ambulance is stocked and I'll see you at dinner." Big Jim says, a sly smile beginning to cross his face.

"Um, OK." is all I can say as I turn to leave, my cock quickly rising to full mast, tenting out my own slacks, as I make a mad dash to the restroom. I practically ran Tim over as I run into the bathroom.

"Whoa! What's the rush?" Tim says.

"Nothing!" I shout back as I head for the first stall. I yank my pants down, sit on the toilet and, as quietly as I can, start stroking my cock. It doesn't take long for me to shoot my load as I replay the vision of Big Jim's semi-hard cock tenting his slacks. I wipe my cock off, flush a couple of times to make sure the evidence is gone and as I head out the stall stop dead in my tracks as I see Tim standing there.

"Did you just jack off?" he whispers to me. I look around to make sure we're alone, we are, so I quickly walk over to Tim and kiss him.

Tim pulls me off and scolds me, "Not here jackass. What if someone walks in?"

"Big Jim was briefing me, on what I have no idea, anyway, I went into a fantasy about him." I tell Tim.

"When he was done briefing me, he stood up and Tim, I swear to the God's of sex, he had a freaking hardon!" I continued.

"You shitting me?" Tim asks, his hand running down to grab his cock.

"No man, I'm not shitting you. His cock was tenting out his pants plain as day. Isn't he like totally straight and totally devoted to his wife?" I ask.

"Yeah, but you don't know what he was thinking about, hell he coulda been thinking about banging his wife for all you know." Tim said. "Don't get your hopes up Craig, 99% of the men in this station are totally hetero and completely hands off and if you value your job, you'll leave it that." Tim said.

"Yeah, you're right, what the hell was I thinking!" I exclaimed, walking over to the sink to splash some cold water on my face.

The door to the bathroom opened and in walked the Captain. Nodding to both of us, he walked into the stall I'd just been in, newspaper in hand. He stood there for a few minutes as he heard the rustle of his pants being lowered. Tim nodded for us to leave and headed out the door. I hung around for a few minutes and soon heard what I thought was the tell tale rustling of clothes as a cock is being jacked off.

I quickly left to let the Captain do his business and headed to the ambulance to make sure everything was stocked and ready to go. I'd no sooner finished doing my inventory when the fire alarm rang, we were being called to an auto accident on the freeway. As I and the other two EMT's climbed in, the radio crackled to life and started giving us what few details were known.

I was in the back of the ambulance and sighed as it sounded like this was a bad one and we could expect a fatality. This was the part of the job I hated the most and no matter how seasoned you get, it still hits you whenever a life is lost. We arrived on scene and were instantly relieved to find that everyone was, for the most part, going to be OK. There were a couple of broken bones and one suspected heart attack but no fatalities.

We went about our business and within a few hours were rolling back into the station. I was flying high on the adrenaline and decided a long hot shower would feel pretty good and would relax me.

The hot water cascading over my tense muscles felt good. I hung my head and just stood under the spray of the nozzle letting the hot water wash over me. I heard the shower room door open and was soon aware of someone standing at the nozzle next to me. "Odd, why would someone stand so close to me when there a twelve other nozzles around the shower." I thought to myself. I opened my eyes and turned to see the Captain standing next to me, staring right at me as he lathered his hair with shampoo.

"Shit! Do not get hard, do not get hard!" I screamed to myself as I quickly took in the Captain's body. The Captain had his own shower, I found it rather odd that he was in here, especially with me.

"Shower's broke." was all the Captain said to me as he continued to stare at me, his eyes soaking in my wet nude body. I glanced down at his cock again, he was getting thicker and it was obvious that he was on his way to a raging hardon.

"Like it?" he asks me, I say nothing, trembling with a mixture of excitement and hesitancy.

I soak in his body while he rinses the shampoo out of his hair. His chest is covered in the same salt and pepper hair that is on his head. He manscapes as it is neatly trimmed, his dime sized nipples are hard and jut out from his pecs. Hair covers his ripped abs and leads into a neatly trimmed bush. His cock is rock hard and swaying with the movement of his hands, he's thick, the mushroom head of his cock the same angry purple that I fantasized about. His balls are medium size and completely shaved, thick hair covers his massive tree trunk thighs that taper into well defined calf muscles. He turns his back to me and I marvel at the firm globes of his ass.

The Captain bends over, his ass cheeks parting, showing me his shaved pink pucker, he makes it wink at me. "You're married." I finally manage to say.

"I'm bi." He responds back as he soaks in my naked body and raging hard cock.

"I locked the shower door." he says to me, indicating that the Captain wants his privacy.

"How'd you know I was into men?" I asked him as I reach over to rub my thumb around his hard nipple.

"Just a feeling," he says as he soaps his body up. My hands join his and I reach down, caressing his cock, he groans his appreciation and shoves my face into his freshly washed arm pit. "Lick it!" he orders as I start lapping at the hair in his pit, taking in the fresh clean scent of his skin. My hand reaches down and grabs his balls and I squeeze gently. His cock flexes as a drop of clear fluid forms at the tip and begins to fall to the shower floor.

I pull off his arm pit, look at him as he rinses the rest of the soap off his body and say, "So you really were half hard when I was in your office weren't you?"

He turns to me, kisses me, his tongue making love to my mouth and after a few minutes, pulls off and says, "I've been wanting to do that since you first came to work here."

I groan, slide to the floor and suck his cock into my mouth, my hands caressing his ass, searching for his hole. I get no resistance as I rub my finger along his pink pucker so I start to push in. The Captain closed his eyes, gasping as my finger enters him, his cock flexes in my mouth and I'm rewarded with a stream of his clear nectar.

"Oh yeah, fucking feels good." He whispers to me, pulling me to my feet he shoves his tongue back in my mouth again and begins to hump me with his hard cock, his own fingers quickly finding and penetrating my tight hole.

"Mmm..." he moans in my mouth and I return my own fingers to his ass and begin playing with him. He bucks into me as I gently shove two fingers into his pouting hole.

"Oh fuck! Yeah, stretch my hole Craig. Stretch my daddy hole with your fingers. Keep that up and I may have to take a ride on your hot cock!" He says to me. My cock flexes and my own clear juice runs out, coating the underside of his cock, mixing with his own clear juice.

"Eat my hole!" the Captain whispers to me. He turns around and bends over, offering me his sweet delicious hole. I squat down and begin eating his muscle ass out. I no sooner started fucking his hole with my tongue when the alarm when off again.

"Shit!" Big Jim shouted, "guess we'll have to put this on pause." as he stood up, turned off the showers and headed out to dry off.

"Fuck!" I said, standing there, panting, trying to regain my composure.

"Hurry up pup! No time to waste, we need to roll!" Big Jim shouts at me and I scurry to get dried off and dressed.

As I walked past him, he slapped my ass and promises that we'll finish this up later. My cock jerked and a rope of cum shot out, landing on the floor. No time to wipe it up though as I quickly dressed and followed the Captain out, practically mowing Tim over as he was rushing in to grab something out of his locker.

Right before the door closed, I heard him say, "Son of a bitch!" and I couldn't help but giggle, knowing that he must have seen the rope of cum on the floor that I'd shot out. Within a matter of minutes, we're in our vehicles and on our way to a three alarm fire in an abandoned warehouse that was being used by transients.

CHAPTER 4

The fire we responded to had completely engulfed the abandoned warehouse. Ladder Company 19 was already on scene and was working hard to get the flames under control. Two of their firefighters had pulled a couple of transients from the building and were treating them for smoke inhalation. They asked if our crew could take over so they could get back to the fire and we obliged, to include taking them to the local hospital for treatment and observation. By the time we had returned the flames were under control and our firefighters were busy putting their equipment away and getting ready to head back to the station.

An hour later and we're all back at the station and going through the process of cleaning up. The showers are packed as I remove my uniform and stuff in my laundry sack to be sent out for cleaning. Towel wrapped around my waist, I sit on the bench in the locker room and wait for the crowd in the showers to thin out. My cock has kept reminding me that there was unfinished business between the Captain and I. I'm afraid it will betray me if I enter the showers now. I'm afraid that the casual touch or sliding of skin as we bump into one another will cause my cock to rear up, giving my secret away. I scan the locker room and see Tim, draped in a towel, talking with Matt. Tim's absentmindedly rubbing his left nipple and I wonder what must be going through his head as he chats Matt up. I notice Matt is running his hand up and down his firm stomach and I let my mind fantasize about these two for just a few moments. My cock plumps and twitches beneath my towel and I quickly put my imagination on hold.

There's only four men in the shower so I head over, removing my towel and hanging it up on the hook. I take the shower head closest to me and keep my eyes closed as I begin to wash the smell of smoke and sweat from my body. The noise level in the locker room lessens as one by one the men, dressed in casual clothes, heads out to the day room or other parts of the fire station. Our fire station is a relatively new one, the Captain has his own private one bedroom suite just behind his office while the rest of the men share their living quarters on the second floor next to the garage area. I soon realize I'm the last one in the shower and think maybe I can get in a quick jerk off session just to keep my cock satisfied. I reach down and grab my cock just as I hear the door to the shower room open. I turn my back to the entrance, afraid someone will see my semi-hard cock.

"Craig, when you're done, come see me in my office." Big Jim says.

"Roger that sir." I respond, my cock rising to full mast now as my brain and cock connect, hoping and thinking we can finish what we started. I quickly rinse off, check to see I'm alone, grab my towel to hide my hard cock and quickly head to my locker to get dressed.

I decide to throw on my jock strap and in a matter of seconds, or so it seems, I'm dressed in a t-shirt, shorts and my cock is happily tucked away in my jock strap. I close my locker, spin the dial on the combination, check to see it's locked and quickly head to the Captain's office. My hands are shaking as I knock on his closed door. His office has windows and I notice he's closed the blinds, not unusual, he normally does this time of the evening. It's an indication to us that, unless it's an emergency, he's not to be disturbed. The door opens and I stare into his dark brown eyes surrounded by his thick lashes. My mouth waters, my pulse quickens and my cock does it's best to rear up in its pouch as he grabs my hand and leads me into his office, closing and locking the door behind me. He reaches up, grabs my shoulders, spins me around and shoves his tongue into my mouth. I kiss him back with the same urgency that he's kissing me with and I groan.

He pulls off of me, looks me over and tells me, "Damn! You look even better out of that uniform. C'mon, let's go to my room and pick up where we left off."

Grabbing my hand he guides me around his desk and through the open door that leads to his apartment type room. He closes and locks his door behind, "Can't be too careful." he whispers as he begins to kiss and lick the back of my neck, his hands groping my ass, pushing the back of my shorts down.

"Mmmm...I love an ass in a jock strap!" he purrs in my ear as his finger seeks out my hole. I'm already wet and moist with anticipation as he begins to lightly run his fingers around the lips of my pucker. I groan and a shiver runs through me.

"Bend over, let me taste that sweet ass." He says, gently pushing on my back, I oblige and bend over. Big Jim pulls my shorts all the way to the ground and I manage to step out of them before he begins to feast on my pink rosebud. I sigh and groan when his tongue darts out and connects with the sensitive flesh around my hole. His hand is reaching up and fishing for my balls and cock. He massages the area between my hole and my balls while his tongue continues to lap and flick around my hole.

"Oh fuck that feels good Big Jim. Yeah, fucking get your tongue in my ass, eat my hole daddy, eat my hole!" I say, louder than I should.

He slaps my ass and I groan. "Ssshh, this room isn't sound proof!" he scolds me.

My cock is pouring out it's clear honey and the front of my pouch is wet. He reaches in and pulls my cock back so that the head of my dick is pointing back at him. It hurts but in a good way and I groan again, rewarding him with a drop of clear nectar. His mouth covers the head of my cock as he darts his tongue in and out of my piss slit, lapping up the clear fluid. I manage to remove my T-shirt and let it drop on the floor.

"Oh yeah, fuck yeah, your cock is so delicious. Hmm...and your ass, your ass is one of the finest I've seen in a long time." He growls.

He pulls my cock back further, further than I think it can go and I soon feel the head of my dick brushing up against my hole. It feels good and I wonder if he's going to try and fuck me with my own dick. I feel him pressing the head into my hole, I groan at the thought that I'm about to fuck myself in my ass. My cock twitches, a stream of clear liquid runs out and he uses that to lube up my hole as he continues to push the head of my dick into my ass.

"You like that? Huh pup? You like the feel of your own cock inside your ass?" He asks me as I feel my cock enter me.

"Oh GOD yeah!" I groan, "OH fuck, how much is in me?" I pant.

"Almost your whole head, I think I can get all of the head of your cock in your ass." He pants back and he pushes and pulls, forcing my ass to swallow more of my cock. I cry out as I feel the head of my cock move past the ring in my ass.

"Oh yeah buddy boy, yeah, fucking look at that. Fucking got the head of your dick in your ass. Oh fuck yeah! Fuck pup! You're gonna make your daddy captain cum!" He squeals as he stands, jerking his cock he nudges the head against my ass and I feel his load blast over my hole and my cock. He pulls my dick out of my ass and finishes firing the rest of his cum on my asshole.

"Fuck! I'm gonna cum, oh fuck, I'm gonna..." I trail off as my cock fires, cum splattering the cheap carpet in his room. Big Jim continues to rub the head of his cock over my hole, smearing his cum. I can't believe he's still rock hard, hell I can't believe I'm still rock hard, after shooting what seemed like a huge load.

"I'll be right back." Big Jim tells me. I stand up and remove the rest of my clothes just as he renters the living room/kitchen area of his room. I gasp as he enters the room, nude, his thick cock swaying and bobbing in front of him, his balls have disappeared and I can't wait to get my face between his legs and chew and lick on his ball skin. He's carrying a bottle of lube, a dildo and a sheet. He sets everything down and spreads the sheet out over the couch so we won't stain the fabric with our play. He walks over to me, sinks to his knees and sucks my cock in to the base. I groan and thrust my hips forward, trying to shove my cock further down his throat.

He pulls off and says, "Not so fast pup, I want this to last." and then begins to lick and suck my balls. My legs are shaking as he expertly works my balls and cock with his mouth, I'm close to cumming again. He senses that and pulls off, standing up he guides me to the couch, lays me on my back and I instinctively bring my legs up to my chest.

"Such a sweet ass, such a sweet delicious ass." He says, slapping my cheeks, making me moan and my cock flex. He dives in, his tongue piercing the lips of my hole. I shout out and am rewarded by another slap on my ass. His tongue is diving in and out of me, fucking my hole, licking the lips of my ass. He chews and gnaws and fucks and sucks with his mouth, tongue and teeth. I'm reduced to a quivering, moaning puddle and I'm begging him to fuck me, to please shove his cock in my ass and fuck me hard. I feel him shift and glance up, he's pumping lube into his hands and rubbing it over the head of the dildo.

"You ready?" he growls, "Yes! Oh GOD yes!" I pant back. I arch my back and have to bite down hard to keep from screaming as I feel the head of the dildo enter my ass.

I'm so worked up by now that my hole starts to suck the head of the rubber dildo into my ass. I pant and moan and buck and writhe as he feeds me more and more of that imitation cock. My stomach is coated with the clear juice of my cock and I know that if I just barely brush my cock with my hand it'll fire. I'm not ready to cum yet, this feels too good, I want it to last. I sense movement and realize he's laying on his back, legs up, our feet touching. It's the first time I notice that the dildo is double headed and he's quickly working the other end into his own ass. I feel the heat of his skin as he inches himself closer and closer to me, the dildo going further and further into his own ass.

Our ass cheeks make contact and I'm amazed that he's filled his entire gut with the rest of the dildo. He reaches between us and begins pulling up and down on the rubber cock, causing the dildo to move in and out of our asses. We cry out together as our asses are simultaneously fucked, I reach forward searching for his hard cock and he pulls it up and places it into my fingers. I moan as I feel the thickness of his uncut cock in my hand, his cock honey streaming out his piss slit, coating my fingers. I let go of his cock and it slaps his stomach and I quickly lick the sweet clear juice from my hands.

"God Big Jim! Oh GOD! I want your cock in my ass, please, please fuck me. I can't take anymore, I gotta feel your hard cock in my ass!" I groan and pant.

"Yeah? You want your Captain Daddy to fuck you? Fuck you with his big daddy cock?" He pants back.

"OH GOD YES! FUCK ME!" I shout out. He pulls off the dildo and gently removes it from my ass. I'm panting, on the borderline of hyperventilating as I feel the head of his cock rubbing up and down the slit in my ass. I shove forward, trying to impale myself on him. He pulls back, teasing me.

Another slap on my ass and I groan. "Yeah pup, you want my daddy cock up your ass don't you. Wanna feel my hot hard cock pound you, my hot cum shoot deep in your guts don't you!" He says as he clamps his mouth down on one of my nipples. I cry out again, I've never experienced pleasure on this level before and I just know I've died and gone to cock heaven. He slaps my ass again, my cock jerks, painting the fur on his stomach with my clear juice. He starts kissing me again and I can feel his hard cock between my legs. I start humping, trying to get my ass around that dick of his.

Pulling off my mouth he says, "Ready for my big daddy cock? Huh? Are you pup?" and slaps my ass.

"Fuck yeah, oh fuck yeah, fuck me with that big daddy cock of yours, fuck me hard, please, oh please!" I beg and pant. I feel the head of his cock at my backdoor again and again I hunch myself forward, trying to get him inside me.

"Not so fast pup. Patience, patience." He whispers.

"Fuck Big Jim! Give me your fucking cock and stop fucking teasing me with it!" I shout, slapping him on the ass. A look of shock and surprise spreads across his face.

"You just slapped my ass!" he says. He looks down at me and I'm not sure if he's turned on by it or pissed off and for a few seconds, I'm afraid it's the latter of the two and he's going to stop what he's doing and send me on my way, frustrated, turned on, but not satisfied.

"You want my cock? You got it!" he says and he thrusts the full length of his cock into me. I arch my back and cry out, not in pain but in pure pleasure. I begin to tremble and shake, my eyes rolling in the back of my head. My cock rears up, flexes and my cum shoots out, coating his hairy stomach. Tears roll out the corners of my eyes as I'm overcome by one of the greatest orgasms I've ever had. Big Jim is pounding my ass as I continue to cum. I can't control my breathing and I pant and huff and groan, my head rolling from side to side. I begin to calm down and realize he's slapping my ass and telling me over and over that I have a sweet ass, a tight ass.

"Yeah my big daddy cock loves fucking your ass pup!" he says, grabbing and twisting my nipples. He leans forward and kisses me again, hard, his tongue is like a flash of lightening and speed as he tries to fuck my throat. I groan and pant and whimper, I can't talk, I'm too far gone, too wrapped up in the rapture of this man and his magic cock to find words to tell him how great I'm feeling. Big Jim knows though, he's seen the same looks and received the same actions on both men and women who've taken a ride on his wild cock.

He fucks me nonstop and I can't believe how long he's lasting. He quickens and slows his pace, pulling his cock completely out and ramming it back in. I have no idea how long we've been at it and yet my ass continues to beg for more of his thick hard cock. I realize that at some point he's moved me on my side and he's fucking me from behind now, his hand wrapped around my cock, holding my dick, keeping me from cumming again. He's talking dirty to me but I'm lost in my sex filled fog and can't hear what he's saying. I'm only aware of that massive cock buried deep in my guts, reaching areas and hitting spots in me I never knew existed. I cry out, buck back against him, stiffen and fire another load, coating his hand in my cum. He lets my cock go, brings his fingers to my mouth and tells me to lick my cum off his hand. I nurse and suck on his fingers, cleaning my cum off his massive hand. I lean back to kiss him, my load still in my mouth.

He covers my mouth with his and I share my cum with him. "Oh fuck pup, getting close, getting close, oh fuck I'm getting close!" he says, his pace quickening even more.

"I'm gonna paint your face with my load!" He cries out, yanking his cock from my ass and sitting up. I fall on my back and he straddles me, jacking his cock, the head pointing at my face.

"Get ready bitch, here it comes!" He groans. He stiffens and arches his back as the cum shoots out of the end of his cock. I open my mouth, trying to take most of his load in my mouth but he's got his cock aimed so that the first volleys of his cum land on my forehead and cheek. I feel shot after shot cover my face as he howls with his orgasm. He quickly places the cum covered head of cock in my mouth and I nurse and lick it clean, the last few spurts shooting down my throat.

He falls back on the sofa, panting, sweat pouring off his forehead and chest. I sit up and lay on top of him, my head on his chest, listening to his rapid breathing and his pounding heart as he comes down of his orgasm induced high.

"Fuck pup, you are one wild fuck!" He pants, rubbing my back with his hand. My hand runs down his chest and stomach and I grab his deflated cock. It flexes and a dribble of cum runs down the tip, covering my fingers. I bring it to my mouth and clean my fingers off and grab for his cock again. I can't believe I'm still horned up and my cock is rock hard again.

"Pup? You ready to go again?" He asks me. I say nothing as I scoot down and suck his cock into my mouth, my hand reaching between his legs, my fingers seeking out his wet hole.

"Oh fuck pup, damn, give me...ohhh yeah." He moans as I nurse his cock back to life while my fingers enter his hole. "Let me have some of your cock." Big Jim says and he pulls me into a sixty-nine position, my cock hanging over his head.

I suck and nurse on his cock, flicking the head with my tongue and running the tip of my tongue over the sensitive area underneath the head of his massive cock. "Oh shit pup, shit that feels good, oh you're gonna make your Captain daddy cum quick if you keep doing that. God yeah!" He says as he goes back to sucking and nursing on my cock.

I groan and the vibrations run through his dick, he groans and thrusts his cock into my mouth. I add two, three then four fingers to his ass. He's grinding his hips on my hand and moaning, the vibrations tingling through my own cock, coaxing me closer and closer to another cum.

"Fuck buddy boy, oh fuck yeah, I'm gonna cum pup, gonna blast my load!" He mutters as his back stiffens and his cock fires what cum is left in his balls in my mouth. I groan around his spasming cock and I shoot another load down his throat. He pulls me cock out of his mouth and takes the rest of my load on his face. His cock softens in my mouth and I turn around, amazed to see the amount of cum I've painted his face with.

"Come clean me up!" Big Jim barks and I begin to lick the cum from his face, offering it back to him as we kiss. Satisfied his face is clean he pulls me to him and we cuddle.

"God Big Jim, I have never been fucked like that before!" I purr.

"Umm, you are one hot fuck Craig. I can't believe how you were taking my cock, I've always wanted to do that with a guy but no one's been able to ride me like that." he purrs back.

"I was literally slamming my dick in and out of your ass and you were begging and crying for more." He continued.

"Well, I don't quite remember all of that, I sort of went into a fog but I know my ass enjoyed it, hell it's still tingling and begging for more." I giggled.

"Yeah, well, you need to tell it to calm down, I'm spent, between your ass and your mouth, I don't think I could cum again if my life depended on it!" Big Jim giggled back.

We laid there for a few more minutes and decided it was time to get dressed. I looked at the clock, I'd been in his office, getting fucked for two straight hours. Dressed, I walked out of his office and headed for my bunk. I had to piss so I stopped at the restroom, Tim was coming out as I walked in.

"Where the fuck you...you bitch! Who you been fucking? I warned you about..." Tim said.

I cut him off, "The Captain and I had some private coaching to do." I said as I continued to head to the urinal. "...and if you're a bad bad boy, you might get some too!" I giggled over my shoulder, winking at him as he approached.

"God you wreak of cum! So tell me, was he good?" Tim asked, rubbing the front of his shorts.

"Fucking A he was good. Two solid hours he pounded my ass!" I replied.

"No way!" Tim said, pulling the front of his shorts down to show me his hard cock.

"Way!" I replied back, "Check it out for yourself!" I continued, dropping my shorts and moaning as I felt Tim run his finger down the crack of my cum soaked ass.

"Awe shit!" He said, stroking his cock. Tim looked around the restroom and said, "Wanna suck me off, we'll take the last stall."

"Tim, honey, I'm fucking worn out." I said.

"C'mon man, please? I'm so fucking horny." Tim said, stroking his cock faster.

"Sorry buddy." I replied.

"Let me stick my dick in your wet ass, it won't take long for me to cum, I promise." Tim begged, "I'm so fucking horny!" he continued to whine.

"C'mon then you big baby." I said as we headed for the last stall. We walked in, Tim spun me around, bent me over and shoved his hard cock in my ass. I winced as I was now beginning to feel the soreness of getting fucked for two hours.

"Awe fuck man, fuck. I'm in your ass, fucking you with Cappy's load still in there. Hang on baby, hang on, I'm gonna cum." Tim growled as he thrust into me, stiffened and shot his load. He was true to his word, he was quick. We quickly cleaned up, pulled our shorts back on, stepped out of the stall and stopped dead in our tracks.

Standing there, rubbing the front of his pants was Matt Billings. "I knew you two were a couple of rump rangers." He said.

"Matt, look man." Tim started to say.

"Shut it, so we have a problem here don't we?" Matt said. "Wonder what we're going to do to make sure no one else knows about this." Matt continued, stroking his now rock hard cock through the front of his jeans.

CHAPTER 5

Tim and I stared at Matt, watching him grope and work the hardening cock in his shorts. "So, looks like I got you two by the balls. What ya gonna do huh?" Matt sneered at us. I looked at Tim and then back at Matt.

"Nothing" I started, "we're going to do absolutely nothing. What the fuck are you trying to do Matt? Are you trying to blackmail us?" I said. I walked over to Matt and grabbed his crotch, a shudder went through me as I felt his sizable hard cock and imagined him on his knees in front of Tim and I sucking our hard cocks.

"The fact of the matter is Matt, you aren't going to do or say a damned thing because in the big scheme of things, no one in this fucking department gives a rats ass what any of us do in our off time. Even more factual is I'd bet money that 90% of the men would kill to have their cocks sucked off because their wives won't." I said, standing in front of Matt, my finger pointing into his chest.

For a brief second I caught a glimpse of fear in Matt's eyes, fearful of what, I couldn't tell you, but fear nonetheless. I leaned into Matt as though I was going to kiss him and continued my rant, "Now listen to me and listen to me good you little cock bite. You are going to keep your mouth shut and if you truly want to find out what it's like to take a hard cock up your ass, be at my place at five o'clock on Saturday. Tim and I will be more than happy to show you what man to man sex is all about and we'll let you suck our hard cocks, drink our cum and take turns bouncing your tight little ass up and down on our cocks." I had continued to squeeze Matt's cock while I lit into him. I felt his cock twitch as I finished my sentence, a groan escaped his lips and his cock bucked as he dumped his load into his shorts.

"Now fucking go clean yourself up bitch boy!" I snapped, slapped him on his ass and headed for the door. I didn't look back as I heard one of the doors to the stalls slam shut and a sly grin crossed my face as I heard the quiet sobs of a man who'd just had his ego thoroughly shattered.

Tim caught up with me as we headed out of the rest room, slapped me on the back and said, "Bravo! Well done Craig! DAMN! I had no idea you could be that forceful."

"Me neither!" I giggled back, "But it was fun!"

"So what are you going to do if he shows up at the house on Saturday?" Tim asked.

I turned and looked at Tim and said, "You did not just ask me that. Please tell me you did not just ask me that. What the fuck do you think I'm gonna do? I'm gonna tap that gorgeous sweet ass of his and fuck him until he's begging for me to stop. Sounds like you and I have a date Saturday!" I said, winking at Tim and heading upstairs to catch some sleep.

Walking into the barracks room the usual sounds of a room full of men sleeping greeted us. I could faintly pick up the rustling of cloth and figured at least one of our firefighting brethren was yanking on his cock. More than likely it was as a result of some wild sex dream or maybe he was just plain horny and figured in the still of the night no one would know what he was up to. I quietly climbed into bed and thought about our encounter with Matt.

"Would he really go through with this or was this just a ruse, an attempt to get us to satisfy a curiosity that he didn't have the balls to approach us with?" I absentmindedly toyed with my left nipple as I began to think about the possibilities. I heard a soft groan followed by a grunt and smiled as whomever it was that was jacking off reached his orgasm. "Awe men!" I thought, smiling to myself as I dozed off.

The remainder of the week was pretty quiet. A few minor traffic accidents and a couple of small kitchen fires was all we responded to. The Captain and I hadn't been together since that first night and I was quite hungry for more of him. Tim was busy working and training with some of the new fire recruits, Matt being one of them, so he and I hadn't been able to sneak off together. My balls were full of cum and aching to be released and I couldn't seem to keep my mind off of sex. Judging by the half hard cocks I saw in the showers from time to time, I'm guessing my firefighting brothers were experiencing the same frustration as a result of a quiet week. Thursday rolled around and I watched as the new shift rotated in. I was sitting in the dayroom, trying to watch some TV when Tim came in.

"Hey, see ya on Saturday?" he asked.

"You bet buddy!" I chimed back.

"Think he'll show?" he asked again. I shrugged, "How was his attitude with you this week while you were training?" I asked, staring at Tim's crotch my mouth watering as I wanted nothing more than to shuck his jeans down and dive on his cock.

"It was OK, he was pretty reserved, pouty." Tim said. "Catch ya later." Tim said as he headed out the door.

My cock was hard and leaking and I positioned myself so that if someone should walk in, they wouldn't spy my boner. A few of the men from the other shift came in, asked if I was watching the TV and if they could turn it to the baseball game. I nodded that it was OK, sighed, and proceeded to check them out. I wasn't familiar with these two as they were new to our team, I hadn't gotten the chance to know them yet but would love to see what they looked like nude, with hard cocks pointing at my face.

"Dude! You OK?" one of them asked me.

"Hmm?" I responded back coming out of my sex induced fog.

"You looked like you were far away and staring at my crotch!" he said, nudging the other guy in the ribs.

"Oh sorry, no I wasn't staring at your crotch." I said defensively, "LIAR!" I screamed in my head. "It's been a long week and I'm wiped out, ready for my shift to end." I responded back.

"Uh huh. SHIT! You damn umpire, what are you, fucking blind, that guy was out by a mile!" he shouted at the TV, his attention obviously no longer focused on me. I decided to go see what Big Jim was up to and maybe get a quick one in.

The door to his office was open so I walked in only to find that he wasn't there. I looked at the door to his suite and noticed it was slightly ajar and could hear faint sounds coming from his suite so I decided to investigate. I walked in and heard soft moaning and sighing coming from his bedroom. My cock immediately sprang to life as I imagined Big Jim laying on his bed, nude, stroking his hard cock. I turned the corner and stopped dead in my tracks. The Captain was bent over his bed while Michael McKinley was busy fucking this shit out of him. Their backs were

41

to the door and neither apparently heard me enter. Michael McKinley was the shift supervisor, also married, and was a gorgeous red head.

His family was 100% Irish and he was third generation. He had lost the Irish brogue, however, every now and then it would come out, usually around the Holidays when he would spend a great deal of time with his family. I stared, I couldn't help myself, as I watched his powerful ass flex and move and his hips grind his irish cock into Big Jim's back side. They both were panting and softly moaning, movement from the Captain's right arm indicated that he was jerking his big hard cock in time to Mike's thrusts. Mike's back and ass cheeks were covered in a soft sheen of sweat and I licked my lips at the thought of being able to lick that from his back. I heard the Captain grunt a couple of times as his cock emptied it's load all over the bedspread, the smell of fresh cum greeted my nostrils and I sighed, quietly.

I heard Mike whisper to the Captain, "Get ready, I'm gonna fucking blow my load!" and watched him slam into the Captain a couple of times, stiffen and then heard him groan as he emptied his cock into the Captain's ass.

"Fuck this is hot!" I screamed in my head and turned to hurry out of his suite before my presence was detected. I was rock hard and there was no way I was going to hide this boner from any of the other men. I almost felt like the proverbial trapped rat, I couldn't think of a place I could hide in until my cock softened where I wouldn't be noticed. I decided to head to the bathroom and take the chance that no one was in there, maybe I could at least jack my cock.

There are four stalls in the bathroom along with three urinals. The urinals are not divided, so it's a perfect chance to get some eye candy whenever you're taking a leak. The only stall that wasn't being used was one in the middle, so I headed for that one. I closed and locked the door, shucked down my jeans and sat on the toilet. I reached for some toilet paper and noticed that the toilet paper holder was slightly ajar. Figuring it was a loose screw, I started to straighten it when the whole thing came off the wall in my hands.

"Holy shit! How long has THIS been here?" I screamed to myself as I looked at the glory hole someone had drilled through the wall. I looked through it to find the other side was open as well and sitting on the toilet was another fire fighter, I couldn't see a face, stroking a rather sizable hard cock. I watched as the fist belonging to the faceless man slowly stroked the hard cock up and down. He was uncut and I watched in fascination as he twisted and pulled on his foreskin. It didn't take me long to realize that he was putting on a show and it was just for me. I grabbed my own hard cock and stroked as I continued to watch the man play with his cock. He'd completely removed his pants, and now he spread his legs and ran his hand over his ample bull balls. I watched and stroked as he caressed his balls, forgetting his cock for the moment, he pulled and tugged on the skin of his ball sack. I had to taste this mans cock, had to have him down my throat so I put my mouth up to the glory hole and stuck my tongue through the opening. I pulled back to see if I was going to get any sort of reaction, I received none.

I continued to watch him stroke his beautiful cock, it was at this point that I realized he was completely shaved, his pubic hair was gone entirely. I sighed as I continued to imagine what his cock would taste like. I heard a groan in the on the other side and quickly realized that there must be another glory hole over there too.

"Holy fucking shit!" I screamed in my head. "This shift is one giant orgy!" I concluded. My faceless performer stood, walked over and poked his hard cock through the glory hole. I immediately dove on it with my mouth, moaning as I took my first taste of uncut cock, my taste buds exploding in delight over the musky taste of his foreskin. I lapped at his piss slit, coaxing his cock honey out and was rewarded with a steady stream of the sweet nectar.

"Yeah, suck my cock." the faceless voice whispered to me. "Make me cum in your mouth." he continued. I heard a groan and a grunt from the stall next to me and realized the man in that one had just lost his load. I continued to nurse and suck on my uncut friend as he continued to quietly urge me on to getting him off. I was sucking his cock like a mad man, determined to bring him to a quick cum, my hand flying over my own cock as I felt my nuts tighten in preparation of my approaching orgasm. The faceless cock was thrusting into my mouth, faster and faster, he shoved his cock in and out.

The head of his cock thickened and I knew he was close to cumming.

"Get ready, I'm gonna shoot!" He grunted as he slammed his hips into my one last time and cum started shooting out of his cock. I cried out, cum dribbling down my chin, as my own cock started shooting my load. I nursed and sucked his cock clean and would have kept right on sucking him had he not pulled out. I saw movement and put my eye back up to the hole. He bent over to grab his underwear and I was able to catch the side profile of my faceless cock.

"You! It's you!" I screamed to myself as I recognized the newbie from the TV room. He quickly dressed and hurried out of the stall. I sat back down on the toilet, my cock soft and leaking after cum.

"FUCK! I wonder if I can get transferred to this shift?" I thought to myself as I grabbed some toilet paper and started to clean up the cum I'd shot on the floor. Once that was done, I pulled up my jeans, flushed the toilet and headed out of the bathroom.

"Wait till I tell Tim about this!" I thought to myself. I walked back into the TV room, sitting there, cheering and shouting at the TV was the man who's uncut cock I'd just serviced. He was alone so I approached him, leaned down and whispered in his ear, "Nice fucking cock and I love the taste of your cum!".

He froze for just a few minutes, blushed, looked back up at me and said, "That was you?" I nodded in agreement, "Man! You sure know how to fucking suck cock! Thanks buddy!" he smiled and slapped my ass as I turned to go sit back down.

"So, is your whole shift like this?" I asked him.

"Pretty much." He said.

"Holy fuck - I gotta transfer!" I said to myself as I began to imagine the trouble I could get myself into.

CHAPTER 6

Friday finally rolled around and I prepared for the shift change. I was inventorying the medical supplies in the ambulance when Marc Johnson poked his head in the rear door.

"Hey buddy! Ready to head out for a few days?" he asked.

"You bet! What's up?" I asked.

"Awe you know, same same." He replied as he hoisted himself into the rear of the ambulance. Marc Johnson and I had attended EMT training together. He was aspiring to be a doctor and was putting himself through med school. Marc and I had quickly hit it off during our training and done quite a bit of partying and studying together. Marc is a giant of a man, he stands six foot eight and is built in all the right places. He's also black and judging by the sizable mound in his crotch, is rather hung. Marc is also a gentle giant and one of the best EMTs I've had the pleasure to work with. I've often wondered and fantasized about what it would be like to have sex with him. Marc could also have any girl (or guy) he chose, I would watch the stares of both sexes as he would cross the bar, making his way over to our group, while we were in training.

I finished up the inventory of the supplies, turned to Marc and asked him if he was ready to inventory the medicine. He said sure and we back the required cross checking, me telling him what was on hand prior to the shift, what had been used during the shift and him checking the inventory off and verbally telling me if something was being restocked or there were enough on-hand. I must have seemed somewhat distracted, once we had verified our inventory Marc turned to me and asked me if everything was OK.

"Marc, let me ask you something. Is there something particular about this shift?" I asked, realizing just how vague my question sounded.

"Unusual? What do you mean?" He asked back.

"Well, I noticed something out of the ordinary in one of the stalls today." I responded. Looking at Marc I realized he still wasn't following me so I continued. "I'd gone into one of the middle stalls to take care of some business and noticed that one of the toilet paper holders was crooked, when I went to straighten it..." I stopped my sentence as I watched a big smile cross over Marc's face.

"Oh you mean THAT um, unusual stuff. Yeah, there's some really interesting shit that goes on during this shift." Marc said, squirming a little on the bench in the ambulance. Marc looked around, for what I don't know, it was pretty obvious that there was some serious man on man action happening here, looked back at me and asked, "So, you get into that stuff?"

I looked in his eyes for a few minutes before I responded. I noticed that maybe he had either a certain curiosity about this stuff or he was like the rest, balls deep into the action.

"Why do you ask?" I coyly responded.

Marc reached down and adjusted his crotch, "Man, don't be toying with me bitch. You know what I'm talking about, do you get into that stuff?" He asked again. I didn't respond, I waited for his reaction.

"Shit man, c'mon. You know what it's like being here four days straight, no pussy. I mean, yeah, we find ways to get our nut." Marc said.

"So, do you?" I asked him.

"Do I what?" he asked.

"Now who's toying with whom? Do you get off on the man to man action?" I asked point blank.

"Whoa wait buddy, I don't take it up the ass or anything like that, I ain't no one's bitch, but yeah, I've let my cock get sucked a time or two." he said.

"Ever thought about taking it further than that?" I asked him, noticing that he was readjusting his cock again. "Ever thought about fucking another guy in the ass?" I asked again. Marc didn't respond so I figured I'd either hit a nerve and this wasn't boding well for him or I'd hit a nerve and he had given this serious consideration, maybe even taken it to that step already.

"It's time for you to hit the road buddy, maybe we can pick this conversation up again later." Marc said as he began to shut and lock the cabinets.

"Yeah maybe but I'm thinking either you've taken that step or you want to take that step just not sure how far or with whom. Judging by the way you keep adjusting yourself, I'd venture to say I've got your curiosity peaked." I said, hoping like hell that I hadn't crossed a line with him that I ought not cross. Marc was a good friend of mine and I valued that friendship.

"We'll see." Marc said to me. "Hey, before you head out, I'm only on shift tonight, taking a couple days off, you doing anything tomorrow night?" Marc asked.

"Umm, not sure, have some tentative plans in the works but nothing concrete." I replied back, thinking about what I had told Matt.

"Mind if I drop by then?" Marc asked. "We can pick this conversation up and clear the air. I have a feeling you and I walk the same path." Marc said.

I smiled, and said, "Deal! Sevenish?"

Marc smiled back and nodded yes, I patted his thigh as I made my way out of the ambulance, packed my stuff up and headed for home. I walked in the front door, checked the answering machine, four messages from my mother, leafed through the mail and headed to my bedroom to dump my dirty laundry and change out of my uniform. Once that was done I grabbed a beer, popped it open and stood in front of the fridge trying to decide what I wanted for dinner. I opted for a peanut butter and jelly sandwich and quickly devoured it. I decided to call Tim and reached for the phone and dialed his number. After a couple of rings a woman's voice answered and I asked for Tim.

"Hello?" Tim said into the receiver.

"Hey, it's me, who the hell is that?" I asked him.

"Nunya" he responded.

"Nunya?" I replied back.

"Yeah, nunya as in nunya business. What's up?" Tim responded.

"We still on for tomorrow?" I asked. "Yup, hey, gotta go, chat with you tomorrow." Tim said, hanging the phone up before I could say anything. I decided to take a quick shower and just as I was turning to head to the bathroom the door bell rang. I answered to door to find Bill standing there.

"Did you forget we had a date tonight?" He asked as he stepped through the door.

"Well kinda." I replied. "Care for a beer? Help yourself, I'm going to take a quick shower and will be out in a few." I said, turning to head back to the shower. I quickly stripped, turned the water on and entered the shower. I sensed I was not alone and looked up to see Bill standing there, nude, his half hard cock pointing at me through the clear shower door.

"Mind if I join you?" He asked. I opened the door and let him come in, he quickly got behind me and I could feel his now hard cock wedge itself in the crack in my ass. "You OK? You seem a little tense." Bill said as he reached up and started massaging my shoulders.

"Yeah, I'm OK, oh man that feels good and so does that." I said, squeezing my ass cheeks around his cock. "Been a trying couple of days at work, oh yeah, feel that knot? Yeah, right there!" I cooed and purred as his magic hands worked on my shoulders.

It really hadn't been a trying couple of days, I was a little tense about Tim and the girl that he'd be banging tonight and maybe a little tense too regarding the stunt Matt had pulled. I closed my eyes and let myself go as Bill's hands worked my shoulders, neck and across my shoulder blades.

My cock was responding to his touch and I reached back and pulled his hard cock down and tucked it between my legs. The head of his cock nudged against my balls and I sighed as my pulse began to quicken. Bill had pulled me to him and was now gently kissing my neck and licking and nibbling on my ear lobes while his hands toyed with my nipples.

"Oh fuck that feels good Bill, feels so fucking good." I said.

"Umm, you taste good too, I like that salty-sweaty taste on a guy." as he continued to nibble and lick my neck and ears. I turned my head and Bill leaned further forward, our lips parting, tongues dueling with one another as the heat from our passion continued to build. While Bill kissed me I felt his cock pull out from between my legs and his finger begin to gently rub my hole. I groaned at his touch and he purred in my ear and told me how he couldn't wait to get his cock back in my ass again. My cock flexed and a drop of clear juice formed at the tip of the piss slit. I turned so that we were facing one another and continued our kissing, our hands roaming up and down over each other's backs and ass cheeks. I decided to get brave and daring and would dip my finger into the crack of his ass, each time eliciting a moan or a sigh from him.

"Turn around I want to introduce you to something." I said, nudging him, hoping he's going to follow my lead on this and not ask any questions. He looked at me and reluctantly turned his back to me.

"Now just relax and let me take you to a new level." I whispered in his ear as I began to kiss his neck, moving lower and lower until I was at the top of his ass. I gently licked and nipped his ass cheeks, occasionally darting my tongue into his ass crack. I continued to be rewarded by his moans and sighs and was even shocked when he started to thrust his ass back towards me. Figuring it was either now or never, I gently pulled his cheeks apart, darted my tongue out and made contact with his virgin rose bud. Bill gasped and jerked, I wasn't too sure he was going to let me finish.

"Oh fuck...yeah..." he groaned. I licked his hole, licked around his hole, down between his legs, up the crack of his ass until he was writhing and moaning, his hips grinding on my mouth as I gave him an expert rim job. I stood up, my cock lodging itself in his ass, the head of my dick nudging against his hole. Bill immediately flexed his cheeks and let me know that the entrance was not open.

"C'mon, let's get out of here and head for the bedroom." I said as I reached to turn the water off. We stepped out of the shower, quickly dried ourselves, and standing in the bathroom resumed kissing. I pulled off his mouth, led him to the bed and had him lay on his stomach. Bill looked at me, unsure as to what I was going to do and I just smiled, patting his ass, I told him to relax that I wasn't going to do anything that he didn't want done. I told Bill to raise his ass up in the air and again, looking at me with an unsure look on his face, did as he was told. I moved in behind him and stroked my cock while I just gazed at his beautiful ass. Bill's cock was rock hard, a thin line of clear juice hung from the tip of his cock as the bead made contact with the bed spread. I leaned forward and went back to eating his ass.

Bill gasped again when my tongue made initial contact and before long he was bucking his ass back onto my tongue, actually fucking himself on my face. His cock continued to pour out juice and I reached between his legs, pulled it back and licked the clear nectar from the head of his cock. I thought Bill was going to cum that very minute the way he groaned and bucked. I then went back to eating his ass, alternating between his hole, his balls and the head of his cock. After a few minutes of that, Bill was panting and moaning his appreciation. I decided he was fired up enough to take the next step so I took the tip of my finger, ran in round the head of his cock, using his pre-cum as lube and gently started rubbing his hole. Bill gasped and bucked and his cock head flared again. Between my eating his ass and his pre-cum, his ass was wet enough that I could start sliding my finger inside him. I slowly and gently worked my finger in him, all the while he bucked and writhed and moaned, biting my pillow to keep from shouting out.

"Yeah Bill, that's it, let it out, scream if you want to. You like that?" I said.

"Uh huh...ohhh fuck..." He whined as his ass continued to accept my finger. Before long I had made contact with his prostrate gland and started pushing down on it. Bill's cock flexed and a stream of pre-cum poured out. He screamed out his pleasure as I rubbed my finger over his love nut.

"Oh fuck, oh fuck!" He continued to moan. I started to add another finger and Bill tensed as he realized what I was doing.

"Shhh...just relax, I'm not going to hurt you." I said as I rubbed the head of his wet cock head with the thumb of my other hand. Bill's thighs were quivering and I knew I was taking him to a level he'd never thought was possible.

I felt his cock harden even more, the mushroom head turning purple and expanding and knew he was close to shooting. I wanted him to cum on my cock so I could use that as lube and hopefully introduce him to anal sex. I rose to me knees and placed my cock underneath his as my second finger continued to enter him. I soon had two fingers in his tight, very tight, hole and once they both started working his prostrate it pushed Bill over the edge. He shouted he was going to cum, reared his ass back on my fingers and I felt the first splash of his hot cum wash over my cock. I continued to rub my thumb around the head of his dick as he came, shouting, whining, bucking, humping my hand Bill let his orgasm wash over him.

"Oh God, please, oh God, oh fuck yeah." Bill shouted and screamed as his cock continued to shoot. I began pulling my fingers, slowly from his ass.

"No, no, don't take them out, please, oh fuck it feels so good, no please, don't take them out, fuck me with your fingers, please oh fuck..." Bill panted and moaned.

"I'm going to fuck you with something better Bill." I softly said as I stroked my cock, using his massive load to lube my dick up. I took the rest of his cum and rubbed it on his hole then leaned in and gave him another rimming. Bill's cock never went soft and he continued to beg for me to be inside his ass.

"Relax Bill, push out while I'm pushing in, you ready?" I asked. Bill nodded his head as he continued to pant and whine and moan. I placed the head of my cock to the entrance of his ass and started to gently enter him.

"Ohhh..." Bill cried out as his lips parted to accept my cock. "Ohhh fuck..." He cried as my head pushed past the ring of his ass. I stopped, letting him get used to me being inside him. "Hurts, it hurts, take it out, please oh GOD it hurts." Bill cried, trying to push the head of my cock out of his ass.

"You'll get used to it, just relax." I said as I reached between his legs and started slowly stroking his cock again. Bill moaned and bucked as he fucked his cock in my fist. I felt Bill's ass relax around my cock so I proceeded to push further into him, going slowly, ever so slowly, allowing his virgin ass to accept the new sensation he was feeling. Bill continued to moan and sigh as I continued to fill his sweet ass.

"Ohhh...Ohhh fuck...oh fuck..." he suddenly screamed out as the head of my cock pushed over his prostrate. "Oh fuck...oh I'm gonna, I'm gonna, I'm...aaaayyyeeeee!!" Bill shouted out as his cock fired another load again. I cupped my hand over the head of cock, catching some of load, I quickly fed it to him. "Umm...Unnnggg..." he moaned as he greedily licked his cum from my hand, sucking my fingers in.

"Fuck me, fuck me Craig. OH shit, I gotta cock in my ass, oh fuck it feels good." Bill cried out as he started bucking his hips on my cock. I quickly flipped us over so that he was facing away from me and on top. Bill quickly spun himself around on my cock and I watched his cock bounce up and down, slapping my stomach, as he fucked himself on my cock.

"Yeah, yeah, oh fuck yeah, fuck me with your cock. Oh God, I got your beautiful hard cock up my ass, oh fuck..." Bill shouted as he bounced and ground his hips on my cock.

"Cum in my ass! I want your fucking big load up my ass! Yeah, oh fuck yeah, fucking shoot that cum in me!" Bill screamed.

"Yeah? You want my load up your sweet ass?" I cried out. "Fucking get ready, I'm getting close! Your sweet hot tight ass is going make me cum!" I screamed.

Just then Bill shoved his ass down on my cock, his eyes widened and he screamed at the top of his lungs as his final orgasm took over. His cock erupted, showering me in ropes of his cum. His ass flexing around my cock pushed me over the edge. I grabbed his hips, pulled him up and shoved him back down on my cock again, shouted, and pumped my own cum inside his ass. Bill whined and cried and shouted out as he felt my cock flood his ass with my cum. He fell forward on top of me and started kissing me hard, his tongue fucking my throat. I felt his cock flex again and another torrent of cum shot out as I fired my last volley of cum deep in his guts. My face was covered with his load and Bill quickly went to work, cleaning it off my face, feeding it back to me.

He moaned and whined and purred and continued to buck his ass up and down on my now wilting cock. "More, I want more, yeah, more." He moaned as he slurped and licked down my body, eventually taking my cum covered cock in his mouth and cleaning me off. "Umm, unngg." He moaned while he managed to suck my spent dick back to life again. His cock was rock hard again and he turned himself around so we were in a 69, his drooling cock poised over my lips.

"More, give me more, cum in my mouth." He begged. I sucked his cock in my mouth, tasting his load, and ran my fingers over his freshly fucked ass. Bill yelped and bucked at the sensation. I could see my load beginning to ooze out of his hole and I used my finger to wipe it around his hole. Bill pulled off my cock, screamed again, and I felt his cock twitch and flex as another orgasm hit him. Nothing came out of his cock though, he'd drained his balls dry. I muffled I was going to cum again and Bill dove back down on my cock, sucking me until my orgasm hit as well. Finally spent, Bill rolled off of me and collapsed on the bed, panting, his forehead covered in sweat. We lay still and quiet for a few minutes, each one of us collecting ourselves.

"Fuck, what the fuck just happened?" Bill panted. "What did you do to me?" He asked.

"Did you like it?" I asked back.

"Shit! Did I like it? Oh my GOD! That's the best fucking sex I've ever had. I had no idea it could feel that good!" Bill exclaimed, reaching between his legs and feeling the pouting lips of his freshly fucked ass.

"Ow!" He cringed.

"Sore?" I asked. He nodded yes, "You will be for a few days my friend. You fucked yourself on my cock pretty hard for a first time." I continued.

"Oh man, fuck, that was HOT!" Bill panted. We laid there a little while longer, got up and headed back to the shower, this time to clean the cum and sweat off our bodies. Bill looked as though he was in a trance the entire time. I kept asking him if he was OK and he kept reassuring me he was, just overwhelmed with what had happened. We cleaned ourselves up, and once we were dried threw our clothes back on.

"I should go." Bill said as I walked him towards the door.

"You don't have to." I said back.

"No I really do, I, I..." He stopped, looking at me he leaned in, kissed me, turned and then headed out the door. I closed and locked the door behind him and smiled, "I think I could fall in love with him." I thought, frowned, shook the thought from my head and sat down to watch some TV before turning in for the night.

CHAPTER 7

I was awakened on Saturday morning in the normal way, rock hard cock and full to bursting bladder. Funny things start happening to your body around the age of 40, one being that it seems that your bladder shrivels to the size of a thimble, another being that the days of sleeping until noon seem to come to an end, at least for me they did as my bladder wakes me sharply at five in the morning daily. I got up, emptied my bladder and crawled back in bed, not quite ready to get up. Closing my eyes, I toyed with one of my nipples while I stroked my cock, playing several different scenarios in my imagination on what Tim and I were going to do to Matt.

I finally settled on making Matt the filling in a man sandwich and stroked my cock to orgasm. I quickly cleaned up, showered and greeted the day of errands before our evening encounter were to begin. One thing I definitely needed to do was call Tim and run over a few things with him about tonight. I would also need to try and get a hold of Marc and push his visit to tomorrow. I no sooner had reached for the phone when it rang.

"Hello?" I answered.

"Hey buddy!" Tim's voice responded back.

"S'up?" I asked. "Oh man, I banged the hottest chick...oh you probably don't want to hear about that do you?" Tim said.

"Um, no not really, we still on for tonight?" I responded back.

"Shit yeah! Can't wait to knock that arrogant mother-fucker down a peg or two." Tim shouted back.

"Well, we told him to be here around five, wanna come over say about four? We can grab a quick bite to eat, better yet, stop on your way over and grab a pizza!" I said.

"Sure thing buddy, shit, my cock's hard just thinking about nailing that little shit!" Tim said.

"Easy buddy, settle down! See ya tonight!" I replied back and hung the phone up. I realized I didn't have Marc's phone number and called the station to see if the Captain would give me that information. He did and I quickly dialed his number.

"Hello?" Marc answered, sleepily.

"Marc? Hey, it's Craig. Did I wake you?" I asked.

"Yeah, it's freaking seven in the morning dude!" He replied back, sounding rather annoyed that he was woken up this early.

"Sorry, forget that not everyone is an early bird. Say, can we get together tomorrow rather than tonight?" I asked.

"Huh? Wha...oh yeah, yeah, um, sure, I'll give you a call." Marc said and then hung up the phone.

I set the phone back in the receiver and headed out to take care of my morning chores. I saw Bill heading out of his garage on his bike, he pulled up and we casually chatted for a few minutes before he took his leave and rode off. "Umm umm umm...gorgeous, gorgeous ass..." I thought to myself, my cock stirring in my own shorts.

I spent the morning running my errands and was back at the house by noon. I decided to quickly tidy things up, not that I'm a slob, I'm a rather neat housekeeper, but there were some things I'd left out that needed to be put away and a light dusting wouldn't hurt either. I'd just finished dusting when the doorbell rang. I answered the door and was greeted by a man, holding his arm in one hand, a gash on his forearm.

"Hi, listen my name is Mark, Mark Andrews and I'm your other neighbor. Can you help me out? I know you're an EMT and I was trimming some of the shrubs in my backyard and, well, looks like I cut myself." he said.

I'd seen my other neighbor, but only in passing and usually as we were both heading out the door to work. I invited him in, telling him that he really should have called 911 if he thought his cut was that bad. I escorted him to the kitchen, had him sit down while I grabbed my EMT bag.

"I'm Craig, Craig McFadden by the way, nice to meet you!" I chirped as I proceeded to clean his wound. Once his wound was cleaned I quickly realized he really should have gone to the ER. "Buddy, you're going to need some stitches, I'll get this dressed then will drive you over to the ER." I said.

He hissed as I applied some peroxide to the cut to flush out any debris. I quickly bandaged him and making sure his house was locked up and he had his keys, locked my own house and off we went. We arrived at the ER and they took him in right away, the ER was empty for a change, normally it's full and there is at least a three hour wait for non-life threatening injuries or illnesses. I took this opportunity to check him out. He was absolutely gorgeous, sandy brown hair, thick, neatly trimmed, square set jaw, aqua blue eyes with a Roman style nose, full lips. I was already half hard and still hadn't finished checking out the rest of his body. He was wearing a wife beater that showed off his well defined bi-ceps and broad shoulders. A tuft of reddish brown hair peeking out from the top of his shirt. His chest was just as muscular as the rest of him, his pecs and hard nipples clinging to his shirt. I followed his abs down to his shorts. They were the type of shorts that I remember our gym teachers wearing, the kind that were of a polyester type blend but that clung to the thighs, ass and emphasized the crotch. He was sitting down on the gurney so it was difficult to tell how big his package might be, but this thighs and calves were also well sculpted and coated in the same reddish brown fur as what was peeking out of the top of his shirt.

"OK, you're all set. Go home, take it easy, make sure you change your dressing a couple times today. Do not get it wet, use a grocery bag or saran wrap and cover it when you shower. You don't want those stitches getting wet. We're phoning in an antibiotic to your pharmacy, just in case, along with some pain killers for you. Follow up in a week with your primary care physician." The attending ER resident explained.

Mark thanked him, hopped off the gurney and said "let's go." I let him pass by me so I could check out his ass and what a great ass it was too! Two beautiful melon like globes, firm, pouty, just begging to be parted to reveal the pink treasure hidden inside. "Oh fuck! Note to Craig, feel this one out, see if he's available." I thought to myself as I thanked the ER doctor and followed after him. We got into my car and started to head back to the house.

"Thanks. Thanks a lot for helping me out, I really appreciate it." Mark said.

"No problem!" I responded back, looking at him and taking a quick glance at his crotch, "DAMN! Still no indication!" I screamed inside my head. I pulled into my driveway and he hopped out, thanking me again, and headed back over to his house. Glancing at my watch I realized it was now a quarter till four and Tim would be here in a few minutes. I ran inside the house, took a quick shower to get the hospital smell off of me and threw on a pair of shorts and T-shirt and anxiously waited. Tim arrived on time and we drank a beer and ate the pizza he brought with him, both of us brushing our teeth afterward to make sure we didn't have garlic or onion on our breath.

Matt arrived right on time and as I opened the door to let him in, was rather shocked to see he was dressed in a simple T-shirt, bib overalls and boots of some sort. "Bibs?" I snorted. "Ya thinking you're going to a ho-down?" I giggled as he passed by me.

Matt was not the same, arrogant, flippant person he was at the fire station. He seemed quite subdued, almost as if he really didn't want to go through with this. "Look, let's just get this over with." Matt said, blushing with what seemed like embarrassment as he reached to unsnap one of the straps on his bibs.

"What crawled up your ass?" Tim asked.

"NOTHING!" Matt snapped back as he unfastened the other strap and let his bib overalls fall to the ground. Matt was not wearing any underwear and was rock hard, his cock jutting out. He wasn't nearly as thick as I thought, in fact, his cock was slender, a tip of clear juice forming at the slit in his mushroom head. Tim approached him and he flinched as he reached out and wrapped his hand around his cock. I quickly pulled my shorts down and off, revealing my own hard cock and walked up behind him, nudging my cock between his legs. Matt stiffened again as he felt the head of my cock slide between his legs and nestle against his balls, stimulating the area between his ball-sack and his pucker.

I looked at Tim and we exchanged a knowing glance, that being that Matt was being forced to go through with this but some unseen and unknown pressure. I had a pretty good idea I knew who was making him go through with this. Tim and I quickly helped him get completely undressed and we did the same, both us resuming our previous positions. Matt sighed as Tim bent forward and started licking one of his nipples while his hand caressed his cock. I heard Matt sigh again as I went to work, licking and kissing the back of his neck, giving him goose bumps, as I worked my way up to his ear lobes.

Tim and I caught each other's glance and Tim winked at me as he placed his hands on Matt's shoulders and pushed down, indicating to Matt that he wanted him to start sucking his cock. Knowing Tim's quick trigger on the first go around, my pulse quickened as my mind quickly played out Tim filling Matt's mouth with his initial load of cum, which by the way, was always a big load. Matt was on his knees, staring at Tim's hard cock. He opened his mouth and, sticking his tongue out, took a hesitant lick on Tim's head.

"Oh buddy boy, you're going to have to do better than that! Suck it, c'mon, open up and suck my cock!" Tim growled. A shudder went through Matt as he opened his mouth and took just the tip of Tim's cock into his mouth.

"Take it all bitch!" Tim growled again as he thrust his hips forward, shoving the head of his cock completely into Matt's mouth. Matt groaned and I watched his cock flex and twitch as he took Tim's cock into his mouth. Matt pulled back a little then moved his head forward again, taking more of Tim's cock into his mouth.

"Oh yeah boy, that's it, fucking suck my cock!" Tim moaned. I watched Tim's balls draw up in their sack and knew he was going to blow his load at any moment. Matt pulled back again and had half of the head of Tim's cock in mouth when he came. Matt started coughing and sputtering, backing completely off of Tim's cock and letting cum shoot in his face.

"You fucker!" Matt shouted at him, cum running down his chin and foaming around his lips. "That shit's nasty!" Matt cried as Tim shot the rest of his load on Matt's chest. Tim and I just chuckled as Matt stood, wiping the cum off of his face with the back of his hand and smearing it along his thigh. "I can't believe you did that!" Matt cried again.

Tim and I looked at each other, nodded to one another and sank to our knees at the same time. Tim sucked Matt's now deflating cock into his mouth and quickly went to work while I pulled the cheeks of his ass apart and started eating his freshly washed pink hole. Matt cried out at the sensations that his body was sending him, not sure which area he liked the best, having his cock sucked by an expert or his ass eaten by another expert. Either way, his body sensation was in overload and within a few minutes Matt had his head thrown back and was panting and whining, mumbling how good it felt. Matt suddenly stiffened, thrust his cock down Tim's throat and shot is load, Tim swallowing and sucking, coaxing his full load out of his balls.

"Oh fuck!" Matt panted as his orgasm ended just as quickly as it hit him. "Well, thanks guys, guess I better go." Matt said.

"Not so fast!" I replied. "We aren't done with you yet." Tim added.

"But...I don't think I can...oh...oh fuck yeah..." Matt groaned as we both went back to work on him, Tim on his cock, me on his ass. Matt was quick to recover and his hard cock was again sliding in and out of Tim's throat. Tim pulled off his cock and led Matt to the couch.

"Wha...what are you going to do?" Matt asked nervously as I stood in front of him, turned around, bent over the couch and offered my ass to Matt.

"You're going to eat my hole!" I squealed.

"But, I..."Matt stuttered as Tim pushed him into a squatting position, his face right at my ass. Matt stuck his tongue out and took a quick taste of my ass. He paused a few seconds, trying to decide if he liked it or not, then started giving me an expert rim job.

"OH yeah bitch! Look at you, fucking eating my ass! Yeah, fucking feels good!!" I shouted, surprised that for someone who seemed to be so reluctant could be doing such a great job at eating me out. While Matt rimmed and licked me, darting his tongue in and out of my hole, fucking me with it, Tim crawled underneath him and proceeded to rim him out along with suck his balls and work on his cock. Within a few minutes, Matt was going to town on my ass and bucking and grinding his hips on Tim's mouth, groaning and panting the entire time. Tim decided Matt was ready for a few fingers and Matt stiffened and groaned as Tim started sliding two fingers into his well eaten and wet ass. Matt took Tim's cue and started to do the same to my ass, my cock responding by releasing a river of clear juice.

"Oh fuck yeah Matt, yeah, fuck me, fuck my ass!" I groaned as he added two more fingers to my ass and was now fucking me with three fingers.

"Give me your cock Matt, c'mon, slide that fucking cock of yours up my ass!" I panted. Matt removed his fingers and I heard him spit and slick up his cock. I moaned as I felt the head of his slender cock begin to enter my ass. Matt gently fed me his cock and I sighed and panted as he slowly slid his fuck stick inside me.

"Oh fuck yeah Matt, goddamned but that cock of yours feels fucking good up my ass." I shouted. Matt remained still and I soon heard him grunt and realized that Tim must be sliding his cock into Matt.

"FUCK! It hurts, it fucking hurts, take it out, take it out!" Matt cried out.

"Ssshh...just relax, push out, like you're taking a shit." Tim purred and cooed in his ear. "God your ass is so fucking tight, so fucking tight." Tim continued.

"No, please, no, I can't, take it out, take it...oh...oh yeah, oh fuck, what's happening, oh fuck, feels, feels, so good!" Matt cried out as Tim had now buried his entire cock up Matt's ass and was standing still letting Matt get used to it.

"Oh God, oh fuck, I got my cock buried and I have a cock, oh shit, shit, shit, shit." Matt panted as he began to thrust in and out, each time he would groan and cry out as he experienced the sensation of his cock fucking a tight ass while another cock slid in and out of him. Tim remained motionless and let Matt do the work, fucking my ass while at the same time riding Tim's cock. Within a few minutes Matt was fucking and riding us like a mad man. Slamming into me and thrusting himself forcefully back on Tim, crying out and shouting as he did this. Tears streamed down Matt's face as the feeling of the new experience overwhelmed him. My cock was rock hard and threatening to shoot, I kept reaching between my legs and wiping the clear juice from the head of my swollen cock and licking it from my hand and fingers.

"Oh fuck yeah, c'mon Matt, pound my fucking ass! Fuck me hard you young pup! Yeah, slam that fucking cock into me, c'mon bitch, fuck the cum out of my cock!" I screamed as my orgasm approached. Tim was groaning and his hips were shaking as he continued to let Matt ride his cock, his own cum building up and threatening to spill out.

Matt's eyes opened wide and he shouted, "Fuck, I'm gonna cum, I'm gonna fucking cum!" He slammed into me one last time and my cock erupted as I felt the first bolt of jizz shoot out of his cock deep into my guts. Tim screamed and slammed his cock into Matt as he flooded the inside of his ass with his own load. The three of us bucked and groaned and shouted as we came, Matt pulling out of my ass and letting the last of his cum shoot on my back.

This was undoubtedly one of the hottest fuck sessions I'd had and judging by Tim and Matt's responses, theirs too. Tim pulled his softening cock out of Matt's ass and Matt fell to his knees, resting his cheek on my ass, panting as he came down off his orgasm.

"Uh Matt, I need to move, my back is fucking stiff!" I moaned as I rolled over and collapsed on the couch, my dripping cock making contact with Matt's forehead.

Matt leaned up and sucked my cock back into his mouth, groaning as he tasted the remnants of my load. Matt's cock quickly hardened again and he started stroking his cock, his other hand reaching between his legs, his fingers rubbing the cum into the lips of his freshly fucked ass. Matt continued to slurp and lick on my cock, as powerful as my orgasm was, I knew I was done for the night so I let him suck on my cock like a baby sucking a pacifier. Tim's cock was hard again and he stood over Matt, stroking his dick while Matt sucked my cock and furiously stroked his own cock.

"Yeah Matt, suck his fucking cock. C'mon, let me see you shoot your fucking load." Tim said as he moved his cock closer and closer to Matt's mouth. Matt groaned and sighed as he nursed on my cock.

"Shit Matt, that's fucking hot, yeah, c'mon fucker, shoot your load. I'm fucking close bitch, real fucking close and I want to see you shoot while I cum on your face!" Tim shouted.

Matt spit out my cock, arched his back and shot a load all over his stomach. Tim stiffened, groaned and then shouted as Matt sucked his cock into his mouth and started swallowing what little cum Tim's cock shot out.

"Shit yeah! That was fucking hot!" I said as Matt continued to nurse and lick and suck the cum out of Tim's cock. As Matt came down off his experience, what had just happened to him started settling in his mind.

"Fuck guys, shit man, I'm sorry!" Matt said as he burst into tears. "I'm so fucking sorry I did that to you, I just, I mean, oh fuck I'm sorry guys." Matt continued to sob, his shoulders heaving.

"Matt, dude, it's OK." I said.

"I fucked up, I fucked up big time." Matt cried. Tim and I just let Matt cry it out, whatever it was he felt he needed to cry out anyway. Matt quickly got himself collected, looking at the both of us, his cock half hard he asked if we could do this again.

"Tonight?" Tim asked, looking at Matt like he was out of his mind.

"Matt, not tonight, but yeah, we can do this again if you want." I replied as Matt finished getting dressed.

"Thanks guys! See ya at work on Monday Tim." Matt said.

"You bet!" Tim replied, slapping Matt on the ass as Matt headed out the door.

"PHEW! That was fucking HOT!" I said as I put my arms around Tim and kissed him. "Tim, no more, I'm fucking wiped!" I said as I felt Tim's cock start to jut out and snake it's way up my crotch.

"Hey, I'm wiped too but obviously, someone has a mind of his own!" He said, pointing to his cock.

"Well, put it to fucking sleep!" I said as I playfully batted at his now hard cock.

"Ungh!" Tim shouted, stiffened as another orgasm took hold of him, this time though his cock was dry, his balls drained from the load he'd dumped into Matt's ass.

"Well, THAT was interesting!" Tim panted as his cock quickly softened.

"C'mon bitch, let's go to bed!" I said, grabbing Tim's hand and leading him to my room. We both collapsed on the bed and quickly fell asleep, our cocks waking us up a few hours later. I cried out as Tim entered me from behind and he quickly fucked me again, our orgasms quickly overtaking us, neither of us producing any cum. We fell back asleep, Tim's cock still buried in my ass, his head nestled in the crook of my neck.

CHAPTER 8

Tim has this uncanny way of sneaking out in the middle of the night and tonight was no different. I woke up and quickly realized that Tim had left at some point and I'd spent the rest of the night alone. I was thinking of my neighbor next door and soon realized that I'd been neglecting my own trees and shrubs and decided to make good use of my Sunday morning.

It took me a couple of hours to trim the shrubs and had set up my step ladder to reach the trees. I climbed up the ladder and started working on thinning out some of the overgrowth. I always make it a point to keep my cell phone on me, usually in one of the pockets of my shorts, when I'm working in the back yard. I do this mostly in the event I get called in to work, which happens from time to time, but also as a safety precaution in the event I fall or something happens. Today would be the day I'd get to put that theory to work. I hadn't been more than 15 minutes into my trimming project when I heard a sharp crack as the step on the wooden ladder I was standing on gave way. I fell off the ladder with the ladder landing on me, fortunately not landing on the side that my cell phone was.

"Shit! OW, FUCK!" I cursed as I tried to kick the ladder off of me, suddenly aware of a sharp pain in my right arm. I fished out my cell phone, dialed 911 and proceeded to tell the operator what had happened and where I was at. She stayed on the line with me, just in case I might have a concussion, until I heard shouts coming from the gate.

"It's open! I'm back here! Can't miss me, I'm the guy on the...oh hello!" I said as the EMT made his way over to me.

"Thanks operator, they are here." I said as I hung up the phone. "Hi! I've fallen and I can't..." I started to say, noticing the annoyed look on the EMTs face, you can just imagine how many times we hear that, and quickly shut up.

"So, what happened?" the EMT said. The name tag on his shirt read Mike.

"Craig, Craig McFadden, nice to meet you..." I said.

"Mike, Mike Ormsby, what happened Craig?" He said as he began to take my vitals. I filled him in one what had happened as he took my vitals, checked me for a possible concussion and satisfied I didn't have one, helped me sit up. Mike hushed me as he listened to my lungs, taking the required deep breaths in and out, I let my eyes roam over the lone EMT. He was very well built, dark brown hair, cropped short on the side and spiked on top, crystal blue eyes set in a round face with thin lips. I took in Mike's body, his EMT shirt fit snugly, brown hair poked out of the top button. I could tell he was very well built, his pecs firm and solid, his waist narrow as I followed it down to his, shorts? He was wearing shorts? That's odd for an EMT, safety precautions...and then my eyes made contact with his crotch and my mouth instantly began to water. He was squatting and his shorts had ridden up enough that his crotch was perfectly outlined. I had no idea what he was packing but judging by the fullness of his crotch, I wanted so bad to find out.

"Hello? Craig, Craig, you with me?" I heard him say, snapping me out of my sexual coma.

"Huh?" I said. "I asked you where your pain is." Mike responded, a slight smile crossing his face as he surely had just busted me checking him out.

"Oh uh, my OW! FUCK!" I said as he grabbed the arm I'd been favoring.

"C'mon, let's get you up and in the house." Mike said as he gently lifted me to my feet, I glanced down again and now his crotch seemed even fuller. My cock began to stir in my own shorts, and since I hadn't bothered to put on any underwear, hoped that he hadn't noticed the tenting that my cock was now doing.

I looked at him, sighing internally as I stared sideways at him, "You're by yourself?" I asked him.

"Yeah, freaking newbies, they both called in today." Mike said as we made our way inside the house. I groaned as he helped me sit down on the couch and then screamed out again as he bumped against my arm while he was laying me down on the couch. "Sorry about that." He said as he squatted down again next to me and started checking the glands in my throat, for what I don't know, this wasn't part of the normal routine.

"What's up with the shorts?" I asked. "Safety precautions dictate…" I was interrupted.

"I know what the safety precautions are, I'm by myself today so won't be responding to anything major. It's too freaking hot for pants so there you go, write me up if you like, don't really care." Mike snapped back.

"Whoa dude, sorry, didn't mean to make you mad. I was just asking." I snapped back.

"Sorry Craig, really sorry. It's been a helluva fucking month and I guess today was just the straw the broke my back. I need to cut this shirt off of you so I can check for broken ribs." He said as he grabbed his scissors and started cutting my T-shirt up the center.

I thought I heard him gasp a little as he opened the front of my T-shirt, revealing my chest and firm stomach muscles with a pleasure trail of fur leading into the waist band of my shorts. I winced as he began to work my arm again, moving it in different directions, checking to see if there were any fractures.

"Well the good news is I doubt very seriously your arm is broken, more likely a bad sprain." he said, standing, I stared at his crotch, noticing that it definitely was much fuller than before. "I'm going to leave you a sling and you'll need to follow up with your primary care physician at the earliest. If I take you in to the ER, you'll wait forever for nothing. I'm also going to leave you some pain pills…" he didn't get to finish as I cried out in pain, fake pain I might add.

"My thigh, my thigh, oh it hurts." I cried out.

"All right, let's check this out too. Um, gotta remove your shorts." He said.

"I can't, oh I can't, the pain, it's just too much." I put on my best act. He shrugged, grabbed his scissors and proceeded to cut my shorts off. My hard cock reared up and slapped my stomach, Mike gasped as the head of my cock brushed against his lips.

"I think I see the problem." Mike said as he took hold of my cock and guided it towards his mouth. I groaned as his lips closed over the head of my cock and he began to suck my hard cock down his throat. Mike moaned as he deep throated me, the vibrations sending ripples of pleasure down my cock.

"Oh yeah, feeling much better now, much better." I groaned.

Mike spit out my cock, looked at me and said, "I think I know something else that would make you feel better." as he stood and proceeded to remove his shirt. I gasped as he revealed his chest. His pecs were rock hard, as were his dime sized nipples. Hair fanned out across his pecs and down across his ripped abs. My cock flexed and a bead of clear sweet juice formed at the tip. Mike kept his blue eyes on me as he unbuttoned and unzipped his shorts, letting them fall to his feet, kicking them off.

I moaned as I saw his cock sticking out over the waistband of his low cut bikini briefs. His rock hard cock throbbed and I marveled at how thick he was and how even thicker the beautiful mushroom shaped head of his dick was. He had to be at least nine inches in length and two inches thick with a plum sized head sitting on top of his sweet cock. He lowered his briefs, revealing two large balls that hung low and heavy in his sack, both churning, building up a load of cum for me. My cock flexed again and I felt my hot pre-cum run out onto my stomach. Mike squatted back down and licked the pool of clear juice from my bush and then returned to sucking my hard cock, his hand searching between my legs for my hole, my legs naturally parting to give him access.

"God you are huge!" I gasped, trying to nudge his thigh so he could feed me his beautiful cock.

"Let's get you more comfortable." Mike said as he proceeded to gently lift me in his arms and head towards where he thought the bedroom was. He was right on course as he entered my room and laid me down on my bed. He got us into a 69 position, the pain in my arm forgotten as he guided his cock to my waiting lips, my tongue darting out and lapping up the sweet nectar that was beginning to ooze from the mammoth head of his cock. I quickly sucked his cock down to my throat and groaned as he returned to sucking my hard cock and playing with my ass. We nursed and sucked on each other's cocks for what seemed like an eternity. I pulled off of his cock and proceeded to take in his ass, my eyes admiring the firm meaty globes of each cheek that naturally parted revealing his sweet pucker. Mike scooted forward, pulling my legs back he planted his mouth on my hole and began to feast on my ass. This put his ass right at my mouth level and I returned the favor, both of us sighing and moaning as our tongues made contact on each other's holes. I licked and tongued his sweet pucker, his cock flexing and throbbing, clear juice running out and coating my chest. Mike reared up and shoved his ass on my tongue and started fucking himself on me.

"Oh fuck yeah, GOD eat that hole! C'mon, fucking eat my tight hole!" He shouted as he stroked my cock. Mike continued to hump and grind his ass on my face as I proceeded to devour him, my tongue opening him up, tasting him.

"Fuck yeah, oh fuck yeah, fucking eat my ass. You like that ass don't ya? Yeah, like fucking eating my tight hole." Mike shouted.

"Uh huh" I grunted as he went back to sucking on my cock. My balls were beginning to draw up in their sack as my orgasm began to build. Mike sensed this and pulled off my cock.

"Oh no, not yet, no, I don't want you to fucking cum yet." He growled at me. "Yeah, oh fuck yeah, eat that ass. I want to fuck the cum out of you, fucking shove my big cock up your ass and fuck you until you shoot." He said, pulling his ass off my mouth and quickly moving in between my legs, the head of his cock poking at the entrance of my hole.

"Yeah, oh fuck yeah, give me your hard cock. C'mon, fucking give me that big hard cock!" I shouted as I felt the head of his dick begin to enter me. Mike entered me very slowly, giving me plenty of time to get used to the mammoth head on his cock. He had the head of his dick about half way in when I felt the first jabs of pain. I winced and pushed out causing Mike to groan as more of my ass sucked him in. I drew my legs back further, allowing him more room to enter me and my ass suddenly relaxed and started sucking his cock in. Mike shouted and groaned as his cock slid into my ass, I sighed as I felt his pubes tickling my taint, knowing I had him completely inside me.

"Fuck, oh fuck." I panted. "Your cock feels so fucking good in my ass, yeah, c'mon, fuck me. Fuck the cum out of me!" I groaned as I began to grind my hips down on his rock hard cock. Clear cock honey was pouring out of the tip of my cock as Mike began to increase his thrusting.

"Oh fuck yeah, your ass is so tight around my hard cock. Oh you're gonna make me cum soon." Mike groaned into my ear.

"No, no, not yet, stop. God this feels good, you gotta cum in my mouth. I want to taste that fucking load of yours." I grunted back as I clamped my thighs around him, stopping him from fucking me anymore, letting his cock calm down.

"Yeah? You want my fucking load down your throat? I cum gallons, think you can handle that?" Mike said as his mouth clamped down over mine and we began to kiss, our tongues fighting with each other, sucking the other's down our throats, nipping each other lips.

I pulled off of him, panting, "Fuck Mike, I'm gonna shoot, I'm gonna fucking coat your stomach with my cum!" I screamed out as my orgasm hit without warning. Mike felt the first shot of my cum fire out and shoot between our stomachs and this fueled him on.

"Fuck that's hot! I've never been with anyone who can cum hands free. Shit, get ready, fucking get ready, open wide bitch, I'm gonna shoot down your throat!" Mike shouted as pulled his cock out of my ass and scooted up to my face. My own cock was still firing and I grabbed it, aimed it and shot the rest of my load on his thigh. Mike threw his head back and howled as he pumped his cock in my face, the first rope of cum shooting out and landing in my hair. The next two fired out and hit my forehead, I managed to grab his cock and guided it to my mouth, taking the rest of his cum down my throat.

His load was massive, extremely massive, and my cock fired another orgasm as I felt his cum fill my mouth and run out the sides of my mouth and down my neck. No matter how hard I swallowed I couldn't keep up with his cock. Mike pulled his cock out of my mouth and let the rest of load shoot on my chest. He immediately began to clean off his load with his tongue and feed it back to me, moving down to my chest and stomach and cleaning off my cum and doing the same.

"Wow! That was fucking hot!" Mike said as he proceeded to get dressed.

"Yeah, fucking hot is right!" I said as I laid on the bed.

"How about I come back later and check on you?" Mike asked.

"Deal!" I purred, watching him leave. I sighed, my cock was hard again and I quickly stroked myself to another orgasm. "Fuckin A!" I said out loud as I wiped myself clean and proceeded to get dressed again. I took the pain pills he'd left, laid down on the couch and didn't wake up again until around five that afternoon. The knock on my door told me Mike had returned.

"It's open." I shouted, smiling as he walked through the door and proceeded to pull his hardening cock out of his pants.

"Ready for another round?" He asked as he stroked his cock in front of my face. "Umm

Hmm" I purred.

CHAPTER 9

Mike kicked off his shorts and underwear, his hard cock bobbing and bouncing as he made his way over to me. "I'm on my dinner break, we'll have to make this fast." he said as he approached me, his cock pointing right at my mouth, begging for me to suck it. "I'll cum faster if you suck me off." Mike said, his voice husky with his pent up sex.

Using my good arm, I reached out for his cock, stroked it a couple of times then guided it to my mouth. Mike sighed as my lips enclosed around the thick head of his beautiful cock. My tongue darted out and licked into his piss slit, tasting a hint of salt as his cock produced the first drop of clear juice.

"Oh yeah, yeah just like that buddy. Oh your fucking mouth feels good on my cock, c'mon buddy, suck me off, suck me off good." Mike panted as I began to slowly bob my head up and down on his hard cock, my hand reaching down and grabbing his balls.

"Yeah you got a good fucking mouth on you. So good, oh fuck this feels so good. Yeah, keep sucking me, just like that." Mike continued to tell me as he growled, threw his head back and started twisting his nipples. I'd just gone down to the base of his cock when the phone rang. I let it continue to ring as I continued to work on this magnificent cock that was now rapidly fucking my mouth.

The answering machine clicked on and the Captains voice rang out through my living room. "Craig, Craig you there? Pick up!" the voice paused, "I need you to get your ass down to the station as soon as you get this message!" followed next, followed by the dial tone as he had hung up.

"Shit!" I said as I pulled off of Mike's cock.

"Oh buddy, don't stop now, I'm almost there, c'mon buddy, finish me off." Mike cried out, grabbing his cock and trying to pry it back into my mouth. I batted his leaking cock away, looked at him and said, "I'm sorry Mike, but I gotta call him back. He sounded pissed and when the Captain's pissed you don't keep him waiting."

Mike sat down next to me and started stroking his cock off while I reached for the phone. After dialing the Captain's work numbers, I held my breath while I waited for the call to go through and him to pick up. Mike grunted, indicating he was dumping his load, just as the Captain answered.

"Craig?" he asked. "Yes sir, sorry I missed your call, I was..." I started to say.

"I don't give a good damned rat's ass what you were doing, get your ass down to the station now!" He barked into the phone and then hung up.

"Fuck, now what?" I said out loud as I hung up the phone and tossed Mike a hand towel so he could wipe up his mess.

"Sorry buddy, but you need to wipe and run, the Captain is pissed and wants a piece of my ass." I said as I headed for the bathroom to run a comb through my hair and change my clothes.

Mike had already left, throwing the cum rag into the kitchen sink. I grabbed my cell phone, keys and headed out to the station. Just as I was locking up the house, my cell phone rang. "Hello?" I answered, not bothering to check to see who was calling.

"Craig, it's Tim, did the Captain call you?" he asked.

"Yup, I'm on my way now. Ouch! Fuck!" I screamed into the phone as I bumped my sore arm on the steering wheel.

"You OK?" Tim asked.

"Yeah, I fucking fell off a ladder today and sprained my arm." I said back. "Look, I can't drive and talk with one arm, I'll see you in a few." I said and hung up, not giving Tim a chance to respond. I pulled into the parking lot of the station and was surprised to see Tim.

"Tim? What the..." I started to say. "I got the same phone call." Tim said. "I've been waiting for you to show up, I'm not going in there alone. What do you think this is all about?" Tim asked as he started walking to the station entrance.

"I have no idea and you're nothing more than a chicken." I answered back. We walked to the Captain's office, his door was shut and the blinds in the window were drawn close. Tim and I both looked at each other, sighed and I knocked on the door. "It's open!" The Captain's voice shouted. Tim and I walked in, closed the door behind us and realized as we saw Matt sitting there what this was all about.

"Matt here was just telling me that the two of you forced him into having sex with you. That true?" The Captain growled at us.

"Captain, sir, we didn't force Matt into doing anything Matt didn't want to do." Tim shouted back, sounding like a frightened child having just gotten caught by his father, doing something he shouldn't have. Tim also missed the Captain's wink and before he could say anymore, I nudged him in the ribs, wincing as I'd used my sprained arm to do that.

"What the fuck happened to you?" The Captain asked, looking at me.

"I fell of the ladder in the back yard this afternoon and sprained my arm." I said. "Humph." was all the Captain said, Tim and I didn't say anything more.

"Well? I'm waiting, what the fuck did you two knuckleheads do to this boy?" The Captain shouted at us, standing as he did. I let my eyes travel down to this crotch, whatever it was that Matt had told him had gotten him fired up as his cock was clearly hard and threatening to break the zipper on his slacks.

"Captain, Matt caught Tim and I fooling around in the bathroom. He was trying to blackmail us with it and was threatening to tell you as well as the other men. I told him to shut the fuck up and if he really wanted to know what man to man sex was all about to be at my place on Saturday." I explained.

The Captain turned to Matt, "That true son? And don't you fucking lie to me boy!" he snarled at the new firefighter.

"I, uh, well..." Matt stammered interrupted by the Captain to continue telling him what had transpired. Tim and I both took turns, and our time, in explaining to the Captain was happened. I even made it a point to go into great detail on what we had done as I knew the Captain was already rock hard and that this would make him even harder and we might get the opportunity to get some of his cock.

When we had finished telling the Captain, he got up from his chair, walked over to the door and locked it. He headed back to his desk, making sure he brushed his crotch into my thigh as he gingerly stepped around me, not wanting to bump my arm. I took notice that his cock was still rock hard and he'd managed to adjust it in his slacks so that it was sticking straight up. My mouth watered as I realized we had had the desired effect on him and would soon be getting nailed by this beautifully massively built stud.

"Sounds to me like someone needs a good ass whooping." The Captain said.

"Matt, get up, drop trou and bend over." The Captain said as he reached in one of his desk drawers for a wooden paddle.

"But sir, I, they, and then..." Matt whined, "Now boy, drop em now!" The Captain snarled.

Matt looked at the three of us, tears welling up in his eyes as he reluctantly did as he was told. Matt dropped his trousers and his underwear in one swift movement and bent over the chair he'd been sitting in.

"You're gonna act like a spoiled brat, I'm gonna treat you like one boy." The Captain said as he began to paddle the young mans ass. Matt cried out with the first slap, the Captain turned his head, smiled at Tim and I, winked and then let him have another paddle.

"That's for trying to fuck over your team", slap, "that's for fucking lying to our Captain", slap, "and that's for being a brat", slap. Matt's ass cheeks were a bright pink and he was whimpering as the Captain put his paddle away.

"Damn cute ass you got boy!" The Captain said as he began to massage the sting out of Matt's ass. Matt swung his head around, his eyes wide with fear as he figured out what was going to happen next.

"You tight boy? Ever had a cock up your shit chute?" The Captain asked as he reached between Matt's legs and, grabbing his balls, pulled them back, just enough to place the right amount of pressure in the right areas. Matt's cock began to respond and slowly started rising and hardening. Tim and I were now groping each other through our jeans, our cocks rock hard and leaking as we watched the Captain feel Matt up. Matt never did respond to the Captain's question. The Captain let go of Matt's balls and quickly got out of his clothes, his hard cock slapping against his belly leaving a dollop of cock juice in his navel.

"Follow me men." the Captain said as he led us back to his suite, closing and locking the door behind us after we'd entered. "Strip!" he ordered as he sat down on his overstuff leather chair. Tim and I were out of our clothes in nothing flat and the three of us waited, cocks hard, as we watched Matt reluctantly get out of his clothes.

"Get over here boy, show me your cock!" the Captain ordered to Matt. Matt walked over to where the Captain sat, his cock rock hard, bobbing and weaving.

"I think you liked getting your ass spanked. You like it rough boy?" the Captain asked Matt.

"N...n...no sir." Matt stuttered.

"Oh but I think you do boy, or shall I call you rookie? Yeah, I think I'll fucking call you rookie." the Captain sneered.

Turning to Tim the Captain asked, "He suck your cock?"

"Yes sir." Tim responded. "He any good?" the Captain asked.

"He's OK sir." Tim responded, reaching over to grab my cock.

"You like to suck cock rookie?" Cappy asked, reaching out and grabbing his rock hard cock and giving a hard tug.

"Sir?" Matt responded.

"I asked you a fucking simple question rookie. It only requires a yes or no answer. Do you like to suck cock?" Cappy asked sternly.

"As long as it doesn't cum in my...ooohhh...mouth." Matt grunted out, squealing as Cappy's fingers brushed against his hole.

"Show me, go fucking suck Tim's cock. I want to see how well you eat dick." Cappy ordered.

"But sir, he cums really fast." Matt whined. Cappy slapped Matt's ass and shouted that he didn't give a good goddamned and he better not fucking spill of drop and then shoved Matt towards Tim and I.

"Suck him good boy and don't you dare lose a drop of that cum. I got plans for it!" Cappy shouted as Matt dropped to his knees and sucked Tim's cock into his mouth.

"Yeah rookie, that's it, wrap your lips around his cock, damn you got a hot little mouth on you don't you boy?" Cappy snarled as he slowly stroked his cock, spitting in the palm of his hand to add lube.

"Oh fuck!" Tim groaned as he stiffened and started shooting in Matt's mouth.

"Yeah, that's what I like to see, a fucking pup taking some cum in his mouth. When you're done, get your ass back over here boy!" Cappy shouted, letting go of his cock and moving up to twist his nipples. Matt was true to the Captain's orders and didn't lose one drop of Tim's massive load. Tim nodded to the Captain indicating he'd finished shooting.

"Get over here boy, let me taste that." Cappy ordered as Matt made his was to him, leaning down, Cappy began to kiss him, his tongue prying open Matt's mouth, causing him to spill Tim's load into the Captain's mouth. Matt tried to pull off the Captain's mouth, somewhat repulsed and yet a little excited that this dominating hunk of a man was shoving his tongue down Matt's throat and licking the inside of his mouth, trying to get all of Tim's cum into his mouth. Tim and I watched in fevered excitement as Cappy continued to work on Matt's mouth, his nipples and cock forgotten as he held the back of Matt's head, forcing him to continue kissing him. Matt groaned and we both realized that he was beginning to get into kissing this man and enjoying even more the exchange of tongue and cum. Cappy pulled off of Matt, growled and wiped his mouth with the back of his hand.

"Fuck that tastes good!" He growled. "Don't tell me you didn't like that rookie, your cock told me otherwise, look at the fucking mess you made on me." Cappy snarled as we looked at the streaks of cum that coated Cappy's chest. Neither Tim nor I had realized that Matt had came, he'd given no indication, in fact his cock was still rock hard.

"Get down there and clean me up rookie!" Cappy ordered, shoving Matt to his knees. Matt had now lost all of his hesitancy and greedily licked the cum from the Captain's chest and stomach.

"Eat my cock rookie! Bite it, bite that fucking big head!" Cappy ordered as he grabbed Matt's head, shoving him down to his cock. Matt opened his mouth and sucked Cappy's cock in.

"God damn it rookie! I said bite it! If I'd wanted you to fucking suck my cock I would have told you to! Now fucking bite the head of my... ooooohhhh fuck yeah boy, fuck yeah. Eat that head, c'mon, fucking chew on the head of my...god damn fuck boy, yeah!" Cappy shouted as Matt began to lightly bite the head of Cappy's cock.

"Oh fuck that feels good, get my balls boy, get on down there and chew on that fucking nut sack!" Cappy ordered, spreading his legs, allowing Matt to position himself so he could go to work on his balls.

Tim and I started kissing one another, we were lost in this homoerotic scene that was playing out in front of us. I had no idea that Cappy was into this level of sex, but he seemed to enjoy a certain amount of pain along with his pleasure. Cappy was groaning and bucking as Matt went from chewing on his ball sack to eating his cock, his hand reaching down and stroking his own wet cock.

"You like that sir?" Matt asked, looking up at the Captain for approval.

"Yeah boy, fucking feels good. Let's see if you eat ass as good as you eat cock." he continued, bringing his knees to his chest, offering Matt his beautiful brown pucker. Matt didn't hesitate, he dove in face first. Cappy continued to groan and buck as Matt expertly rimmed him, occasionally nipping at the folds of skin that made up his pucker.

"Fuck yeah!" Cappy shouted.

"You two, get the fuck over here! I want some cock in my mouth!" Cappy ordered and we were quick to respond, each of us standing on either side.

Cappy reached up, grabbing both of our cocks, "Nice fucking meat here boys, real nice." He growled as he leaned over and sucked Tim's cock into his mouth.

"Ffffuuuucccckkkkk." Tim cried out. Cappy growled and groaned while he sucked Tim's cock, Matt using his mouth, lips, tongue and teeth and going from Cappy's hole to his balls to his cock. Cappy pulled off of Tim's cock and dove on me.

"Unnnnggggg!" was all I was able to say as my hard cock was sucked into the Captain's mouth. Cappy was an excellent cock sucker, knowing just the right amount of suction and tongue play, licking at all the right areas, his teeth occasionally scraping the sensitive head of my cock. It wasn't the least bit painful but was quite the opposite. I found myself soaring quicker and quicker towards orgasm. Cappy knew this somehow, and managed to keep me right at the brink without letting me go over the edge. He would do the same to Tim, take him right to the edge and then hold him there. Tim and I were panting and groaning and begging for Cappy to let us cum. We could tell that Cappy was at that point too, only somehow, he was able to keep himself on the edge without going over. Matt couldn't get enough of Cappy's cock, balls and ass and was mumbling to us over and over how much he loved sucking the Captain's big cock and eating his balls. Matt then surprised all of us as he started begging to get fucked, pleading that we each shove our cocks up his ass and fill him with our cocks and our cum.

Cappy pulled off of Tim's cock, looked at Matt and asked, "You want some meat up your ass boy? Huh? Is that what you want?" Cappy asked.

"Yes sir, please sir, please, fuck me, God I want your cock inside me so bad sir." Matt panted, stroking his cock as fast as he could, his other hand playing with his own ass lips. "Please fuck me." Matt continued.

"Get on the bed boy, doggy style!" Cappy ordered. Matt squealed his delight and did as he was told, disappearing into the bedroom. We could hear him softly cooing and moaning as he waited, his ass thrust up, for one of us to feed him our cocks. Cappy entered the room and walked up to Matt, slapping his ass. Matt groaned, a drop of pre-cum spilled out from the tip of his cock and landed on the bed spread. Cappy squatted down and began to rim Matt's waiting ass, Matt cried out, groaning and bucking his ass on Cappy's mouth as he tongue fucked him.

"Yeah, oh yeah, oh fuck." Matt panted and whined. I sank to my knees and started sucking Tim off while he toyed with his nipples, staring at the Captain as he continued to fuck Matt's ass with his mouth, his fingers darting in and out every now and then. Cappy stood up, spit in the palm of his hand, slicked up his cock and proceeded to shove his rock hard cock in Matt at once.

"OOHH FFUUCCK!" Matt cried out in pure pleasure as the Captain's thick cock tore through him. Cappy was bent over Matt, kissing his neck and ears as he power fucked Matt's ass. I pulled off of Tim's cock and went over to where Cappy and Matt were. Squatting down I pulled Cappy's ass cheeks apart and began to feast on his beautiful hole.

"Fuck yeah!" Cappy shouted as he slammed in and held his cock inside Matt while I rimmed him. I stood up, spit into the palm of my hand, slicked up my cock and proceeded to slide my dick into Cappy's ass.

"Shit yeah boy! That's it, yeah, fucking slide that rock hard cock up your Cappy's ass!" Cappy shouted out. Tim managed to somehow angle himself so that he could offer his hard cock to Matt, which he greedily sucked down. I pulled out of Cappy's ass far enough to let him continue to fuck Matt while at the same time he was fucking Matt. We continued this for a few more minutes before Cappy pulled out of Matt and flipped him over on his back, a loud pop echoing through the room as Tim's cock was pulled from his mouth. He pulled Matt to the edge of the bed and then climbed on top of him. Pulling Matt's cock back, he quickly sat down on Matt's rock hard and leaking cock and then leaned forward. Cappy looked back at me and his eyes told me all I needed to know, he wanted to get double fucked.

I placed my cock at the entrance to Cappy's ass and slowly started sliding in him. Cappy squealed and groaned as he felt the head of my cock open him even more. I groaned as well as I felt my cock slide into Cappy's ass, Matt's cock stimulating the underside of my own cock. I heard Tim groan and as I looked up, saw that Matt was eating his balls while Cappy sucked his cock into his mouth. I cried out at the head of my cock slide over the head of Matt's cock and quickly started to fuck Cappy's ass. The four us moaned and cried out as we continued to move in rhythm with one another.

Cocks sliding over cocks, a tongue licking the underside of a cock while teeth nipped and tugged at the ball-sack. I couldn't believe we hadn't came yet, the sight before me was one I'd only imagined.

Cappy spit out Tim's cock and growled, "Yeah oh fuck yeah, I'm getting close men, getting close. Oh shit this feels good, two cocks inside me and one in my mouth." as he dove back down on Tim's cock. Tim shouted he was going to cum and Cappy started sucking him harder. Cappy pulled off his cock just as the first bolt of cum shot out. He and Matt fought each other over who was going to get the most of Tim's cum, most of his load landing on their faces. Tim stroked the last of his cum out of his cock as Cappy's orgasm hit him. Cappy screamed, stiffened and started bucking harder on Matt and I's cocks as his load sprayed between he and Matt, coating their stomachs with his sweet cum. Feeling his load shoot out and wash over his stomach triggered Matt's load. I was fucking Cappy for all I was worth, my own cum boiling in my balls, begging to shoot out. I could feel Matt's cock spasming, his cum pouring out of his cock, coating my cock and Cappy's insides. I slammed into Cappy one last time and my cock fired, adding to Matt's massive, pent up load. I shouted and screamed as my orgasm raced through my body. Cappy stiffened and shouted as he too came again. The feeling of his ass twitching around both of our cocks triggered another orgasm for Matt and just made mine last even longer.

The four of us, panting, sweating, collapsed on the bed. We all started kissing and licking, cleaning up the sweat and cum. I moved down to Cappy and Matt and proceeded to clean off their cocks, occasionally dipping my tongue into Cappy's ass, tasting the mixture of Matt's and I's cum.

"Fuck that was good!" Cappy panted as I cleaned the last of his cum off his stomach.

"God yes!" Tim whispered back while he continued to kiss Matt.

"Umm hmm" Matt purred back.

"Nice show you put on for us!" a familiar voice broke the stillness of the room.

"Who the fuck?" Cappy said, startled as he sat up to see who was in the room. Marc Johnson and Mike McKinley stood just inside the doorway, both were nude, cum dripping off each other's stomachs.

"How long have you two been there?" I asked.

"Long enough to know that I think we all need to get together one of these nights." Marc answered.

"Yeah? Well why wait, why not now?" Cappy asked, his cock beginning to rise and stir.

"Yeah, why not now." Marc answered back, his own cock rising as he made his way to the Captain.

"Umm...more cock." Matt whispered as Tim opened his mouth and began bobbing up and down on Matt's hardening cock.

"Here we go again." I said as Mike made his way towards me, reaching out for his semi-hard cock I quickly engulfed him in my mouth.

"Oh yeah, fuck, if only my wife could suck cock like this." Mike responded.

"Mmmpppfff." was all I replied with.

CHAPTER 10

I had no sooner swallowed Mike's cock to the base when the alarms went off.

"Fuck!" I said as Mike yanked his cock from my mouth and proceeded into Cappy's office to get dressed.

"Let's go men!" Cappy groaned as we all scurried around putting our clothes back on.

"Not so fast Craig, you stay here, you're in no shape right now to be out on an emergency call with us." Cappy said to me.

"Cappy, I'm not even on this shift." I responded back.

"Well, stay the fuck here anyway, we've got some unfinished business to tend to when we get back!" Cappy snapped at me as he headed to his locker to grab his firefighting equipment. I decided to go watch the trucks leave, it always gave me an adrenaline boost and was surprised to see Tim suiting up.

"Tim, you're not on this shift either!" I said to him. "I know, but the Captain asked me to come along, another cardboard recycling center has gone up in flames, you know what that means." Tim responded as he suited up.

"Yeah, you'll be gone for awhile." I sighed, somewhat disappointed as my cock was still half hard and begging for release. I waived goodbye, said a silent prayer, and watched the trucks pull out of the station, one by one, lights and sirens blaring, horns sounding, warning traffic to move out of the way.

I headed to the bathroom to take a piss and decided to take a short cut through the shower room. I didn't think too much about the fact that the showers were running as I passed through and made a quick mental note to turn the water off on my way back through, as someone, obviously interrupted by the fire call, had forgotten to turn the water off. I did my business, flushed and headed back to the showers, as I approached I heard the unmistakable moans of two men engaged in sex. I quietly snuck in and peeked into the showers. I silently gasped as I saw two of the firefighters that had not gone out on the call locked in a passionate embrace. I don't know all of the firefighters on this shift as I rarely come into contact with them. Their shift change occurs an hour before mine, so by the time I arrive, the first shift has already departed. These two men were truly a beautiful sight to behold.

Both men were around six feet tall, muscular without being grotesque. The first man had jet black hair that was closely and neatly trimmed. His black mustache was thick and full. Square set jaw that led down to a thick neck that sat on broad muscular shoulders. His chest was perfectly sculpted and covered by a thick matt of jet black hair. His abs were firm and led to a narrow waist. I could see his ass from where I stood and it was a beautiful bubble butt covered by a thin coating of jet black hair that seemed to fan out from the small of his back downward across his cheeks. I reached down and groped by hardening cock through my shorts. I couldn't quite make out the other firefighter and decided I needed to somehow find another vantage point to see these two and also check out their cocks. I quietly and quickly made my move and found a spot where I could remain somewhat hidden but was able to get the perfect view of these two men.

The second man was about an inch or two taller than the black haired man. His body was sculpted as a mirror image of the black haired man. He had dark brown hair and a reddish colored matt of hair covered his chest and legs. His ass was much fuller and meatier than the black haired man's ass and my mouth watered at the thought of tasting both of these gorgeous mens asses. They were holding each other close, kissing, tongues darting in and out of each other's mouths, hands caressing faces, backs, asses. I still couldn't make out their cocks as they were too close to one another. I watched as the dark brown haired man's hands roamed across his buddies ass, spreading his cheeks, a finger obviously circling his pucker as he quickly threw his head back, gasped and panted, "Oh yeah." They pulled off of one another's mouth and separated, giving me my first chance to glimpse their cocks. I gasped when I saw them, they were about eight inches long, thick with slender heads on top. Below their cocks hung two pairs of the biggest balls I've ever seen. They were oblivious to my presence so I got bolder, quietly kicking off my shorts and underwear,

I moved to where I now could be seen. I was secretly hoping I'd be caught by these two and they'd take me in whatever manner they saw fit.

I slowly started stroking my cock as I watched the dark brown haired man kiss the other man's neck, down his chest, sucking in and licking his nipples. The black haired man sighed and cooed, no words were spoken between the two. The dark brown haired man continued to kiss his way down the mans stomach, dipping his tongue into his navel before moving on to the man's bush. He kissed and licked around the black haired man's cock and balls.

"Oh fuck! C'mon, suck me, suck my cock!" The black haired man panted and pleaded.

"Uh uh, not yet." the dark brown haired man responded back as he sucked in one of the giant balls. The black haired man hissed and threw his head back, "Fuck, oh fuck yeah." he groaned. The dark brown haired man continued to slurp and lick and eat the balls of the black haired man, causing them to draw up in their skin and practically disappear.

"Oh fuck yeah, you keep doing that and you're going to get a face full of cum. You know that drives me wild!" the black haired man cried out.

"Give it to me, you know I love your cum. C'mon, shoot it on my face baby!" the dark haired man said, looking up into the mans eyes who's balls he had been sucking.

"Tell me you want it, tell me you want my cum!" the black haired man said back.

"God you know I do, you know I love it when you shoot your fucking load on my face!" the dark brown haired man responded back.

"Then set me off boy, c'mon, you know the trigger!" the black haired man replied, taking his cock and slapping the other man's face with it, his cock juice leaving a slimy trail across the bridge of his nose.

"Yeah? You ready to cum?" the dark brown haired man replied as he reached around and pulled the black haired man's ass cheeks apart.

"Yeah, fuck yeah, c'mon, make me shoot! I'm so close now!" the black haired man said.

"Mmmm...ready?" the dark brown haired man asked.

"Oh yeah, fuck yeah, c'mon, fucking make me shoooooottttttt!" the black haired man cried out as his cock erupted, triggered by the dark brown haired man jabbing two fingers up his ass. The black haired man grabbed his spitting cock and held it in front of the other man's face. Cum burst out of his cock, hitting the man in the forehead. He angled his cock down and the rest of the jets of cum landed on the man's cheeks and lips. The dark brown haired man opened his mouth and stuck out his tongue as he furiously stroked his own cock, his cries echoing off the tiled walls of the shower as he too shot his load. Ropes of cum flew out of his cock and landed on the tile between the black haired mans feet, the water sweeping it up and washing it down the drain. My own cock fired and I cried out as my orgasm took over. Startled, the two men looked at me and before I knew it, my shirt was being ripped off my body and I was being guided to the black haired man's still hard cock.

"Fucking spy boy! We'll give you something to cry out about!" he said as he shoved his cock down my throat, making me gag.

"Fucking take it bitch, fucking take this monster cock!" he said as he started to fuck my face, not letting me get used to his cock being down my throat, me gagging and coughing.

I grunted as I felt the other man's cock enter my ass in one swift movement. "Who the fuck are you? And why were you spying on us bitch? Did you like what you saw, huh? Did you boy?" the dark brown haired man asked as he started to power fuck me.

"Mmmmmpff." was all I could respond with as I began to get into rhythm with them and was deep throating the cock that was power-fucking my face.

"God DAMN boy! You suck cock like a pro!" the black haired man panted.

"Yeah and you should feel his fucking ass around your cock. It's like dipping your cock into velvet butter, so tight, so smooth!" the brown haired man said as he continued to pound my ass.

"Uunngghh!" I managed to shout out as my cock erupted again, my cum shooting out, splattering the tops of the dark brown haired man's feet.

"SHHHIIITTT!! You're fucking cumming and your ass muscles clamping down around my cock...ffuuucckkkk!" the dark brown haired man shouted as he slammed into me one last time and his cock started shooting its load in my ass.

"Mmmm...mmmmpfff!" I cried out as I felt his hot cum shoot inside me and then back out and run down the back of my balls. I felt the head of the cock in my throat expand, indicating that the black haired man was going to fire another round of cum. As he pulled out, I managed to take as deep of a breath as I could before he rammed his cock back down my throat and started shooting his cum down my throat.

Both men were crying out as their cocks fired, almost simultaneously. I was in pure heaven, I had a cock shooting up my ass, cum running down my balls and another shooting down my throat. The black haired man pulled his cock out and I collapsed on the tiled floor, landing on my sprained arm, I cried out in pain.

"What the fuck?" the dark brown haired man said, cum dripping off the tip of his cock.

"My arm, my arm, I sprained it earlier today." I panted, trying not to pass out as the pain was intense.

"Shit! Let's get you up and take a look at it." the black haired man said as they very carefully picked me up off the wet floor and carried me into the dayroom. My arm was beginning to swell, worse that what it already was and as the black haired man examined it, moving it this way and that, I cried out in even more pain and blacked out.

I moaned as I began to wake up in the Emergency Room, somehow dressed, my arm in the process of being placed in a cast. "Well, look who decided to join us." the voice said to me.

Opening my eyes, I stared into the bluest eyes I've ever seen. "Dr. Gimble is the name. And you are?" he asked me.

"Craig, Craig McFadden." I replied. Dr. Gimble looked as though he couldn't be more than 21. "How old are you?" I asked.

"Never-mind that, I'm the attending doc. You're buddies brought you in." he said, pointing to the two men who, also dressed, had been fucking the living daylights out of me earlier.

"So, looks like when you slipped and fell in the shower..."the doctor started to say.

"Slipped and fell in the shower? Is that what happened?" I said, looking right at the two men, their eyes cast downward, a slight blush in their cheeks.

"Yes, you slipped and fell and it appears that your sprain was really more than that, it appears that you had a hairline fracture and when you fell and you landed on your bad arm, well, it just finished the job for you." Dr. Gimble said.

"Great! Just fucking great!" I snarled back, pissed that I was not only going to be out of commission job wise, but this was going to definitely put a hamper on things for the rest of the night.

"OK, so, we're done with the cast. I understand you're an EMT?" Dr. Gimble asked.

"Yes." I replied back, pouting and glaring at the two firefighters.

"So then as an EMT, I'm surprised you didn't realize you should have..." Dr. Gimble started to say.

"Blah blah blah, cut the fucking lecture doc. I know the drill and I know the routine for the after care as well." I snapped back.

"Hmm...OK, well, you medical people make the worst patients, anyone ever tell you that?" Dr. Gimble said, winking at me, trying to get my spirits up. Dr. Gimble handed me a couple weeks supply of pain killers and told me to call his office in the morning and they'd set up a follow up appointment for me in a couple of weeks.

I snatched the business card from the doctor and proceeded to get up off the gurney. Looking at the two firefighters, I snarled, "Well, you two dumb-fucks going to just stand there or are you going to take me back to the station so I can get my car and go home?"

"Oh no, no, no driving for you grumpy." Dr. Gimble said.

"And just why not?" I asked.

"Well because we gave you a little shot of Demerol and it should be kicking in right about now." Dr. Gimble replied. I started to take a step forward just as the Demerol kicked in. I stopped, shook my head a couple of times, looked at the two men and then back at Dr. Gimble.

All three seemed to look a little fuzzy, as the Demerol continued to take over, my eyes glazed over, I smiled, looked at Dr. Gimble and said, "Damn, you are one fine hunk of a man. You married?" I asked and then started to giggle.

"C'mon, let's get you home. Thanks Doc!" the dark brown haired man replied as they gingerly placed me in a wheel chair and wheeled me out to the truck they'd brought me in.

"Um, Craig, where do you live?" the black haired man asked as he placed me in the truck.

"In a house." I responded, giggling. "Woo hoo this shit feels gooddd!" I continued to giggle.

The two men took me back to the fire station and as they were getting me out of the truck, the crew started returning to the station. Cappy saw the two carrying me towards the rear entrance and came running up, asking what had happened.

"Cappy, can we get him in, he's dead weight and heavy. Then we'll explain what happened." the dark brown haired man said. They took me to the dayroom and gently laid me down on the couch.

"Hey, black haired dude!" I shouted.

"Yeah?" he responded. "Come here, you're fucking gorgeous, I want to kiss that sweet mouth of yours!" I slurred. He blushed, turned and left to help the rest of the men get their gear off the trucks, stowed and put away. The dark brown haired man stayed with me and within a few minutes both Tim and the Captain returned. The dark brown haired man filled the Captain in on the truth and after getting scolded, chewed out and chastised for a good solid 30 minutes was excused.

"I'm sorry Cappy" I said, "I'm really sorry, but I don't think I can come out and play tonight. See, they gave me some drugs at the hospital and I'm really weirded out right now and...and...the hills are alive with the sound of music!" I broke out into a giggle before dozing off.

"Tim, get him home. Call me tomorrow and let me know how he's doing." Cappy said, patting Tim on the back and then broke out laughing.

"Man, he sure can't handle his narcotics can he?" Cappy said, laughing as he turned to head to the showers. Tim picked me up, took me to his truck and drove me home. I don't remember a thing, not one thing, except waking up the following morning, in Tim's arms. It was the first time he'd ever stayed the night.

CHAPTER 11

While I was sleeping off my Demerol induced fog, Cappy and the men, to include Matt, were back at the firehouse, putting the equipment away, cleaning things up, etc. At least once a week the men of shift one, as they are referred to, come together in a pure expression of their devotion to each other and to display their brotherhood. Tonight was to be a special night as Matt was going to be inducted into the brotherhood and shed his title of "Rookie".

The ritual of brotherhood normally started (and sometimes would finish) in the shower room. There are normally 12 firefighters on the first shift along with two paramedics. Cappy had dispatched one of the firefighters to lay out the special mats in the showers. These mats were soft and had a non-skid surface on them that was not abrasive to the skin. Cappy had already decided that tonight's ritual would start and end in the showers.

One by one the men filed into the shower room to clean up. Once all of the men were clean, one of the firefighters would blow a whistle three times to indicate the start of the ritual. Cappy led Matt into the shower room once he heard the three whistles. The men formed a circle around the center of the shower room and parted to allow Cappy and Matt to proceed. Matt had not yet showered and the stench of smoke and sweat quickly filled the room.

"Men, tonight we welcome Matt into the brotherhood." Cappy said as he guided Matt towards one of the shower heads and turned the water on.

"Matt, tonight we will cleanse you and induct you into the brotherhood of Ladder Company 49." Cappy said as he took the soap and began to gently wash Matt, ridding him of the smoke, sweat and soot. Cappy payed special attention to Matt's erogenous zones, taking his time, he gently lathered and washed his nipples, arm pits, cock and balls and ass. By the time Cappy was done and had rinsed Matt off, Matt had a huge erection and was trembling with sexual excitement.

Cappy then took a rubber cock ring off one of the soap dishes and proceeded to strap it around Matt's hard cock, drawing his balls through, the cock ring nestled against the base of his cock, with another piece of rubber splitting his balls so that they remained tight against the base of his cock. Matt groaned and panted as Cappy fit his cock and balls with the rubber device. Standing, Cappy surveyed the crowd, most of whom were now sporting erections and were slowly stroking their cocks, others were half hard and were either playing with their nipples or the nipples of the man standing next to them. Sexual tension and excitement filled the air.

"Matt, tonight you will drink each man's cum, accepting their offering and further binding you to the brotherhood." Cappy said as he led him to the first firefighter, a short stocky built young man with a six inch cock. Guiding Matt to his knees, Cappy instructed him to open his mouth and suck in his firefighter brothers cock. The sexual excitement in the room continued to rise as Matt sucked in the young man's short stubby cock.

"Unnnggg." was all the firefighter could say as Matt expertly sucked his cock in. Cappy squatted down behind Matt, his own hard cock tucked up under Matt, throbbing against the area between Matt's balls and ass.

"Show him how much you want to be his brother Matt. Suck his cock, nurse it, lick it, drink it's sweet nectar." Cappy whispered in Matt's ear. "Yeah, that's it Matt, suck his dick, there you go boy. Yeah, fucking good boy you are, sucking your brothers cock, making him feel good." Cappy continued, his cock gently thrusting in and out between Matt's legs.

"Cappy, I'm gonna cum." Matt whined.

"No you're not boy, that device you're wearing won't let you." Cappy purred as he started to finger Matt's tight hole.

"You're a good little cock-sucker aren't you boy? You like the feeling of that cock driving in and out of your mouth don't you boy?" Cappy asked.

"Mmmm Hmm..." Matt groaned as he continued working on the short man's cock.

The man who's cock he was sucking was panting, Matt could feel the head in his mouth begin to swell and he knew it wouldn't be long before his cock erupted and he'd be swallowing his brother's seed.

"See that Matt? See how he likes your mouth? You're going to make him cum and you're going to drink his cum and not waste a drop aren't you?" Cappy said.

"Mmmppfff." was all Matt could respond with.

"Oh, I'm gonna cum, holy fuck, holy fuck, oh get ready, get ready boy, here it coooommmeeess!" the stalky man said as he shoved his cock into the back of Matt's throat and started cumming. Matt was prepared, and expecting, a huge load as up until now, that was exactly what he got from the cocks he'd sucked off. This firefighter though only came in two small squirts, pulling his cock out of Matt's mouth, he painted his lips with the remainder of the cum that dribbled out.

"Excellent boy, excellent. Now, onto the next one." Cappy said as he maneuvered Matt to the next cock that was waiting for him.

This cock was mammoth, at least 10 inches long and thick, very thick. Matt wasn't sure he would be able to get the head of this cock into his mouth, let alone the rest of it. The cock on this firefighter was not cut and Matt marveled at how the foreskin slid up and over the head of the cock, masking the true size of the fat bulbous leaking head.

"Open your mouth Matt, suck him in. Taste your brother." Cappy urged, sliding his dick back and allowing the head of his cock to brush against Matt's hole. Matt groaned as he opened his mouth wide, feeling like his jaws were going to unhinge as he sucked in the giant head, his lips closing around the base of the head. Matt started to gingerly suck on the huge cock, letting his lips and teeth skin back the foreskin, releasing a flood a sweet nectar. Within a few minutes Matt was able to get the head past the back of his throat and some of the shaft, but that was it.

"There you go boy, yeah, what a good boy you are. Working on your brother's big cock. Here, give me a taste." Cappy said as Matt pulled off the cock and Cappy dove on it, taking half the shaft down his throat in one fell swoop. Matt moaned as he watched his

Captain deep throat this man. Cappy sensed the man was close to cumming and pulled off his cock.

"Relax your throat boy." Cappy purred in Matt's ear as Matt went back to working this huge cock down his throat. Matt was able to get maybe another inch of his cock down his throat when it erupted, cum spurting directly down his throat and into his gut.

"That's it boy, you're doing good, keep drinking his cum." Cappy said as he nudged the head of his cock against Matt's hole.

Matt pulled back off the mammoth cock to catch his breath, unfortunately he pulled back to fast as the still erupting cock plopped out of his mouth, his cum painting Matt's face.

"Oh fuck that's hot boy, watching you get your face painted with his load." Cappy said as he started to lick the cum from the side of Matt's face. "You like this Matt? Like showing your brothers how much you love them?" Cappy asked, sliding his cock back along the underside of Matt, driving Matt closer and closer to an orgasm that he knew he wouldn't be able to have yet.

"Yeah Captain, yeah, fucking love it, I fucking love sucking cock. Oh Captain, please, I gotta cum, I gotta...gotta...uuunhhh." Matt cried out as an orgasm of sorts washed over him. Cappy held him close while Matt's body was overtaken by an immense sense of pleasure, his cock hardening even more, the head of his dick turning purple, clear juice running out of the tip and flowing down the underside of his cock.

"Yeah, that's it boy, oh go through it, c'mon, you got some more worshipping to do boy before we let you cum." Cappy said as he guided Matt to the next cock.

Matt continued to worship the hard cocks of his firefighting brethren as Cappy guided him from one cock to another. By the time Matt had reached the last cock, he was covered in the cum of his brethren. Matt was panting and writhing as the last cock erupted, firing it's sweet load down Matt's throat, the owner yanking his cock from Matt's mouth and letting the rest of cum shoot on his chest. Cappy was still guiding him, his own cock still rock hard. At one point in the line of cocks that Matt had worked, Cappy had slid his cock into Matt's ass, triggering another wave of orgasmic pleasure to wash over Matt. Matt let the last cock he had sucked fall from his mouth. Panting, shaking, he begged the Captain to please let him cum, he need to cum so bad it hurt.

"Not yet my boy." Cappy said as he pick Matt up in his arms, Matt's legs wrapping around the Captain's waist, the head of the Captain's cock nudging at the entrance to Matt's tight hole. The Captain proceeded to lick and clean off the cum from Matt's face, their tongues making contact from time to time to exchange the taste of each man's load.

"Fuck Captain, oh fuck." Matt moaned.

"Yeah boy, you like this don't you? Like sucking your brother's cocks, drinking their loads. I think it's time you felt your brothers inside you, let them fuck you, cum inside you, feel the tight ass you got." the Captain said. "Is the room prepared?" Cappy asked the crowd.

"Yes sir." one of the firefighters responded. "Good! Follow me men." the Captain said as let go of Matt and led him to the day room. A waist heigh table with another soft matt had been placed in the center of the dayroom and he had Matt lie down on it. Cappy then fitted Matt with a self restraining sling so his legs would be permanently up and spread. Once he was done, he knelt down and began to feast on Matt's ass, getting him wet and ready for the line of cocks that would soon be entering him. Someone placed a large pump bottle of lube on the table next to Matt and when the Captain was done eating his ass, he applied a generous amount of lube to Matt's ass.

"First man, come forward!" The Captain shouted. The first forward was the man with the mammoth cock. Matt saw this and his ass muscles instantly clenched.

"NO Captain! Please! He's too big!" Matt pleaded. "Shhh...relax Matt. He knows how to take care of you." One of the firefighters said.

Matt felt the head of the mammoth cock rubbing up and down his lube slicked hole, massaging and stimulating the lips of his ass. Before long, Matt was groaning with pleasure and his ass lips began to suck on the mammoth head, drawing him in, slowly, inch by inch until Matt soon felt the head slide past his sphincter. Matt arched his back, threw his head back and howled with pleasure as his ass continued to suck this man's cock inside him. Matt's eyes rolled to the back of his head, his head moved from side to side and he moaned and groaned and uttered obscenities as the man began to slowly thrust in and out of him.

"Fuck me, please fuck me, hard, please,oh god please fuck me with that giant cock of yours!" Matt shouted. Cappy came over to the side of the table and fed Matt his own hard cock. Matt groaned and writhed in pleasure as the unknown giant cock fucked him and he nursed on the Captain's cock.

"Yeah boy, that's it, fucking ride his cock! Fucking take that giant cock!" the Captain shouted.

"Captain, oh fuck Captain, I'm gonna shoot. Damn this boys tight!" the firefighter shouted, surprised that he had been able to cum this quickly. Matt spit out the Captain's cock and shouted, "Fuck me hard you mother-fucker! God DAMN get that cock inside me and fill me up!"

"Get ready bitch! Here it comes!" the firefighter shouted as he slammed into Matt, his cock firing, ribbons of hot scalding cum shooting out and flooding Matt's insides. Matt sucked the Captain's cock back into his mouth and started sucking his cock like there was no tomorrow.

"Whoa buddy! I'm not ready to cum yet and you got me close boy!" the Captain said as he pulled his cock from Matt's mouth and watched as the next firefighter took his place and guided his hard cock into Matt's wet ass. Matt howled as he felt the next cock enter him.

"Oh yeah, yeah, fuck me, fuck me hard, Captain please make me cum." Matt whined and purred.

"Not yet, boy, not yet." the Captain said, leaning over and stroking Matt's cock, using the pool of pre-cum that had been steadily flowing out of Matt's cock as lube. One by one the firefighters took their turn fucking Matt's ass. By the time the last one had cum, Matt was delirious, cum leaked from his asshole, cock nectar streamed from the head of his cock.

"You've done great boy, absolutely fucking great." the Captain told Matt. "Now it's time for us to cum together" the Captain said as he climbed on top of the table and over the top of Matt.

"Get me ready men!" the Captain said over his shoulder. "Ah fuck yeah!" the Captain shouted as he felt the hands of one of his firefighters lubing up his ass, fingers being inserted one by one until the Captain had four fingers inside his ass. The Captain groaned and bucked on the unseen fingers that were now fucking him.

"You ready Matt? Ready to shoot?" the Captain asked, leaning forward to shove his tongue down Matt's throat.

"Unnnggg." was all Matt could reply with as he kissed the Captain back.

"Uhhhhh Huhhhhh..." the Captain groaned into Matt's mouth. The unseen fingers had now removed themselves and the head of a double headed dildo was sliding it's way into the Captain's ass.

"Awe fuck yeah! Fucking give me that fucking dildo!" The Captain squealed as he sat back, forcing more of the dildo up his ass.

"Oh fuck, fuck yeah!" Matt cried out as the other end of the dildo was inserted into his well fucked ass. The Captain sat back a little and removed the rubber cock ring from around Matt's cock and balls.

"You ready Matt? Ready to do this together?" the Captain asked.

"Fuck yeah, oh fuck, just let me cum please!" Matt cried out.

"OK, get ready!" The Captain said as he reached back and grabbing the middle of the dildo proceeded to fuck both he and Matt at the same time.

"Ahhh...ahhh...oh fuck Captain, fuck, oh I'm gonna shoot, I'm gonna cum, Captain, oh fuck...I...I'm cummmmiinnngg!" Matt screamed as his orgasm hit.

"Me too! Fuck hang on boy, hang on, here it comes, here it... aaaaahhhhhh..." The Captain shouted out as both of their cocks erupted at the same time, spraying cum everywhere. Several of the firefighters had gathered around the table and had been stroking their cock while they watched Matt and their commander fuck with the dildo. When they saw their cocks erupt, felt the spray of their cum as they released their pent up load, it sent them over the edge as well. As the Captain and Matt continued to cum, covering each other along with the table, the men started shooting their loads too. Cum from their cocks shot out, landing on Matt's chest and face. A couple of them pointed their cocks at the commander and shot their loads on his stomach and erupting cock.

The dayroom wreaked of cum and fucked ass as the men came down off of their orgasms. Cappy had fallen forward back on top of Matt and the two of them were busy kissing and licking the cum from each of their faces. Once everyone had calmed down, the men filed by Matt, welcoming him into the brotherhood. The Captain had removed the harness and was helping Matt off of the table.

"Phew! Man, my legs are weak!" Matt said.

"C'mon, I'll help you to the shower and we'll get you cleaned up. How about rooming with me tonight?" The Captain asked.

"Only if I can fuck that sweet ass of yours sir!" Matt said. Winking at Matt the Captain said, "Deal!" and they headed into the shower, turned on the water and proceeded to get clean.

CHAPTER 12

Cappy rolled over, his morning hardon resting in the crack of Matt's ass cheeks. A low throaty growl escaped his lips as he nuzzled Matt's ear, gently kissing and nipping at the ear lobe.

"Good morning stud." Cappy purred in his ear.

"Mmmmmm." Matt groaned back, backing onto Cappy's hard cock, causing his cock to slide between Matt's ass cheeks. Cappy began to thrust his hips forward, running his cock up and down Matt's ass crack, the already leaking head leaving a trail of natural lube. Cappy leaned forward, kissing Matt on his mouth, their tongues gently caressing the others. Cappy slid his cock down until he felt the already wet head make contact with Matt's ass lips. Matt backed up even further, sighing as he felt the head of Cappy's cock begin to open his swollen ass lips.

"Yeah, that's my good little cock slut. Let your Cappy in boy, let him in." Cappy whispered in his ear as he slowly and gently began to thrust forward, his dick parting Matt's ass lips and beginning to enter his well fucked hole. Matt hissed and jolted upright, knocking Cappy off balance, causing him to fall out of bed and land, with a thud, on the tiled floor.

"Shit! Fuck! I'm sore!! Oh man, it's gonna hurt when I...Cappy?" Matt said, looking for Cappy and seeing only his hand reaching up and grabbing the bed linen to pull him up off the floor. "Cappy? You OK?" Matt asked.

"Yeah, damn it all!" Cappy growled back as he hauled himself up off the floor.

"Cappy, I'm, I'm sorry..." Matt managed to say before he broke out in laughter.

"That's it, laugh it up pup! Go ahead, laugh it up!" Cappy snapped back, then he too broke out in laughter as he imagined what the entire scene must have looked like. Once they were done having a good laugh, Cappy looked at Matt and said, "So, you're pretty sore huh. No wonder, you took twelve hard cocks up your ass and a dildo. I've got something that will help, be right back."

Cappy got up and left, Matt's cock hardening as he watched the Captain's magnificent ass cheeks sway as he watched him walk away and head into the bathroom. Cappy came back a few minutes later with a silver packet in his hands.

"Here, this will help with some of the soreness. Roll over and get on all fours." Cappy barked.

"What is it?" Matt asked as he assumed the position.

"It's Preparation H, it'll help calm down the soreness and the swelling. God damn boy! You're ass lips look like they've been given a collagen injection! No wonder you're sore!" Cappy said as he gently eased the suppository into Matt's ass. "Fine ass you got boy! Fine ass!" Cappy said as he slapped Matt's ass cheeks and reached between his legs to grab his hard cock.

"Umm, yeah Cappy, your hands around my cock feel so good. I can't believe how fucking horny I still am." Matt groaned as he thrust his cock into the Captain's hands.

I rolled over in my own bed, and sensing I wasn't alone, sat up, rubbing the Demerol induced hangover from my eyes. I glanced over and saw Tim, lying on his side, sheets pulled up to his chin.

"Tim? Tim, wake up!" I said as I used my good arm to nudge Tim.

"Hmm, wha, what? Craig? Fuck! Craig, you OK?" Tim said as he sat up, nearly knocking me out of bed as well. "What time is it?" Tim said.

"Never mind that Tim, what the hell happened?" I asked.

Tim yawned and stretched, the muscles in his hairy chest rippling with his movements, causing my cock to stir. Rubbing his eyes and stretching again, Tim yawned and began to tell me what had happened in the showers. "You feel OK?" Tim asked me as he gently caressed my cheek with his oversized hand.

"Mmm, Tim, when you do that to me, I..." I stopped.

"You what?" Tim asked, looking me in the eyes, searching them to see if he can gather what my thoughts might be.

"Nothing, why Tim, is that a pickle under those sheets or are you glad to see me?" I said as I stared at his morning hard on.

"Oh that's so original there buddy boy." Tim grinned as he gently grabbed me and pulled me to him, his arms enfolding me as I lay my head on his chest and listened to the gentle beating of his heart. I rolled over, rather attempted to roll over, so that I would be laying on him. I got about half way over when I bumped the cast on my arm on the night stand, bolts of pain shooting up through my arm.

"AAAAAHHHH!!" I cried out, "Shit! Fuck, oh holy cow's of, fuck that hurts!" I continued to scream, jumping out of bed and doing some sort of dance. Tim cracked up laughing, got out of bed, his hard cock standing out in front of him, and went into the bathroom to get a glass of water and some pain pills for me. Tears had welled up in my eyes by now and not only was I doing "the pain dance" but was also sobbing it hurt so bad. Tim came back, saw me and gently eased me back down on the bed.

"Baby, look at you. You're a mess!" he chuckled as he handed me the pill followed by the glass of water. Once I had swallowed the pill and washed it down with the water, Tim helped me get a T-shirt on and a pair of shorts and escorted me out into the living room, helping me lay down on the couch while I waited for the medicine to kick in.

I turned on the TV and started surfing, finally settling on the local news. Within a few minutes the buzz in my head told me that the pain killers were starting to kick in, no wonder, I'd taken them on an empty stomach, not a wise thing to do. Tim came back in with some toast and a glass of orange juice that he set down in front me while he sipped on a freshly made cup of coffee.

"That coffee smells good, how come you didn't bring me any?" I slurred.

"Because you need to get something in your stomach first before those pills upset it. Coffee wouldn't be the best thing right now." Tim responded as he headed back down the hallway towards the bedroom to put some clothes on.

The doorbell rang, "Tim? Can you get the door?" I called out.

"Yeah, in a minute." Tim shouted back from the bedroom. The doorbell rang again.

"Jesus Christ! I'll get it!" I shouted to the air as I got up off the couch and made my way to the door. Opening the door, I saw Bill standing there. "Bill! How the hell are you?" I smiled.

"What the hell happened to you?" Bill asked as he looked at my arm.

"Oh, well I broke my arm." I replied back.

"Duh! I can see that, how?" Bill asked.

"Come in Bill." I said, letting Bill pass by me as he entered the living room. "Want some coffee?" I asked, completely forgetting that Tim was in the bedroom still.

"Nah! I drink one cup a day, already had that. So finish telling me what happened." Bill said as he sat down on the couch next to me.

Tim then entered the room so I made the proper introductions and as Tim resumed his spot on the overstuffed chair, I finished telling Bill what had happened.

"Damn dude!" Bill said after he'd heard the story, adjusting his crotch as I'd told him that I fell in the shower while getting ready to get laid by two studs.

There was a brief silence between the three of us as Tim and Bill sized the other up, each silently wondering what the other man would look and taste like. Bill finally stood, the erection tenting out his shorts and said, "Well, I should go." Bill said.

"You don't have to Bill. Looks to me like you could use some relief." I slurred.

"Um, yeah well." Bill said.

"I'm in no condition to take care of that for you but I bet Tim would." I urged, looking at Tim for some sort of reaction. Tim and Bill just looked at each other, a wicked smile beginning to creep across Tim's face as the thought of doing Bill in front of me crossed his mind. Bill walked over to where Tim was sitting and stood in front of him, looking down at Tim he asked, "You like to suck cock?" "You like to get fucked?" Tim asked back as he reached out and started massaging Bill's cock through his shorts.

"Um, only been fucked once, was kinda hoping Craig here would fuck me again."

Bill said looking over at me, a sleepy dopey grin on my face as I rubbed my own hardening cock through my shorts. I looked over at Tim and nodded, indicating that he should take care of my neighbor's needs. Tim scooted forward in the chair and lowered Bill's shorts, letting his cock bounce up, his shorts falling to his ankles.

"Suck him Tim, go on, suck his hard cock." I urged.

"Oh fuck!" Bill moaned as Tim sucked his hard cock into his mouth, his head gently bobbing up and down on Bill's hard cock, his hands cupping his balls, toying with them as they churned and rolled in his hands. I slid my own shorts down to my knees and gently caressed and stroked my hard cock while I watched Tim suck on Bill's hard cock, Bill moaning and groaning his appreciation.

"Let me see what you've got." Bill said as he pulled his cock out of Tim's mouth.

"OK but I should warn you, I cum fast and a lot on the first go." Tim said, standing, dropping his own shorts to his ankles and freeing his rock hard and now leaking cock.

"Mmmmm." Bill growled as he sank to his knees and sucked Tim's cock into his mouth.

"Oh yeah man, work that cock." Tim groaned. My own cock was leaking now; I stopped stroking it and using my finger tip played with the clear liquid that was oozing out of the tip of my cock, rubbing it over the head of my dick, licking it from my fingertips.

"Get ready buddy, I'm gonna blow." Tim panted.

"Mmm mmppff." Bill groaned back as he increased the speed and suction on Tim's cock.

"Yeah, buddy, that's it, that's it, oh fuck, get ready, here it comes, oh fuck!" Tim howled as his first orgasm hit him, his cock bucking and jerking, shooting ropes of fresh cum down Bill's throat. Bill did his best to swallow the massive load, however he couldn't keep up and cum leaked out the corners of his mouth, running down the sides of his mouth and dripping off his chin.

When Tim had finally quit cumming, Bill pulled off of his cock, cleaned the head off and said, "Damn! That was the biggest load I've ever seen, or swallowed."

"Nice isn't it?" I said. "He's not done though." I continued, pointing to Tim's still hard cock.

"So how about it? Wanna get fucked?" Tim asked, stroking his cock.

"He any good?" Bill asked as he looked over in my direction.

"The best!" I exclaimed.

"Tell you what, how about you fuck me while I suck Craig off?" Bill asked Tim, reaching out and playing with the after cum that was dripping from Tim's cock.

"Deal!" Tim shouted. Bill and Tim moved the coffee table out of the way, helped me up into a sitting position and then Bill got in a modified doggy style and started sucking my cock.

"Oh yeah Bill. Suck my fucking cock, yeah that feels good!" I groaned. Bill moaned as he felt Tim's tongue make contact on his tight hole. Bill released my cock and started sucking and licking my balls while Tim continued to eat his ass.

"Yeah buddy, oh fuck yeah, eat that fucking hole. Get me wet buddy. Yeah, that feels good." Bill said and then went back to sucking my cock.

"You ready?" Tim asked as he looked up from behind Bill.

"Mmm Hmm...just go easy buddy. You're only the second person to fuck me." Bill said, looking back as Tim placed the head of his cock at the entrance to Bill's tight hole.

"Just relax buddy, just relax." Tim said as he began to slowly enter Bill's ass, reaching around and grabbing Bill's cock.

"Uh, fuck, unngh, shit, wait, wait, let me get used to it. Damn! That's a fucking big cock!" Bill exclaimed as Tim stopped, not even half of the head of his dick was inside Bill. Tim continued to gently stroke Bill's cock, which in spite of the stimulation, had grown soft while he focused on getting his ass to accept Tim's cock.

"OK, slowly, just go...aahhh." Bill said as his ass suddenly sucked Tim's cock head in. "Oh fuck that feels good!" Bill purred as he gently rocked back and forth on Tim's cock, his cock hardening again in response. "Oh yeah! God DAMN that fucking feels good!" Bill squealed as he eased back on Tim's cock, taking the remainder of his dick and sighing as his ass cheeks came into contact with Tim's pubes.

Bill went back to sucking my cock, this time more urgent as Tim began to slide his cock in and out of Bill's ass. Within a few minutes the sounds of three men enjoying sex were filling the room. I was sighing and panting while Bill worked on my cock, Bill was groaning and moaning while Tim fucked his ass and Tim was panting and telling the two of us what a sweet hot and tight ass Bill had.

"Dude, you keep fucking me like that and stroking my cock and I'm gonna cum real fast. This fucking feels so good, yeah, fucking feels so good. I got a beautiful hard cock up my ass and I'm sucking another beautiful hard cock. Shit man, shit!" Bill moaned as he sucked my cock back into his mouth.

"Fuck! I'm close, getting close!" Tim panted.

Bill spit out my cock and said, "Yeah? You gonna fucking cum in my ass? Huh? Fucking shoot that load up my ass! C'mon stud, fucking give it to me, yeah, my fucking ass is gonna get creamed by your load!"

Bill shouted. I was getting close myself and I pushed Bill back own on my cock, the first sign of my approaching orgasm tingling in my balls.

"Shit yeah, fuck this is hot. Getting blown by my neighbor while I'm watching my buddy fuck his ass. Oh I'm gonna cum, get ready, fucking gonna blow my load!" I shouted and then stiffened as my cock erupted. Bill slurped and sucked, swallowing my load, his own cock firing, his cum spraying on the front of my leather sofa. The feeling of Bill's tight ass lips clamping around Tim's cock while he came triggered Tim's cum and he slammed into him one last time. Groaning, Tim stiffened as his cock unloaded up Bill's ass. Bill cried out as he felt the surge of hot scalding cum shoot deep in his ass, his ass lips clenching around Tim's cock, trapping as much of his load inside him as he could. Tim fell across Bill's back after he was done shooting, his softening cock slipping out of Bill's tight hole, a stream of cum following and landing on the hard wood floor.

The combination of the intense orgasm I'd just had coupled with the pain killers finally overtook me and I drifted off into a pleasant sleep. The cries of Tim cumming again woke me briefly, my eyes barely focusing on the image of Bill pounding Tim's ass on the floor, Tim's legs up and draped over Bill's shoulders as Bill cried out, his cum shooting up Tim's ass. When I woke again, it was late afternoon, my shorts had been pulled back up and I was beginning to feel the throbbing of my broken arm again. I called out for Tim and Bill, neither answered, I got up, stumbled to the bathroom, emptied my bladder and taking another pain pill, fell back onto the bed and dozed off again.

CHAPTER 13

Cappy was not a man who smoked cigars or cigarettes, however, he was known on occasion to light up, especially after having given some young pup a thorough fucking. Matt had thoroughly abused Cappy's ass with his hard cock, leaving the rugged Captain breathless and panting, the remnants of his hands free cum drying on his hairy chest. Matt had cleaned up and left about an hour ago and Cappy was still laying on the bed in afterglow, the smoke from the cigarette hanging lazily around his head as he blew it out.

"Fuck!" was all Cappy said to the air as he got up and headed to his shower to get cleaned up. Cappy had a huge appetite for sex and today was proving to be one of those days where he would need to venture out to the clubs to feed his appetite. Sure, he had a firehouse full of hot men that would fall to their knees and worship his cock at a moments notice, but Cappy needed more today, something much more.

Showered and dressed, Cappy headed out through the fire house in search of his second in command, Mike McKinley. Mike was in the kitchen, setting out the ribs for tonight's dinner, getting the rub ready so they could marinate all day before he threw them on the grill.

"Ribs huh? Mmm Mmm, but you make the best ribs!" Cappy said as he strolled into the kitchen.

"Hey Jim! S'up?" Mike answered back, smiling at the Captain.

"You're in charge tonight, I need to get out and take care of some business." Cappy responded, slapping Mike on the ass as he walked past him to get a cup of coffee.

"Oh I know what that means!" Mike joked back, "Cappy's gonna get his freak on tonight. Lucky guy!" Mike answered back, a slight tone of jealously in his voice.

"You just never mind what Cappy's gonna be doing!" the Captain shouted back, jokingly. "I live in this freaking fire house and sometimes, I just need a night to myself." the Captain continued as he grabbed his coffee and a granola bar from the pantry and headed out of the kitchen and back to his office.

Cappy sat at his desk and went over some paperwork the other men had left for him from the day before. As he was reading the various reports his mind kept wandering to tonight's events. His cock was starting to harden as he thought back to the day that he and David McKellum had met. They were both young men then, 20 years old in fact, and had entered the fire fighter's academy at the same time. They hit it off instantly, both silently exchanging the knowing glances that they "pitched for the same team." It wasn't until they were half way through their training that they were finally able to do something about the sexual energy that had been building between them. Cappy's mind churned as his memory replayed the night they tasted each other's cocks for the first time, so many years ago.

His memory jumped ten years forward, to the night they were both fighting a particular nasty fire. That was the night that ended David's fire fighting career, the night the explosion knocked him off the ladder truck, his back breaking, lucky to be alive as well as not paralyzed. David was able to stay on with the fire department and had gone on to become one of the academy's best instructors. Shortly after David had recovered, he had talked to Cappy about opening a bar in the Phoenix area. There weren't any that catered to his and David's taste, so, each taking a portion of their savings, they invested in an old warehouse in a seedy part of downtown Phoenix and opened their own bar. "Razor Strap" opened a few months later, a levis and leather bar, it catered to the men that Cappy and David were so drawn to. Their joint efforts were an instant success and as the years went by, they managed to keep the bar in touch with the current events, and as the city grew, so did the clientele, they also enjoyed the financial rewards of their success.

Cappy reached for his phone and dialed David's number. "Hello?" David's voice answered.

"Dave! Hey, it's Jim." Cappy responded.

"Big Jim! What the hell you doing man?" David said.

"Awe, just sitting here, reading reports, thinking about the good ole days, rubbing my hard cock in my pants." Cappy replied, laughing.

"Umm, been a long time since I tasted that cock of yours. You coming to the club tonight?" David asked.

"Yup! Think you can hook me up?" Cappy asked.

"Hook you up? My brotha, you don't NEED to be hooked up! You still look like a freaking GOD!" David said.

"Yeah, yeah yeah, thanks for helping out an old man's ego." Cappy chuckled.

"See ya tonight!" David said and hung up. Cappy spent the rest of the day trying to keep his mind off of tonight. He couldn't wait to get into his zone, to be with the men he liked so much to be around, the kind that shared his taste for the darker side of his sex life. The sounding alarm stirred him from his thoughts. He left his office to bid the men in his station a fond farewell and wish them luck.

Watching the last truck leave, he looked at his watch and whistled, "Holy fuck! It's already five. Time to get some food in my belly and get ready to head out." Cappy said out loud, turning to head into the kitchen and see what there was to eat. Mike hadn't yet fired up the grill so he knew his famous ribs wouldn't be on the menu. Settling for some leftover pasta, Cappy quickly ate and then headed to his suite to get ready for his night. Cappy locked the door to his suite behind him, he wanted his privacy tonight, and he quickly shucked his clothes and stepped into the shower.

Cappy took his time cleaning himself up, especially taking care to make sure he was just as clean inside as he was outside. Satisfied, he rinsed off, rinsed down the shower, turned the water off and grabbing a towel began to dry himself off. Once he was dried, Cappy went to his closet and pulled out the plastic blue box that held his prized possessions. Reaching into the back of his dresser drawer, he grabbed his leather jock and moaned as he felt the cold, soft leather slide up this legs and thighs, the pouch softly cradling and caressing his balls and cock, the straps outlining his firm ass cheeks. He pulled the front of the jock strap down and, reaching into the blue box, pulled out a thick metal cock ring that he carefully pulled his balls through as he slid it down the length of his cock, nestling it at the base of his dick.

"Umm, yeah, feels good already!" Cappy groaned as he admired himself in his full length mirror. Reaching in again, he pulled out the metal hoop that he would feed through the head and underside of his pierced cock. His cock jerked as he snapped the locking mechanism in place, a bead of clear juice forming at the tip of his head.

"Yeah baby, umm, fuck..." Cappy whispered at his reflection. The next two items Cappy pulled out were heavy metal hoops that he fastened through his nipples, his cock jerking as he gently tugged on each hoop, a long thin line of clear juice leaking from the tip of his cock and hanging down as it slowly dropped to the floor.

"Fuck yeah buddy boy, you're looking hotter and hotter for an old man!" Cappy said again to the reflection in the mirror. Cappy then reached for a pair of faded and worn levis, holes strategically placed, offering the viewer a glimpse of thigh and an outline of his leather jock, or a hint of his fur covered ass cheeks. Satisfied, he put on his leather harness, the center ring accentuating the pierced nipples and his massive and hairy pecs. Cappy squeezed his nipples, causing them to harden more than what they already were. Cappy then threw a solid white T-shirt on over the harness and tucked the shirt into the waist of his jeans. He reached into the back of his closet and grabbed his leather boots, army style, he laced them up and pulled the legs of his jeans down over the tops. He took one last look in the mirror, turning this way and that, flexing and posing, and headed out of the station.

The cool autumn night air washed over Cappy as he made his way through the streets of downtown Phoenix, catching the obvious stares of men and women as he waited at the various red lights he encountered at the intersections along the way. Each stare, each smirk or slack jawed grin only served to fuel his sexual energy. By the time he pulled into the rear parking lot, he was already in a pheromone induced high. Cappy walked in the back entrance of the bar and into the office the two men shared. He removed his T-shirt and draped across the back of the chair, he could here the loud music coming from the dance floor, the heavy base vibrating his insides as it beat. Cappy debated on removing his jeans but opted to leave them on.

He knew David would be working the bar so he headed out to the main part of the club. Walking in and behind the bar Cappy snuck up behind David who was chatting up a couple of pups who were dressed in nothing more than boots and jocks, the white glowing against the black lights that hung above the bar. Cappy walked up behind David, put his arms around his waist and ground his crotch into David's ass.

"Umm, I'd recognize the feel of that crotch any-day! Big Jim!" David said as he spun around, kissing Cappy firmly on the lips, their tongues briefly touching. Pulling away, David looked at his longtime friend and whispered into his ear, "I hope you saved some of your cum for me baby. You know how much I love working that cock of yours over with my mouth and feeling you fuck my ass!"

"Indeed I do my friend, indeed I do. Don't worry, I'll leave some cum in these balls for you." Cappy said as he kissed his friend back, their tongues caressing one another, tasting the other.

"Fetch me a beer bitch!" Cappy said as he slapped his friend on the ass.

"Not until you get on the other side of the bar, you know the deal! State law, no drinking..." David said, cut off by Cappy.

"Yeah, yeah, yeah, no drinking behind the bar." Cappy mocked back as he headed to the other end of the bar and made his way around. The two leather pups watched Cappy the entire time, both of them were licking their chops as he strode up and stood next to them.

The pup standing closest to Cappy reached over and ran his hand up and down Cappy's chest. "Mmmm, nice, bet your cock is just as nice as your chest." he said as he fingered one of Cappy's nipples.

Cappy reached up and pulled the young pup's hand away, "Didn't your momma teach you any manners?" he snarled at the young man. "Don't fucking touch the merchandise until I tell you to." Cappy continued, his cock stirring as he quickly showed the young pup who was the boss.

"Fucking get down there and clean my boots bitch!" Cappy snapped, reaching down and slapping the young man's jock strap outlined ass. He took a swig of his beer and winked at his friend David as the young man quickly fell to his knees and began licking the toes of Cappy's spit polished black boots. Cappy turned to address the young man's friend only to find that he had disappeared and was somewhere on the dance floor, gyrating to the beat of the music.

"Enough boy, go find your friend!" Cappy barked down to the young man who quickly and quietly disappeared.

"Hahaha! Damn Jim, you fucking amaze me at how quickly you can command!" David said as he returned from helping another customer.

"Those two were practically yelping as they left." David continued to giggle.

"He he, yup! Still got it!" Cappy joked, flexing one of his muscles as he did so. Turning his back to the bar, Cappy let his eyes take in the action that was occurring around him.

The warehouse was two stories. The bottom comprised of the dance floor and bars. The second floor consisted of a metal cat walk surrounding the dance floor with various rooms, in various sizes, branching off the catwalk. There were two more bars on the second floor. David and Cappy had decided when they opened their bar that they would insist on responsible drinking. If someone entered the bar alone, they were asked if they had driven or if they had arrived by cab. If they had driven in, they were required to surrender their car keys. They only got them back if they were able to pass a breathalyzer, if not, their car was secured in a locked parking lot and a taxi was called for them, paid for by David and Cappy.

If a group of men arrived, a designated driver was asked for and whomever was volunteered, a neon green wristband was secured around their wrist and the designated driver was given complimentary water and sodas while they were there. In addition, everyone who entered was required to provide ID to show they were old enough to be there. David and Cappy had hired a couple of excellent doormen, capable of spotting a fake ID from 100 miles, as a result of, they were one of five establishments in the metro Phoenix area that had not been busted on a liquor violation.

Cappy wandered around the outside of the dance floor. He watched the men on the floor dancing and moving, their bodies gyrating and grinding into one another. Someone passed a bottle of poppers under Cappy's nose, to which he deeply inhaled the heady aroma, his head instantly buzzing with the affect, his cock tingling. Cappy had paused in his journey at one point and was staring up at the cat walk when he noticed someone was staring back at him. The gentleman who's eyes he'd made contact with was leaning over the railing, beer in one hand. He wore no shirt, his chest smooth, long dark hair framed his face. He raised his bottle of beer to Cappy, almost as if offering him a toast and then motioned with his head for Cappy to come up.

Cappy headed for the stairs and quickly, taking two at a time, bounded up them and made his way across the crowded cat walk to where the man stood. Cappy's mouth watered and his pulse quickened as he got closer to the man. Standing about six foot tall, the man was dressed in leather pants, a prominent bulge displayed in his crotch. Both of his nipples sported two large, heavy hoops, the weight of which caused his nipples to sag a little. His eyes bore into Cappy as he continued to approach him, his face framed by the shoulder length hair, the smell of sweat and leather hit Cappy's nostrils as he approached. The effect of which was even more intoxicating than a bottle of poppers could ever be.

Cappy saddled up to the strange man, each one sizing the other up. "Jim, name's Jim." Cappy said.

"Zeek, short for Ezeckiel." the other man replied. "Fucking nice chest!" Zeek said to Cappy.

"Fucking nice crotch!" Cappy said back.

"C'mon, follow me." Zeek said as he turned and headed for one of the rooms. Cappy followed, watching the mans ass move in his tight leather pants. We walked through a couple of the rooms, one set up with an old claw foot porcelain bathtub in the center. One of the young men Cappy had barked at lay in the bath tub, his clothes removed, while several men stood around him and pissed on him, his squeals and moans indicating his enjoyment of being used as a human urinal. The second room we walked through had a bank of glory-holes along one side of the wall. Faceless mouths slurped and sucked on faceless dicks, shouts of men echoed through the room as they pumped the faceless mouth full of their cum.

Cappy entered the next room. A leather sling hung, suspended from the ceiling in the center of the room. It was bathed in soft white spotlights and was empty. Various men were lined up along the wall, some quietly talking to each other, some caressing each other, their hands toying with pierced nipples or stroking a hardened cock that had been freed from the confines of its owners jeans. A few turned to look at Cappy and Zeek as they entered, Zeek leading Cappy to the harness.

"Strip!" Zeek ordered.

Cappy moaned as he quickly shucked his jeans and threw them to the side. Standing in his jock strap, his cock aching, Cappy looked at Zeek, waiting for the next step. "I said STRIP!" Zeek ordered as he reached around and slapped Cappy's ass.

"Unngh!" Cappy groaned at the sting of the slap and quickly went about removing his leather jock strap, his cock rearing up and slapping his stomach, leaving a wet spot in the fur of his belly. Zeek snapped his fingers twice and two burly men appeared from the shadows, picked Cappy up and proceeded to place him in the sling, securing his feet and hands. Zeek walked over and gently and carefully removed the hoop from

Cappy's cock head, tucking it into one of the pockets in Cappy's discarded jeans. Zeek snapped his fingers twice more and the same two burly men stepped forward and proceeded to strip Zeek, all he wore now was were his boots. Cappy groaned as he took in the magnificence of Zeek's body. Zeek was a perfect specimen of body building done with taste, his muscles were firm and toned but lack the grotesqueness of a body overworked by weights and steroids. Between his legs hung a thick ten inch cock with two large balls that had to be storing a gallon of cum. Zeek approached Cappy, turning his head Cappy opened his mouth and waited for Zeek to guide the thick cock into his mouth. Instead, Zeek slapped Cappy across the face, Cappy's cock flexed and he groaned.

"Not yet slut!" Zeek shouted, "Not yet!" Zeek walked around the room, checking each man out, finally settling on the two burly guys that had helped strap Cappy in. "You two, prep him!" Zeek commanded.

The two men disappeared back into the shadows and then reappeared, pushing a metal table they stopped once they had reached Cappy. Cappy looked over at the items on the table. "Oohhh!" he moaned, his cock flexing again, cock honey running out of the tip in a steady stream as his eyes took in the assortment of dildos and butt plugs in various shapes and sizes that were on the table. He groaned again as the two men picked up a can of shaving cream and two razors and proceeded to shave Cappy's body until he was completely devoid of any hair, to include his pubic and ass hair. The two men disappeared and then returned with buckets of warm water. Cappy sighed as they two men expertly washed the hair and shaving cream from Cappy's body then applied a soothing aftershave balm to his chest, arm pits, stomach and pubic area. Cappy's cock continued to produce a steady flow of clear cum, which both men took turns licking and lapping off of his hard cock.

"Enough!" Zeek ordered as he walked over to the table, grabbed a butt plug and a bottle of lube and proceeded to get Cappy's freshly shaved ass prepared. Zeek pumped a large amount of lube into the palm of his hand then slathered Cappy's hole with it, his fingers darting in and out as he did. Cappy groaned and bucked in the sling as Zeek continued to play with his ass, eventually inserting his hand up to the last set of knuckles into Cappy's ass.

"Yeah, fuck yeah." Cappy moaned as Zeek fucked his ass with his hand. Zeek removed his fingers and began to feed the butt plug into Cappy's ass.

"Awe FUCK YEAH!" Cappy cried out as his hole was stretched by the base of the butt plug. "Unngghh...fuck yeah..." Cappy panted. "Somebody fucking feed me their cock, NOW!" Cappy cried out. Cappy was soon rewarded with the head of a cock being placed at his lips, he groaned as he sucked the cock into the back of his throat. Cappy bobbed his head up and down, sucking the strange cock like there was no tomorrow.

"Ahhhh! Ahhh! FUCK YEAH!" Cappy cried out as Zeek removed the butt plug from his ass and applied more lube. "Mmmmm...mmmmm..." Cappy groaned as he continued to work on the hard cock that was now frantically fucking his face. The cock fucking his face was now pounding his mouth, he could feel the head in the back of his throat begin to thicken, indicating the man was getting ready to cum. Cappy managed to spit the cock out long enough to tell the man he wanted his cum on his face. The man straddled Cappy so he could lick his balls while he jerked his cock off.

"Aahh yeeahh!" Cappy cried out again as Zeek inserted a vibrating dildo up Cappy's ass, his cock flexing and slapping his stomach.

"Fucking get ready boy! Get ready, I'm gonna paint your face!" the man jerking his cock cried out. Cappy groaned as he felt the hot cum shoot out and splash on his chest. The man above him grunted and groaned as he continued to jerk his cock, painting Cappy's chest with his cum, finally feeding him the dripping, softening head for Cappy to clean off. The man left Cappy's side once he had cleaned his cock off and Cappy gasped as Zeek grabbed his cock, pulled it back and began licking the clear liquid that was flowing out of the tip of Cappy's head.

"Yeah, fucking clean my cock off bitch!" Cappy cried out and was rewarded with another cock nudging his lips. Cappy quickly swallowed the cock and allowed the owner to start slowly thrusting his cock in and out of Cappy's mouth. Cappy moaned as he felt the head of the strange cock hit the back of his throat while at the same time the dildo that was up his ass was slowly removed. Cappy groaned as he felt a tongue begin to lick at the outer lips of his hole. Another cock brushed against the other side of his cheek and, spitting the cock out that he was currently sucking on, he turned his head, only to realize that this cock belonged to Zeek.

"If I'm sucking your cock, who's eating my ass?" Cappy panted. He looked up and stared right into David's eyes.

"Surprise! You like?" David said.

"Oh fuck!" was all Cappy could say as he sucked in the head of Zeek's cock and started nursing on it, the other cock forgotten as he attempted to swallow the ten inch monster. David quit eating Cappy's ass and picked up a metal ring with two wires attached to it and proceeded to gently pulls Cappy's balls through it. Cappy moaned at the soft touch of his balls, unaware of what was going on. David then attached the two wires to the stim unit and turned the unit on, starting at the lowest setting. Cappy was oblivious to the electrical shocks that were beginning to course through his balls, realizing he was unaware of it, David increased the voltage. Cappy soon felt a tingling in his balls and he managed to groan while still working on Zeek's cock. David increased the voltage again and this time Cappy started squirming and bucking in the sling.

"Oh yeah, fuck! Fuck that feels good!" Cappy shouted as he spit out Zeek's cock. "God DAMN David! What the fuck...OH YEAH!" Cappy groaned as David increased the voltage again on the electro-stimulation unit. Cappy forgot all about Zeek's cock as his head thrashed from side to side, moaning, panting, David kept the voltage where it was at, taking Cappy to the brink but not letting him go over the edge.

David got up from where he was at and exchanged places with Zeek. Standing over Cappy, David fed him his cock while at the same time, David sucked in Cappy's cock. Cappy groaned as he sucked his longtime friends rock hard cock down his throat, reveling in the familiar feeling of his dick as well as the taste. Reaching around, David spread Cappy's cheeks, offering his wet pucker to Zeek, who quickly placed the head of his ten inch cock at the opening of Cappy's wet and well stretched ass. Cappy went wild as Zeek fed his cock up his ass, finally settling in at the base.

"Mmmpfff...mmmnnn...mmmppffff." Cappy moaned and groaned while he continued to let David fuck his face. Cappy motioned against David's hip, indicating he needed to pull out of his mouth so Cappy could catch his breath.

David pulled out and Cappy cried out, "FUCK ME BITCH! FUCKING POUND MY ASS...oh David, fuck David, oh fuck!" Cappy panted, "Fucking let me cum David, please, oh GOD, please, I wanna cum so bad!" Cappy cried out.

David continued to suck on Cappy's cock while he removed the electro stim unit from Cappy's balls. Cappy had grabbed David's cock and was now jerking his friend off, his cock pointed right in his face. Zeek was slamming his cock in and out, pulling his dick completely out, rubbing it along the crack of Cappy's ass and balls before shoving it back in.

"FUCK ME BITCH! Oh GOD DAMN FUCK ME!!" Cappy shouted as his balls began to draw up and his orgasm started to build. "David, I'm gonna cum David, I'm gonna fucking cum." Cappy panted as he started licking and nursing on the head of his friends cock. "David, I'm close, I'm getting close, tell me when!"

Zeek panted as he continued to jack hammer Cappy's ass. "I, oh fuck, I, David here it comes, I'm..." Cappy cried out as his orgasm hit, shooting jet after jet of built up cum down the back of David's throat. Zeek cried out, slammed into Cappy one last time, stiffened and emptied his load deep into Cappy's guts. David pulled off of Cappy's erupting cock, shouted he was cumming too, then dove back down on Cappy's cock as he unloaded, painting Cappy's face and lips with his cum. Shouts of other men, who'd been watching, jerking their cocks, echoed throughout the room as they too came, their cum splattering on the floor. Cappy nursed the rest of the cum out of David's cock as David collected himself from his orgasm. Zeek had already pulled out of Cappy's ass and was busy getting his own ass fucked in another part of the room.

"David?" Cappy panted.

"Yeah?" David responded.

"I fucking love you buddy, fucking love you!" Cappy said as the two men stared at each other. David removed Cappy from his restraints and held his friend up until his legs became stable. The two of them looked around the room and, watching the other men involved in the various stages of sex, looked back at each other and David said, "C'mon, we got a bar to run. Help me?"

"You bet buddy, anything!" Cappy responded and the two men embraced again. Finding his clothes, Cappy quickly dressed and both he and David left the other men to their own vices as they headed back downstairs to tend bar. The remainder of the evening they kept grabbing at one another, slapping an ass, groping a crotch.

"Hey, you two lovers?" one patron asked. David and Cappy looked at each other, laughed, and went on about their business.

CHAPTER 14

"But Cappy!" I shouted, standing in Cappy's office.

"Don't but me boy! I said no and I mean no, you're a liability right now and I can't afford that!" Cappy shouted back.

"You're being unfair! I'm not asking to go out on any calls, just put me to work, light duty, I can do other stuff around here besides be a paramedic." I argued back.

"NO! And I don't want to hear another word about it!" Cappy shouted back. "You're on worker's comp right now, getting 45 days continuation pay, go home, rest and recover. I don't want to see you back!" Cappy continued, his finger pointed at me, his face flushed with anger. The entire fire station heard the two of us going at it and remained hidden, including Tim. It was Friday, the start of my normal shift and I was reporting to work, only the Captain was having nothing to do with it and was wanting to send me home.

"Fuck Cappy!" I started to say, "Boy! I am you're Captain and if nothing else, you WILL respect that." Cappy shouted back at me, I knew I was crossing that line with him.

"You're a fucking hard head, you know that Cappy? Huh? Do you? Anyone ever fucking tell you that?" I shouted back. Cappy slammed his fist down on his desk, hung his head a few minutes to collect his thoughts and then, very calmly, very pointedly said to me, "I am not having this conversation with you anymore. You have five minutes to unass the area or I will, and I emphasize will, write your ass up and suspend you so you don't get jack shit! Do I MAKE myself clear?" Cappy glared at me, his nostrils flaring with his anger, his chest heaving. I knew that if I said another word, I'd be done for and so I threw my hands up in the air, sighed and turned around and left his office.

"Craig, wait up." Tim called to me as I stormed out of the fire station and headed to my car.

"What Tim?" I snapped back.

"Are you fucking crazy man? Do you have any idea how fucking pissed off Cappy is with you right now?" Tim lectured me.

"Tim, I don't give a flying fuck about Cappy and his feelings right now. That man is a stubborn jack ass, there is a lot I can do around here, HE just doesn't want me around!" I shouted, just like a five year old who'd just been told he couldn't ride his bike for a week.

"Craig..." Tim started to say, grabbing for my good arm. I yanked away, told him to just leave me the fuck alone, got into my car and sped out of the parking lot, narrowly missing the trash cans that were placed at the curb for tomorrow mornings trash pickup.

The flashing blue lights in my rear view mirror soon caught my attention. Looking at my speedometer, I realized I'd been clipping along at a brisk 60 miles per hour, in a 45 mile per hour zone. I slammed the palm of my good hand down on the steering wheel as I looked for a place to pull over. Once stopped, I dug around my glove compartment for my registration and insurance, retrieved my driver's license from my wallet and had my window rolled down and ready when the police officer stepped up to the driver's side of the car.

Leaning down he looked at me and said, "Son, do you know how fast you were driving?"

"Yes officer, I do." I replied back, looking forward instead of making eye contact with the police officer.

"Wanna tell me why you were going 60 when the speed limit is clearly marked as 45?" The officer growled at me.

"No excuse officer." I replied, dead pan.

"Son, you mind stepping out of your car?" he asked. I sighed and waited for him to step back before I opened the car door. Climbing out and standing up I made my first assessment of the police officer that had pulled me over. It was hard to really check him out, it was dark out and he was wearing a black police suit with a bright orange safety vest.

"You been drinking?" he asked me as he looked over my license.

"No sir." I replied back.

118

"Son, would you mind stepping to the back of your vehicle and placing your good hand on the trunk of your car, I'll need you to spread your legs too." the officer politely asked. I obeyed and waited while the officer phoned in my plates and registration. Coming back a few minutes later he laid his clip board on the trunk of my car and proceeded to pat me down.

"You realize you were more five miles an hour short of criminal speeding?" The officer asked me while his hands roamed over my back and then up the front of my shirt.

"No sir." I responded, my dick starting to tingle and stretch as the officer paid what seemed like extra attention to patting down my ass.

By the time the officer finished patting down my ass and the back of my legs, I was rock hard and suddenly terrified as I realized he was now going up the front side of me, starting with my ankles. His hands moved up my legs, brushed against my hard cock and then returned momentarily, squeezing my hard crotch, making sure it was a hard cock he felt and not a weapon.

"I take it you liked the frisking." He said, slapping me on the ass. I felt my face blush as he instructed me to stand up and turn around. He positioned himself so that he was standing off center of me, I could feel his crotch against my thigh, could feel his own semi hard cock through the polyester jodhpurs he was wearing.

"Open your mouth son." He commanded as he flipped on a pen light and began looking inside my mouth. "Got any weapons?" He asked, telling me I could now close my mouth.

"No sir." I responded.

"Is the address on your license and registration correct?" the officer said as he handed everything back to me.

"Yes sir." I responded.

"Tell you what, because you are on our side, I'm gonna let you off with a warning. Slow it down and be safe." He smiled at me as he handed me the paper warning, slapping my ass as I turned to head back to my car. I got in, started the car back up and slowly pulled back onto the street to finish my journey home. I pulled in my driveway and parked the car in the garage, closed the door and headed into the house. The front of my underwear were now soaked with my pre-cum and I hadn't realized how much the cop frisking me had turned me on. Putting my keys in the kitchen I grabbed a beer from the fridge and headed into the living to watch some TV. The image and feeling of the cop wouldn't escape my mind so I decided to see if I had any cop porn in my stash I could throw in. Give myself a quick yank, finish my beer and then head for bed, that was my plan anyway. I'd no sooner sat back down when there was a knock on my front door. I flipped off the movie and headed to answer the door, opening it I saw the police officer who'd just pulled me over standing at the door way.

"You forgot this." He said, flashing me my driver's license. I opened the screen door, took the license from the officer and thanked him.

"Mind if I come in? I'm off duty, another reason why I didn't give you a ticket. Too close to quitting time." he said.

"Yeah, I suppose." I said, stepping aside to let him pass. The officer walked into the center of the living room, removed his hat, turned and said, "I'm officer Kyle Corkins." and he extended his hand to shake.

"Pleased to meet you Officer Corkins, Craig, Craig McFadden." I replied, taking his hand and giving him a firm hand shake. "Ummm, nice big paw he has." I thought to myself. "So, sit down, can I offer you a beer, soda, water?" I asked.

"Water would be good." he replied as he sat down on the couch while I went into the kitchen to get him a glass of water. I stopped dead in my tracks as I re-entered the living room with his water.

It would seem that I had neglected to hide the cover box for the porno I was just about to watch. Kyle had picked it up and was now closely studying the front cover, which showed a police officer, shirt unbuttoned revealing a muscular hairy chest, and his hard cock was poking out of the fly of his uniform trousers.

"Hole Patrol?" he asked, looking up at me. "Sounds cheesy." he continued as he laid the box back down on the table.

"Mind if I take this thing off?" He asked, pointing towards his weapons belt.

"Uh, yeah, sure." I responded as I sat down next to him. Looking at me, he said, "I'll cut to the chase. We both know why I'm here and since you were getting ready to watch some cop porn, why don't I just give you the real thing." Standing he walked over so that his crotch was at face level with me.

"C'mon, get it out, suck it for me." He said, lust filling his voice. I reached up and unfastened his uniform pants, unzipped his trousers and proceeded to pull them down to his knees. His hard cock pointed up in his white bikini briefs.

"Not bad," I thought, "definitely party size." I continued to think as I leaned forward and inhaled the muskiness of his crotch, rubbing my face up and down the length of his hard cock.

"Eat it." Kyle ordered. I began to lick and chew on his cloth covered cock, reaching up to the tip of his dick that was just poking out of his waist band and then gnawing my way down to the base of his cock, trying to suck his balls in my mouth through his underwear. Kyle removed his uniform shirt and pulled his T-shirt up and over his head. His nipples were rock hard and he moaned as he toyed with them while I continued to chew on his dick.

"Get it out, I wanna see your lips wrap around my cock." Kyle said.

I obliged, pulling his cock out of his underwear and shoving those down to his knees as well. I licked the tip of his cock, tasting the saltiness of the sweat and piss that had accumulated during the course of his shift.

"Yeah, feels good." Kyle sighed as he continued to play with his nipples.

"C'mon, suck it." He pleaded. Kyle hissed as he sucked in air into his lungs, throwing his head back, sighing he said, "Oh yeah, fucking eat my cop cock." I continued to bob my head up and down his hard and leaking cock, letting my tongue slide along the underside of the tip of his cock, licking at the sensitive vein that bulged under the head of his dick. I grabbed his balls and started tugging on them while I continued to suck my new cop friend off.

"Yeah, fuck yeah, that's it, suck my cock, pull on those balls. Mmm, feels so fucking good." Kyle panted as he began to thrust his hips, fucking my face with his hard tool.

"Hang on a minute." Kyle said as he pulled his dick out of my mouth, kicking his boots off and removing both his pants and his underwear.

"Lay back." Kyle urged as he moved the coffee table to one side and squatted down between my legs. I groaned as I felt his tongue dart out and start licking the underside of my own cock.

"Yeah Kyle, fucking feels good." I moaned as he worked his mouth up and down the underside of my cock. Kyle then sucked my cock into the base in one swallow and proceeded to give me an expert blow job.

"Yeah that's it Kyle, fucking suck that cock, suck me off officer." I groaned.

"Mmmmm..." Kyle responded. Kyle continued to work on my cock with his mouth for what seemed like an hour, bringing me close to the brink then taking me back down again. Kyle pulled off my cock and asked me if I had any lube. I got up and retrieved the lube from the bedroom.

"Sit down on the couch again." Kyle said and I complied. Kyle came over, straddled my legs and proceeded to grease up my hard cock, wiping a generous amount on his sweet pucker. Kyle placed the tip of my cock at the entrance to his ass and gently and slowly started lowering his ass down on my cock.

"Oh yeah, you're fucking tight officer." I groaned as I felt my cock slide in to the base.

"Oh fuck. I've been wanting a cock up my ass for a long time now. Can't tell you how long it's been since I've gotten fucked." Kyle moaned as he began to bounce his ass up and down in my lap.

"Oh yeah Kyle, God your ass around my cock feels so good. Feels damn good, yeah, keeping riding my hard cock Kyle." I panted as I reached up with my good hand and started playing with Kyle's nipples. Kyle's eyes were closed, head tossed back and he was moaning while he bucked and ground his ass on my cock.

"Oh fuck yeah, Craig, I'm not gonna last long. Feels too good, I can feel the cum starting to climb up in my cock and I'm not even touching it." Kyle moaned as he increased his speed.

"Yeah? You gonna cum? Oh yeah, fucking shoot it copper, fucking shoot that cop spunk all over me." I shouted as I felt the first signs of my own climax building up in my balls.

"Craig? Oh fuck Craig! Oh fuck, I'm gonna shoot, I'm gonna cum!" Kyle shouted as he slammed down on my cock and ground his hips on my rock hard cock. Kyle's cock jerked and cum streamed out of the head of his dick, running down his cock and onto my pubes. He didn't shoot, it just ran out, like a river of cum, coating my pubes, some of it now running back and underneath my balls. I started bucking my hips into Kyle, slamming him up as I fucked him.

"I'm gonna fucking cum up your ass bitch! Get ready! Get ready, here, it, comes!" I shouted as I bucked up one last time, throwing Kyle forward my cock coming out of his ass just as it started to spray. His ass cheeks caught my cock just in time and held it there at the entrance to his ass while I shot my load. My cum shot out, hit his hole and then sprayed back down over the head of my dick. Kyle hopped off my lap and shoved my cock into his mouth while I finished cumming. The last few jets of cum he swallowed then proceeded to lick my crotch and cock clean.

The ending was very short and unceremonious. Once he had my cock cleaned off, he thanked me, quickly dressed and left the house just as quickly as he entered. "Huh?" I thought as I pondered over what had just happened. My cock was still not satisfied, so I flipped on the movie, grabbed the lube and proceeded to jack myself off to another cum just as the cock on the screen unloaded, covering the face of the cop he'd been fucking with his load. I groaned as I shot another load, wiping my cum off of my stomach and licking my hand and fingers clean.

The phone rang, I answered it and it was Tim. "You OK?" Tim asked.

"Yeah, just finished eating my load off of my stomach." I teased.

"Bitch!" Tim said back.

"Where are you?" I asked.

"I'm still at the station, Cappy is so fired up pissed off at you that he's got all of us working like dogs." Tim said.

"Awe Tim, I'm sorry." I replied back.

"So besides jacking off, what else did you do tonight?" Tim asked.

"Fucked a cop up the ass." I said matter of fact.

"You're funny, seriously, what did you do?" Tim asked again.

"Seriously! I fucked a cop up the ass!" I responded back. I filled Tim on what had happened and as I relived the moment, my cock hardened so I start stroking it again.

"Tim, you hard?" I asked. "Fuck yeah! I'm in the john, jacking my cock off." he continued.

"Yeah, me too. Wanna cum together?" I asked.

"Fuck buddy, you know I do!" Tim said back.

"Let me know when you're ready buddy, I'm almost..." I started to say then was cut off my Tim's groan as he obviously started shooting his load. I stroked my cock a few more times and I groaned in Tim's ear as my cum flowed out, pooling in my pubic hairs.

"Umm, that was fun." Tim said as he was licking the cum off his hand.

"Feel better?" I asked while I did the same.

"No, won't feel better until I got my cock planted in your ass again." Tim responded. "Hey, gotta go, Matt just walked in." Tim said and then hung up. I put the phone down and finished cleaning the cum off me and then headed for bed. I dozed off, my thoughts turning to fantasy as I imagined Cappy and I having make up sex.

CHAPTER 15

"Ssshh Matt. We don't need the other guys hearing us." Tim whispered to

Matt.

"Why not? Ever think they might want to join us?" Matt said as he stroked Tim's cock in the tight stall of the men's room.

"Oh man, dude, I'm close." Tim quietly groaned. "Matt, turn around, I want to cum on your hole and then slide my cock up your ass." Tim whispered in Matt's ear.

Matt let go of Tim's hard cock, dropped his pants to his ankles, turned around and did his best to offer his tight ass up to Tim. Tim had to squat down a little, grabbing his cock he rubbed the head of his dick from behind Matt's balls and up until he felt the lips of his hole on his cock.

"Fuck yeah." Matt groaned as his ass lips twitched at the sensation of Tim rubbing his cock head across them. "Mmmm, feels good already." Matt purred.

"Fuck, I'm gonna shoot, get ready. When I start I'm going to cream your hole and then slowly slide my cock in OK?" Tim whispered.

"Yeah, do what you want. Just feed me your cock." Matt groaned. Tim slid his cock along Matt's hole one more time before it erupted, a giant glob of his cum splatting up against Matt's rosebud. "Yeah, feels good, c'mon Tim, slide that bad boy inside me." Matt urged, groaning loudly as Tim slowly slid his spurting cock up Matt's ass.

"Ssssshhhh." Tim scolded.

Jason Denton had walked into the men's room to take a leak when he heard the whispered sounds of Tim and Matt coming from the center stall. "What the fuck?" Jason thought to himself as he quietly snuck into the first stall and stood up on the toilet so he could peek down into the stall that Matt and Tim were fucking in. "Fuck me!" Jason thought to himself as he watched Tim slowly sliding his cock in and out of Matt's ass, Matt groaning his enjoyment in hushed tones. Jason's cock twitched and began to harden. "What the fuck? What the...this shit can't be turning me on! I love my pussy and I love my wife!" Jason thought as he was surprised to feel his cock hardening at the sight of two men fucking. Tim was now bent over Matt and was kissing and nibbling on the back of his neck. Matt had reached between his legs and was jacking his cock in time with Tim's pelvic thrusts.

Jason reached into the waist band of his sweats and rubbed the front of his underwear. It was at this moment that he started feeling like he was having an out of body experience, as though he were hovering above himself, watching himself get off on watching two men fuck. Tim was beginning to increase his pace, a light sheen of sweat on his back. Matt was moaning his appreciation of the ass fucking he was getting and telling Tim how good his hard cock felt up his tight ass and that he couldn't wait to feel the cum shoot out of his cock and right into his ass. Jason pushed down the front of his underwear, freeing his hard and leaking cock. Pulling the drawstring on the front of his sweats, he allowed them to fall to his ankles, freeing his cock.

"Oh yeah buddy boy, fucking take his cock up your ass, damn, you're fucking your man like my woman fucks me!" Jason screamed in his head. "Yeah, you're making my cock hum and feel good boy!"

Jason continued as he began to frantically stroke his cock. "I'm getting there Matt, wanna eat my load?" Tim said as he slowed his thrusts somewhat, delaying the approaching orgasm. "FUCK! Boy's gonna shoot his cum on his buddy's face! Damn! Even my woman won't take my load anywhere near her face!" Jason continued to think as he pounded on his cock. "Yeah, fucking shoot it in my face Tim!" Matt said, standing up and letting Tim pull his cock out of his ass so he could turn around and drop to his knees.

Matt dropped to his knees, opened his mouth and nodded that he was ready for the load Tim had to offer him. Tim placed the tip of his cock right on Matt's tongue as he jacked himself off to his orgasm. Cum shot out coating the back of Matt's throat and onto his tongue. Matt groaned his own cock unloaded, dumping his load on the tiled floor of the bathroom. Matt placed his lips around the head of Tim's cock and took the last of his load and swallowed it, using the back of his hand to wipe the few stray strands of cum from his lips. Jason, afraid he might be seen by the two men now that they had cum, squatted down on the toilet, awkwardly, and finished stroking his cock. Ropes of cum flew out of the tip of his cock and landed with a splat on the tiled floor. Matt had his head bowed down while he collected himself and saw the cum hit the floor, a large pool beginning to develop.

Looking up at Tim he motioned that someone was in the next stall. The two of them remained motionless while they waited to see if the person next to them was going to leave. Jason looked down after his cock was done spitting and an alarm went off in his head as he surveyed the puddle of his spunk that was now on the tiled floor, clearly visible to anyone in the stall next to him. "Shit!" Jason thought. "Now what do I do?" he continued as a sense of panic began to take over. He quietly stepped down from the toilet, opened the stall door, hoping it wouldn't squeak and made a fast exit out of the men's room.

Tim quietly opened the stall door and peeked around the corner to see if they were alone. Satisfied they were, they pulled their pants back up, wiped off any tale tell signs that sex had just occurred in that stall and quickly left the rest room as well. They both beamed as they casually walked out of the bathroom, content with the knowledge that they'd just had a great fuck session and obviously one of the fire men had enjoyed as well, judging by the size of the load he dumped on the floor. Jason ran back to the sleeping area and crawled into bed, somewhat dazed by what he'd witnessed yet still excited.

Shortly after the three men left the restroom, Mike McKinley, the second in command entered the restroom. "Smells like cum and freshly fucked ass in here." Mike thought to himself. He entered the first stall and slipped in the puddle of cum that Jason had left behind. "What the?" Mike said out loud. "For fucks sake, you'd think these assholes would clean up their mess when they are done jacking off." He sighed as he grabbed a wad of toilet paper and proceeded to wipe the cum up off of the floor. Mike dropped his trousers and sat down on the toilet. Mike also had a pierced cock and loved to have the piercing tugged and pulled on.

Over time, it had stretched enough that if he tried to use a urinal, he would piss all over his pants. Mike relaxed his muscles and sighed as he let his bladder empty, enjoying the feeling of emptying an over-full bladder. Jason had heard someone enter the bathroom and was freaking out that they would spot the puddle of cum he'd left. He got out of his bed and headed back to the restroom in hopes that whomever it was had not taken the first stall. He froze as he walked in the door and saw the door to the first stall shut, indicating it was occupied. He tried to lean down enough so he could see in the stall without being seen and freaked again when he saw that the puddle of cum had been wiped up. Clearing his throat, why he didn't know, he entered the center stall and decided he needed to jack his cock again as it was already hard and throbbing again. Jason dropped his sweat pants and sat down on the toilet, slowly and quietly rubbing his cock, waiting for the person next door to finish up so he could shoot another load.

Jason glanced over to the wall that separated the two stalls and saw the hole where the toilet paper holder should be. He ran his fingers around the edge of the circle, causing the toilet paper holder to rattle on the other side. To Jason it was purely an innocent action, to Mike though, it was a tell tale signal that someone wanted to suck some cock. Mike placed his foot just slightly under the stall that Jason was sitting in and tapped his foot three times, a signal used to indicate he was there for some man to man action. Jason, again acting out of innocence rattled the toilet-paper holder, sending the signal to Mike that he wanted to suck some cock. Mike stood up, his cock already half hard, removed the toilet paper holder and stuck his cock through.

"Oh my God! What did I just do?" Jason thought to himself.

"C'mon, suck it man." Mike whispered as he wagged his cock back and forth.

"Shit! Shit! Shit!" Jason thought.

"C'mon man, stop being a cock tease. You told me you wanted it, now get on it!" Mike said, shoving his hips into the wall of the stall. Jason closed his eyes, leaned forward, stuck out his tongue and took a tentative lick at the tip of Mike's now hard cock.

Jason's cock flexed and reared up as he did this, "Holy fuck!" he thought to himself, surprised by the reaction his body was giving him.

"Bitch, fucking suck it!" Mike insisted. "Don't fucking get me boned up then leave me with nothing!" Mike continued. Jason got a little braver, this time, licking the entire head. "Yeah that's it, fucking lick my cock like an ice cream cone!" Mike whispered. A shudder of pure pleasure went through Jason's entire body and a drop of cum trickled up and out of his cock head, dropping to the floor. "Here goes nothing." Jason thought to himself as he began to slowly suck Mike's cock, starting with just taking the head of his cock into his mouth.

"Fuck yeah boy, good boy, suck that cock." Mike panted. Jason stroked his cock a little harder and started taking more and more of Mike's cock into his mouth, eventually swallowing him down to the base of his cock. "I can't believe I'm doing this," Jason thought as he bobbed up and down on Mike's cock. "I SHOULDN'T be doing this!" Jason screamed in his head.

"Fuck yeah boy, oh you are a born cock sucker. Your mouth on my meat feels so good boy. You keep sucking my cock like that and I'll be filling your belly with my seed real soon!" Mike panted and groaned. "What did he say? WHAT DID HE SAY?" Jason's inner voice screamed at him. "Did he say he's going to cum in my mouth?" Jason continued. "What the fuck do I do now? I've never swallowed cum before, never even sucked a cock before." Jason thought as his hand continued to stroke his cock.

"Yeah boy, fuck yeah, let me fuck your face boy." Mike said as he began to thrust his cock down Jason's throat, deeper than Jason thought was possible.

Jason gagged a few times, "Swallow it boy! Need to learn to relax that gag muscle." Mike scolded.

Jason's orgasm was beginning to build, he could feel his nuts drawing up tighter and tighter against his body. The head of his cock was beginning to swell and his balls had that wonderful tingling in them, indicating he was about to bust a nut. Jason also sensed the head of Mike's cock begin to swell. Suddenly aware that he was about to swallow his first load, something clicked in his mind and he began to really suck on Mike's hard cock, hard and deep.

"Get ready boy, gonna paint your tonsils with my cream. Get ready, here it comes boy, oh fuck, I'm cumming boy, get ready, fuck yeah!" Mike shouted as he slammed his hips into the wall of the stall and his cock unleashed a torrent of cum down Jason's throat. Jason gagged and started coughing, spitting Mike's cock out, the rest of his load landing in Jason's chestnut colored hair. Jason groaned and shot his load as well, creating another puddle on the floor of the bathroom. Mike had finished cumming and, shaking the last drops of cum off his cock, flushed the toilet and headed out of the rest room.

Jason had collapsed on the floor, panting, in shock at what he'd just done. His fingers were tracing circles in the puddle of cum he'd left on the floor. As if on auto-pilot, he brought his fingers to his mouth and tasted his cum. Jason ran his fingers through his cum again and licked it off of his fingers. Like a starving man, tasting food for the first time in a long time, Jason crouched forward and began to lap the cum off the floor, not stopping until he'd cleaned up every drop of it. The reality of what Jason had just done hit him like a ton of bricks. "My God, what have I done? What have I done?" Jason said to the empty air and began sobbing. Sitting on the floor, cum drying in his hair, pants still down around his ankles Jason cried over the guilt of what had just transpired.

"What am I going to do? I know, I know, I'll transfer, yes, that's what I'll do. I'll transfer to another station, where no one knows me and no one knows what I just did, no one but me, and I'll, I'll, I'll..." Jason stopped thinking and sobbed, heavy, chest heaving sobs. He finally collected himself, pulled his pants back up, checked himself in the mirror, ignoring the dried cum that was in his hair, and headed back to his bed. Jason tossed and turned the entire night. He knew what he'd have to do the next day, he'd have to talk to the Captain about transferring. The sun was just beginning to rise when Jason finally dozed off.

CHAPTER 16

Jason was nudged awake by one of his firefighting brothers. "C'mon Jason, time to get up. You've already missed breakfast. Jesus Jason, what the fuck is in your hair?" the firefighter said, heading back to the dayroom, not giving Jason a chance to respond. Jason stumbled out of bed, instantly felt sick to his stomach, and ran to the bathroom to vomit. Jason flushed, walked over to sink and splashed cold water on his face.

Looking at his tired worn face in the mirror he said, out loud, "Jesus Christ, what's happening to me?" "I don't know Jason, what IS happening to you?" a voice answered from behind him.

Jason screeched and spun around and stared right into the eyes of Mike McKinley. "What? Oh, Mike, hey, nothing, I was just, well gotta go." Jason stammered as he started to dart past Mike.

"Jason, you OK? You look like shit this morning!" Mike said.

"Um, yeah, fine, stomach's a little rocky this morning is all, fine, really, just fine, I mean, it's not like I was planted with some strangers seed last night and now I'm pregnant or something, I mean, well, you know what I mean..." Jason just shut up at this point, sighed, hung his head, and quickly left the restroom. "I wonder..." Mike thought as he watched Jason leave.

Tim and Matt entered the rest room to shave, brush their teeth, shower etc., and Mike started up some small talk with them. "Say, you two weren't in here last night were you?" Mike asked.

"Why? Why do you ask Mike?" Matt answered nervously.

Mike leaned in close to the two of them and said, "Because I slipped in a puddle of cum when I walked in here last night."

Before he could say another word, Tim chimed in, "What stall?" Mike looked at the two with a puzzled expression on his face and said, "First one..." and before he could say anything else Matt sighed and, without thinking, said, "Oh good, we were in the second one." Matt realized what he'd said and started to back peddle.

"Chill out Matt, think about who you're talking to here." Mike said, getting a good chuckle out of it. "Listen," Mike started, "Someone was in stall two and proceeded to suck my cock like I've never been sucked before."

"Yeah?" Tim and Matt both said at the same time, reaching down and rubbing their cocks through their underwear.

"Well, I ran into Jason this morning and not only does he look like shit but he's acting awfully guilty. How much do you know about him?" Mike asked.

"I don't know, he's happily married, or so he says anyway, usual stuff, sports, cars, hicks, pussy, that kinda thing." Tim said.

"You know Mike, someone was watching us get it on in the first stall. There was a puddle of cum on the floor when we got done. You suppose it was Jason and now he's all weirded out like?" Matt asked.

"Matt, if you knew the cum was there then why the hell didn't you clean it up?" Mike asked.

"I dunno." Matt said, shrugging his shoulders.

"Just keep an eye on him, something's not right." Mike said and left the restroom.

Matt looked at Tim's reflection in the mirror while he shaved, "You suppose it was Jason in here last night?" he asked.

"I don't know Matt, why?" Tim responded.

"I dunno, he's cute, looks like he's got a nice cock. Wouldn't mind..." Matt said and was then interrupted. "Cool it Matt. Don't be thinking you can convert this guy. You don't know who it was, number one, and number two, we aren't a freaking recruiting team for man to man sex." Tim said.

"Yeah yeah yeah..." Matt said, the two of them continued getting ready in silence.

Jason was fully dressed and had been mentally rehearsing his speech to why he wanted a transfer. Taking a few deep breaths, he closed up his locker, locked the combination lock and headed to Cappy's office.

His door was open when he got there and the rear door that led into his suite was also open. Gathering his nerve, Jason barged in through both doors.

"Cappy, I need to talk to you." Jason said. Cappy had finished his shower, shaved, brushed his teeth and was in the process of ironing his uniform, clad in bikini briefs, when Jason barged in.

"Don't you know how to knock son?" Cappy growled as he continued to focus on ironing his shirt.

"Sorry sir." Jason said as he left the room and proceeded to knock on his door.

"That's better, come in son." Cappy said.

"Cappy, I..."Jason started to say, suddenly realizing that Cappy was wearing only his underwear. He'd never seen Cappy out of his uniform and was shocked at the sight of his body. What shocked him even more was the size of the pouch that was packed inside the crotch of his underwear. Jason couldn't take his eyes off the full bulge of Cappy's cock and balls.

"Well, spit it out so!" Cappy ordered.

"Cappy, I...I...I want to...I want to suck your cock!" Jason exclaimed.

"Wait? What did I just say?" Jason screamed in his head. "Your what?" Cappy asked.

"Cappy, I...I. want to... I want you to fuck me." Jason said again. "Oh my God! What am I saying?" Jason silently thought, as he continued to stare at Cappy's crotch, noticing that the fullness caused the elastic in the waist band to pull away, exposing the neatly trimmed bush.

"Jason, you OK?" Cappy asked, setting the iron down and turning it off.

"Huh?" Jason asked, his gaze still on the Captain's crotch. "I mean, Cappy I want to suck your cock!" Jason blurted out again. "Holy fuck what am I saying, what am I doing?" Jason screamed to himself.

"Jason, this isn't like you. What's going on?" Cappy asked, walking towards Jason and putting a hand on his shoulder. Jason was trembling as he suddenly realized he was rock hard and filled with lust for this man. "Jason, listen to me. Everything going OK at home?" Cappy asked, concern on his face as he looked into the young man's troubled eyes that were now welling up with tears.

"Jason, you and Peggy have been married for what, seven years now?" Cappy asked. Jason just nodded his head yes, his eyes cast downward again, transfixed on Cappy's underwear clad crotch. "Is it getting bigger? Is he getting hard?" Jason's inner voice asked. "Stop it! Stop it!" He silently screamed to himself.

"I know how things can change in a marriage over time, especially in the bedroom." Cappy was saying to Jason. "Should I just reach out and yank 'em down and start chewing on his cock? Oh fuck, what is happening to me?" Jason thought to himself.

"Did something happen with the men last night Jason?" Cappy asked, placing both hands on the young mans shoulders, pushing Jason closer and closer to the edge.

"No, nothing that a load of cum in my mouth didn't resolve." Jason said flatly. "Oh God, I'm screwed, somebody shut me up!" Jason yelled to himself.

"Is that what you really want Jason? To suck my cock?" Cappy asked.

"Yes sir, and fuck my ass sir, please?" Jason said, looking into the Captain's eyes for a sign, something to tell him he wasn't going crazy. Cappy released Jason's shoulder's and turned his back to Jason. Jason stared at the firm globes of Cappy's underwear clad ass, his mouth watering. He was on auto pilot again as he dropped to his knees and inched himself closer to Cappy's ass, inhaling the clean fresh smell of him and the soft hint of fabric softener coming off his underwear. Jason reached up and pulled the back of Cappy's underwear down. Before Cappy's mind could register what was happening, Jason had spread his cheeks and shoved his face in between the globes of Cappy's ass, his tongue darting out and licking his freshly washed hole.

Cappy turned around and staring at Jason asked, "If this is what you really want, then..." Before Cappy could say another word, Jason had reached out and had yanked the front of his underwear down and was now sucking on the Captain's flaccid cock. Cappy groaned as his cock started to respond to Jason's mouth and tongue. "Oh yeah." Cappy said, "you're a fucking born cock sucker." he continued as he started to gently pump his hips into Jason's face.

"Cappy I...whoa!" Mike said, stopping dead in his tracks as he saw Jason on his knees servicing his Captain's cock. Cappy was oblivious to Mike's entry and continued thrusting his now rock hard cock down Jason's throat. Jason, moaning and panting, unbuttoned his uniform shirt and was playing with his nipples through his T-shirt.

"Yeah boy, eat that fucking cock." Cappy said, motioning for Mike to close and lock the door and join he and Jason. Once Mike had closed the door, making sure it was locked, he quickly stripped and walked over to stand next to his Commander, his cock rock hard, pointing out in front of him. Cappy reached over and started stroking Mike's cock while he continued to enjoy the servicing that Jason was giving him.

"Wanna taste another cock?" Cappy asked Jason. Without saying a word, Jason moved over to Mike's cock and started sucking on him.

"Holy fuck boy! That's a great mouth you got on you!" Mike exclaimed as he and Cappy began to exchange kisses.

"Let's see what you're packing Jason, get out of those clothes boy!" Cappy commanded. Jason groaned as he spit Mike's cock out and proceeded to strip out of his clothes at break neck speed.

"Phew! Look at that cock he's packing!" Mike whistled and exclaimed. Jason's cock was long and thin, with a perfectly sized tapered head at the end that sported a drop of cock dew at the tip. His balls were not very large at all, in fact they almost looked as though he was still at the starting stage of puberty.

"Come on Jason, let's get a taste of your cock now." Mike said as he picked the young fire fighter up and carried him to the bed. He gently laid him down and while he was still bent over, Jason reached up, grabbed Mike's head and sucked his tongue into his mouth. While he and Mike kissed hard and passionately, Cappy went down on Jason's cock, his tongue flicking over the tip of his cock, licking the honey from the piss slit.

"Unngghh." Jason groaned as he kissed Mike.

"Fuck Cappy! This boy's hot for cock!" Mike said.

"Yes he is!" Cappy agreed as he moved from Jason's cock to his underdeveloped balls.

"Oh fuck Cappy, yeah, that feels good." Jason panted. "Aaagghh!" Jason shouted out as he felt Mike's lips close around one of his nipples and his tongue dart out and flick across it. "Fuck me, fuck me please." Jason panted and whined. "Oh God, feels good, so good, please..." Jason continued. Cappy quit licking Jason's balls and went back to sucking on his cock. Jason shouted when he felt Cappy suck his cock back into his mouth, his cock releasing a single shot of cum into Cappy's mouth.

"Ummm...you taste good boy!" Cappy purred as he continued to nurse and lick on Jason's hard and quivering cock. Mike moved around Jason so he could feed Jason his cock while he moved down to share Jason's cock with Cappy. Cappy licked and slurped on the base of Jason's cock while Mike worked on the head of his dick. His cock was pouring out clear juice and Cappy and Mike would kiss from time to time, exchanging the sweet flavor of his young pre-cum.

Jason continued to work on Mike's cock, licking and sucking, letting Mike fuck his face with his sizable tool. "Unngg...Unngg!" Jason screamed with a mouthful of cock as his orgasm suddenly hit him. Cappy sense he was cumming and pulled his cock back as the first shot of cum bolted out of the tip of his cock, shooting over Mike's head and landing in the center of Mike's back.

"Yeah boy! Way to go! Fucking shoot that load on us!" Mike shouted. His cock erupted several more times, spraying Mike and Cappy's face with his cum. Cappy leaned forward, letting the rest of Jason's load coat his lips while Mike licked the cum from Cappy's face. Mike and Cappy kissed again, Mike's tongue darting out and cleaning the white liquid from Cappy's lips. The two men continued doing this until Jason's load was licked clean from each other's face.

Jason continued to groan as Mike fucked his mouth, his spent cock not going soft. Jason pulled off of Mike's cock and begged them to fuck him, to please feed him their cocks up his ass. Cappy was all too willing to oblige as he thought about his cock entering the young man's virgin ass. Mike grabbed Jason's legs and pulled them towards him, exposing his ass. Cappy dove in and started eating the young man's ass, his tongue licking around the lips of his freshly washed hole and darting in, tasting the muskiness of his insides. Cappy groaned and Mike encouraged him to continue.

"Eat his fucking hole Captain, yeah, show him what it's like to have his Commander's tongue up his shit hole. Oh yeah Cappy, fucking eat it, fuck his hole with your tongue." Mike said.

"Mmmm..." Cappy groaned as he pulled off his ass and starting running his finger around the tight hole. Jason bucked and let out a muffled scream as he felt his ass start to get penetrated with Cappy's finger. His ass sucked his finger in to the first knuckle and Jason's instincts took over. He spit out Mike's cock and, panting, starting telling Cappy to fuck his ass, shove his finger up his ass and fuck him good. Cappy inserted as second finger and Jason cried out and slammed his hips down on the two fingers.

Panting he said, "Oh fuck Cappy, stop teasing me and get that fucking rock hard cock of yours up my ass!" Cappy removed his fingers, grabbed his cock, spit on the head of his dick and started rubbing it around Jason's ass lips. "Yeah, oh yeah, oh fuck, fuck me daddy, fuck me hard with that daddy cock!" Jason cried out. Cappy very slowly and very gently started feeding Jason's ass his cock. Inch by inch he slowly inserted his dick into his ass. Cappy felt the resistance on the head of his cock as he started to push past Jason's ass ring.

Jason moaned and panted and cried out as the pressure of Cappy's cock inside him increased. "Does that hurt?" Mike asked Jason. "No, feels good, fuck me please, oh god, this feels so good." Jason said, his head writhing and moving from side to side, eyes closed as he centered on a feeling inside his body he'd never felt before. Cappy had about half of the head of his cock inside Jason when his ass ring relaxed. The rest of Cappy's cock slid in, Cappy groaned as the tight virgin ass sucked his cock in. Jason cried out, his cock jerked up and he shot another load.

"Give me your cock Cappy, Mike, fuck me too, I want you both inside me." Jason begged as his cock stopped shooting but still didn't go soft. "Jason, that's not a good idea, this is your first time." Mike said. "I don't care dam-nit! I said fuck me and I mean fuck me! HARD! Get your fucking cock up my ass now!" Jason screamed.

Cappy removed his cock from Jason's ass, Jason whimpered as he suddenly felt a void inside him. Cappy and Mike then explained to Jason how this would work and how it would probably hurt like hell since he wasn't used to having one cock up his ass let alone two. Jason didn't care though, the only thing he was focused on right now was the feeling of having two cocks inside him. Cappy had Jason get off the bed and had Mike lay down on his back.

"Now, I want you to straddle Mike but let me feed you his cock, OK?" Cappy asked.

"Yeah." Jason said as he straddled Mike, his ass poised at Cappy's face. Cappy took a few more minutes to eat his beautiful tight ass out before getting the lube out of the nightstand. Cappy applied a generous amount of lube to both Jason's ass as well as Mike's cock. Grabbing Mike's cock, Cappy placed it at the entrance to Jason's ass and instructed Jason to start lowering his ass down on Mike's cock. Jason groaned and bucked as he lowered his ass onto Mike's cock, groaning and sighing once he hit bottom.

"Now, lay forward so that you're completely on top of Mike." Cappy instructed. Jason did as he was told and he and Mike immediately began kissing while Cappy lubed his own cock up. Cappy then climbed up on the bad and straddling both Mike and Jason, started to slide his cock into Jason's ass.

"OH FUCK!" Jason cried out as Cappy's cock began to slowly enter his ass. Jason bucked and his body began to shake as another orgasm overtook him, yet his cock produced nothing, it just thumped and flexed on Mike's belly. "Yeah, feed me your cock, oh GOD! I've got two cocks in me at the same time, fuck me, please, oh fuck me, feels so good." Jason cried out. Cappy was now fully inserted into Jason's ass. Neither he nor Mike could believe that his virgin ass was taking two cocks at the same time and where he should be howling in pain, he was, instead, howling in ecstasy. Cappy began to fuck Jason, his cock traveling over Mike's causing Mike to moan and tremble.

"Shoot it, fucking fill me with your loads." Jason begged. "I want your cum in me so bad, let me have your cum, oh fuck this feels good, feels so good." Jason said before he elapsed into a sexually induced rambling that neither Cappy or Mike could understand.

"Cappy your cock rubbing over mine feels so fucking good!" Mike said. "Yeah it does, god your cock feels so big like this. You like this Mike?" Cappy asked. "OH YEAH!" Mike growled back. Cappy increased the speed of his thrusts again and both Mike and Jason cried out.

"I'm gonna cum, I'm gonna cum!" Jason shouted.

"Yeah boy! Let it go, shoot your spunk all over Mike!" Cappy shouted. Jason screamed out and collapsed on top of Mike.

"Fuck! Fuck Cappy, he ain't cumming! He's fucking pissing on me!" Mike shouted. "The boy's taking a piss on me!" Mike continued, finding it rather exciting.

"I'm probably bumping into his bladder, either that or he's so stimulated that what he thinks is cumming is something else." Cappy panted, the thought of someone getting a golden shower really turned Cappy on and brought him closer to his orgasm. "You like it Mike? Feel good?" Cappy groaned as his speed increased again.

"A little I suppose." Mike panted. "Oh fuck Cappy, you're getting me close, yeah, keep fucking us like that and I'll be shooting up his ass in no time!" Mike panted.

"Yeah? You gonna cum in my ass? Yeah? Come on Mike, fill me up with you cum!" Jason groaned.

"I ought to fill you up with my piss boy! That's what I ought to do!" Mike snarled back. Jason and Cappy both thought about Mike taking a piss inside Jason's ass and it threw them over the edge.

"I'm fucking cumming! I'm gonna shoot!" Cappy shouted as he slammed into Jason's ass, his cock erupting, coating the underside of Mike's cock with his cum.

"OH I feel it, yeah I feel you shooting in me. I'm gonna cum again, oh fuck here I go!" Jason shouted as his cock erupted, this time coating he and Mike's stomachs with cum.

"God DAMN! I'm there too! Hang on, gonna blow, gonna fucking bust my nut! Aahhh!" Mike cried out as his cock erupted, coating both he and Cappy's cocks in cum.

"Oh, I can feel your cum running out of my hole and over my balls." Jason said as he reached back, trying to dip his hands in their cum.

Cappy slowly pulled out of Jason's ass. His ass lips were puffy and bruised looking. "Boy, you are going to be sore tomorrow!" Cappy said as Jason began to lift himself off of Mike's cock, cum spilling out of his ass and flowing back down over Mike's cock.

"I can't believe you fucking pissed on me!" Mike said.

"I'm sorry Mike, I thought I was cumming." Jason said, trying to work the stiffness out of his legs.

"Mike, that's enough. We need to get these sheets into the wash and I need to obviously head out and get a new mattress, this one is soaked." Cappy said. Jason was laying on the floor, legs spread wide and fingering his ass, the cum that was still seeping out he would scoop up in his fingers and lick them clean.

"What did I just fucking do?" Jason asked.

"Well son, you just had your first initiation into man to man sex and I'm thinking you liked it." Mike said.

"No I didn't" Jason responded, "this wasn't my first time. I sucked someone's cock off last night in the john!" he continued, giggling like a little school boy.

"Were you in the second stall?" Mike asked.

"Yup!" Jason replied.

"Holy fuck! That was YOU last night that sucked me off!" Mike said. "You little shit!" he continued.

"Hey, I wasn't planning on doing that, I actually was going back to clean up the cum I left on the floor from watching two guys fucking in the stall, but you beat me to it." Jason said. "So, you serious about pissing in my ass?" Jason asked, looking at Mike and holding up his cock which had hardened again.

"Grrrr...you boys!" Mike said, "C'mon, let's get this taken care of." he continued as he headed for Cappy's shower, Jason right on his heels asking him how much he had to pee and was he really going to do it.

"Boys will be boys!" Cappy said as he started to pull the mattress out of his suite.

CHAPTER 17

It had already been a month since I'd been told to stay home by Cappy. I hadn't forgotten the heated words we'd exchanged and felt rather badly about being so pissed off with him. I had just gotten back from the doctor's office, follow up appointment, and would have my cast off within another week. I decided to call Cappy and let him know my status, so I reached for the phone and dialed his number.

"Hello?" Cappy's husky voice answered.

"Hi Cappy, it's Craig." I responded.

"Craig, how the hell are you doing? What's the latest with you? We sure miss you around here." Cappy said with obvious excitement in his voice.

"Cappy, I want to apologize for my outburst awhile back." I started, "and to also tell you that my cast comes off next week and I'll be able to return to work the following Monday." I finished.

"Excellent news Craig, excellent news!" Cappy responded. "I'll put you back on the schedule. You gonna be home tonight?" he asked.

"Yes." I responded. "Good, I'll pay you a visit, say sevenish?" he asked.

"Seven is good for me!" I replied, saying my goodbyes and hanging up.

I'd been so blessedly horny over the past month. Tim was busy banging Matt so I hadn't heard anything from him at all. In fact, I couldn't help but feel a little jealous whenever I'd think about him plugging Matt's tight ass or Matt, on his knees, sucking Tim's thick cock. I'd grown tired of watching porn and jacking off so it'd been a week since I last popped a load. Thinking about Cappy coming over and paying me a visit tonight was causing my cock to stir. I laid back on the couch and started rubbing my crotch thinking about the last time Cappy and I had been together. I loved worshipping his cock, loved feeling it's thick velvety head slide down the back of my throat. I was just starting to pull my cock out of my shorts when the phone rang.

"Hello?" I said.

"Buddy! How the hell are you?" Tim's voice said on the other end.

"Tim? Where the fuck you been buddy? Wait, don't answer, you've been busy tapping Matt's ass haven't you?" I asked.

"Yeah, but he went back to fish buddy boy. Been two weeks since I got my rocks off." Tim said.

"Two weeks and you haven't come to see me or get a chick to take care of you?" I asked.

"Nah, to tell you the truth, I've realized I'm not bi, I love cock and fucking ass too much." Tim said. "Guess I've been in a funk, that's why I haven't called. You free tonight? Hey, how's the arm?" Tim rattled.

"Arm is good, get the cast off next week. Hell yeah I'm free tonight, Cappy is gonna come over around seven. Get your fucking ass over here and I'll relieve you of your pent up load then we can have a three way with Cappy." I panted in the phone.

"Fuck! That'd be hot! OK, it's four now, I need to shower, I'll be over around five." Tim said and hung up the phone.

I was rock hard and leaking now. I couldn't believe my luck! In a span of fifteen minutes, I was going to get to see my two favorite men in the same night AND have them both at the same time. I climbed off the couch and set about making sure everything was ready for tonight, to include making sure

I was absolutely 100% clean inside and out.

Five o'clock rolled around fast and within a few minutes, Tim was ringing to door bell. I got up off the couch and let Tim in. Tim said nothing as he closed the door behind him and I dropped to my knees, unbuckling his belt, unbuttoning his 501's and pulling them and his underwear down in one swift motion. Tim's cock was already half hard as it flopped out of his underwear, smacking me in the chin.

I quickly sucked in his cock, remembering that Tim's first load was fast in coming. Tim threw his head back and groaned as I deep throated his rock hard cock, feeling the thick mushroom head nudge past my gag reflex. Tim put his hands on my head and started shoving my head up and down on his cock. I tightened my throat and lips as best I could and reached up to play with his big balls. They were already beginning to tighten in their sack and I could feel the head of Tim's cock beginning to swell, letting me know his load was just a thrust or two away.

"Oh buddy, I've got two weeks of cum stored up in these balls. Sure you can take my load?" Tim panted.

"Unngghh Hunnngghhh." I responded back as best I could.

"Get ready, I'm gonna blow!" Tim grunted as he shoved his cock to the back of my throat and let loose with his cum.

I could feel each round of cum that he fired hit the back of my throat and slide down. My instinct was to swallow but there was no need to, he was firing directly into my throat. Problem was, my breathing was cut off.

Choking, I pulled back slightly to get my breath. That was when his cock really started unloading and flooded my mouth instantly with his cum. I swallowed as fast as I could in between breaths but couldn't keep up.

Before long his cum was flowing out of my mouth and running down my chin.

His hot, scalding cum dripped off my chin, landing in my pubes. I stroked my cock as fast and as hard as I could and within minutes blasted my own load over my stomach, adding to the cum and that was still dripping from my chin. Tim finally quit cumming and pulled his spent cock from my mouth. I licked the last of his load from the head of his cock and the two of us moved from the floor to the couch, panting, our legs weak and barely able to carry our weight. I collapsed against Tim's chest, sliding down, laying my head on his stomach. Tim looked down at me and I saw the same spark in his eyes that I'd seen several times before. Tim smiled, ran his hand through my hair and suggested we get cleaned up before Cappy arrived.

We spent the remainder of our time cleaning up our mess and getting some munchies out in case Cappy might be interested in eating before we got to fucking. Seven o'clock rolled around a few minutes later the doorbell rang. Tim answered the door.

"Tim! Wasn't expecting to see you here but the more the merrier." Cappy said as he walked through the door.

"Smells good in here, what's for dinner?" Cappy asked.

"Nothing, just some munchies for us. Good to see you Cappy!" I said as I walked over and started french kissing our Captain.

"Save some for me!" Tim said as he pulled me off the Captain and dove in on his mouth as well. By the time he and Tim were finished kissing, there was a noticeable lump in Cappy's jeans.

"OK you two, c'mon, let's eat and get caught up." I said. We stood in the kitchen, around the island, and feasted while Tim and Cappy filled me in on the happenings of the fire station. Nothing much had changed, except for

Matt going back to women and then transferring to another station. Our bellies were soon full and, as we'd also been drinking beer, our heads were beginning to buzz when we all three headed for the living room. We quickly shed our clothes, our semi-hard cocks swaying in front of us as we rearranged the furniture to make room for our three some. Cappy and Tim had just finished moving the coffee table and were now standing side by side, stroking each others cocks.

I walked up to them, my own hard cock in hand and sank to me knees and started taking turns sucking the two men off. I started with Cappy, licking the head of his cock, feeling it flex and twitch on my tongue while I stroked Tim's. Both men let out a groan and a sigh as I continued to service Cappy with my mouth. I soon moved to Tim's cock, only instead of stroking Cappy's cock, I decided to reach around and start fingering their asses at the same time. I received another grunt and groan, indicating their approval of what I was doing. I moved back and forth from one cock to another and as I serviced each man, I'd let my fingers sink further and further into their asses. Tim's was still wet from his cleaning and Cappy had obviously applied some lube before he came over as my fingers slid into each of their asses easily. I worked their cocks as I added two fingers to their asses. By now they were moaning, each man kissing the other and twisting and pulling on each other's nipples while I sucked their cocks and fingered their holes.

Without warning, they pulled apart and grabbed me, lifted me up and carried me to the bedroom where they laid me down, on my stomach. Tim and Cappy started taking turns eating my ass, sucking my balls and licking the tip of my cock. I cried out as their mouths ravished my hole, balls and cock. I soon felt the coolness of lube being applied to my hole, followed by the sensation of two fingers rubbing the lips of my hole. I felt the pressure as they eased their fingers inside me, stretching the ring of my ass. I groaned and bucked my hips. Before long I felt two more fingers rubbing my hole as they too started to ease into me. I winced as my ass ring was stretched, the fingers waiting, letting me relax and get used to the sensation. My ass relaxes, allowing the second set of fingers to begin to penetrate me.

"Think he's ready?" I hear Cappy ask Tim.

"Naw, not yet." Tim responds and I feel fingers remove themselves from my hole.

I whine at the feeling of emptiness they leave but soon groan as I feel a tongue caressing my hole again. Within a few moments, a bottle of poppers is passed under my nose. I inhale deeply, letting my head spin and my ass relax. The two fingers insert themselves again and wait. I relax again.

Another whiff of poppers and before I know it, more lube is being applied to my hole. Four fingers are inside me, motionless and I soon feel two more fingers knock at my back door. They begin their entrance, stretching me to the point where I cry out in pain now. The poppers are passed under my nose and I inhale and soon lose myself as they stretch me beyond belief.

I might as well have an entire hand up my ass at this point. I'm stretched beyond anything I can ever imagine. I can feel my cock pouring out the clear fluid of pre-cum. I feel as though I've left my body and am watching from a distance as Cappy and Tim basically fist me. I have no idea they are preparing me for what will be my most powerful orgasm. One by one the fingers leave my ass and I feel myself being moved on the bed. I feel the weight of the bed shift as Tim and Cappy take their position. I'm rolled over on my back like a rag doll and sat up.

"Craig? You OK?" Tim asks me.

"Yeah, fine." I mumble back.

"You wanna try two cocks up your ass at the same time?" I hear Cappy's voice ask.

"Fuck yeah!" I say.

I watch as Tim and Cappy lay lengthwise on the bed, Tim's head resting on a pillow to avoid the foot board hitting his head. They position themselves, legs interwoven within each other, they scoot forward on the bed until they are cock to cock, balls to balls.

"Straddle us." Tim says as he holds his and Cappy's cock together in his hands. I pass the bottle of poppers under my nose again and move myself so that I'm now straddling the two. Cappy applies another generous helping of lube to my ass as I squat down. I feel the heads of their cocks nudging at my hole, begging for entrance and I squat lower as I revel in the feeling of the poppers. The heads of their cocks separate the lips of my ass as I ease myself down on them. I hit the point where they are at the ring of my hole and I don't think I can go any lower. I inhale the poppers again and as they take affect, I continue to lower myself. The pain is exquisite as their heads stretch the ring of my ass and I can't help by yell out in pain. I stop, panting, sweat breaking out on my forehead. I'm not sure I can do this, but part of me wants this, wants these two cocks inside me. I breathe out, close my eyes and lower myself some more. Their heads push past my ass ring and I immediately sink as low as I can on their cocks. I cry out, not in pain, but pure ecstasy as I feel their cocks fill me up.

Tim and Cappy also cry out as they experience a feeling they've never felt before. Each man can feel the underside of the other's cocks while the tight lips of my hole surrounds the outer portions of their cock.

I rest, letting my hole get used to this and within a few minutes I begin to slowly lift myself up. Tim and Cappy moan again as my ass sucks in their cocks while my legs lift me off of them. I rise just to the point where I think their cocks may plop out and I lower myself again. Twisting my nipples with one hand, stroking my rock hard cock with the other, I can't help but cry out as well as I feel their cocks fill me up again. I do this several more times, all three of us crying out with the exquisite pleasure we're giving one another. We each take a hit from the poppers and

I quickly increase my speed, the three of us moaning at the feeling of our joint fucking. The pressure of the two cocks against my prostrate is causing a continuous stream of clear fluid to run from my cock, I'm so lost in the feeling of riding two cocks at the same time that I'm oblivious to this.

"Fuck Cappy, his cock is flowing pre-cum, it's coating our balls Cappy. I don't know how much longer I can last. I didn't think it'd be this fucking hot or this fucking tight!" Tim cried out.

"I'm with you buddy boy, I'm with you. Wanna fucking fill his ass with our load at the same time?" Cappy panted.

"Oh fuck yeah, fuck yeah Cappy! I wanna feel your cum shooting against my cock while I blast his ass with my fucking load." Tim groaned back.

"Shit I'm close! Can you cum with us Craig?" Cappy asked.

"Fuck, just start shooting in my ass and I'll fucking start shooting my load. Fuck yeah, oh fuck yeah, this feels so fucking good!" I cried out as

I increased my pace. We continued to fuck like this for what seemed like an eternity. All of us shouting that we were gonna cum but then losing that edge. My legs were beginning to get sore and tired and I wasn't sure how much longer I was going to be able to do this. I kept going as I want to feel their cocks fire up my ass at the same time.

"Oh God, Oh fucking God, I'm gonna cum, I'm gonna fucking cum!" Tim suddenly cried out.

"Me too! Me too!" I echoed as my cock hardened even more, the head swelling and turning an angry purple.

I felt Tim's cock flex and shudder and felt the first volley of cum shoot in me.

"FFFUUUCCCKKK!!!" Cappy cried out as he felt Tim's cum wash over the head of his cock.

I soon felt Cappy's cock begin to fire and I let loose with my own load as

I felt their cocks flex and jump inside of my ass. Their cum firing deep in my guts and then running back out, coating their cocks with their loads.

I pounded my ass on their cocks as I shot my load, my cum oozing out of my cock, running down the underside, coating my balls and dripping onto theirs. We were a howling, bucking, screaming mess as we fought through our orgasms.

I finally quit cumming and eased myself off of their wet cocks. Cum was everywhere on Tim and Cappy and had even managed to pool underneath them on and on the sheets. I quickly went about cleaning their cocks off, sending each man into another orgasm and being rewarded with a small, but tasty, load. We untangled ourselves and maneuvered ourselves into a position so that we were each on our side. My cock nestled in the folds of Tim's ass while Cappy had managed to work his still hard cock up my ass. Holding onto one another, Cappy started fucking my ass again. Tim had already dozed off and my cock was spent but I still worked my ass, taking Cappy to another orgasm. I dozed off, hearing Cappy grunt and feeling his cock shoot another load in my ass.

CHAPTER 18

The day finally arrived that I was going to get my cast off. I was so excited I couldn't wait, I must have jacked off ten times the night before trying to get myself to doze off and get some sleep. I sat in the examination room, patiently waiting for the doctor to show up. Dr. Coffey had been my primary care doctor for the past five years. An older man, I'm guessing in his 50's, he had always taken great care of me and never seemed uncomfortable with the fact that I'm gay. He certainly kept himself in great shape and although he had average looks, he had what appeared to be a well sculpted and toned body under his scrubs.

I'd already waited about a half hour past my appointment time when there was a soft knock on the door as the door handle turned and was soon opened.

Dr. Coffey did not walk in the room.

"Hello, Craig is it?" the deep voice asked.

"Yes." I replied.

"I'm Dr. Wasson, pleased to meet you. I'm filling in for Dr. Coffey while he's on vacation." He said, looking directly in my eyes and flashing me a pearly white toothed smile that made my legs quiver and my cock twitch. I gawked and gazed as my eyes traveled the length of Dr. Wasson's body. His hair was jet black with just the start of grey at his sideburns and temples. His eyes were a beautiful emerald green with long dark lashes. A roman nose led down to a jet black mustache, perfect lips, square set jaws and a cleft chin. I stared intently at the bobbing Adam's apple while he talked to me, oblivious to what he was saying. I stared at the tuft of hair that jetted over the neck of his white T-shirt. He was wearing a baggy style blue pin striped shirt and as I tried to imagine what his chest must look like, he reached up to my throat and started feeling the glands in my throat.

"Craig? Hello? Craig?" I heard him say.

"Hum? What? I'm sorry, I faded out." I replied back, blushing slightly.

"I asked how the arm's been doing and inquired about your appetite along with your overall general health." He said.

"Oh, all's been good, really good." I replied as he moved from my neck to my arm pits, making me giggle as he hit my ticklish spots while he checked the glands in my arms.

He continued his overall exam, making notes as he went. He did that part in silence and I took that time to finish my inspection of his body. He wore navy blue pleated front pants. I gazed at the mounded pouch that tented his fabric covered crotch and tried to envision what his cock and balls must look like tucked into his underwear.

"I'm going to have the tech wheel in the portable X-ray, well get a shot of your arm and go from there. Sound good?" I heard him ask.

"Uh huh." I responded back.

"Good then, they'll be in in a few minutes and when their done and the film is developed, we'll take a look." Dr. Wasson smiled as he turned and left the office. I about fainted when I saw his tight, small, round bubble butt jutting out through his pants as he left the office. The portable X-ray soon arrived, snapping photos of my arm, the technician placing my arm in different positions. She said nothing to me as he took the x-rays and within a matter of minutes was done and had left the room. Dr. Wasson arrived a few minutes later.

"Craig, I've been looking through your chart. You're due for your physical next month, wanna get it done today and then not have to worry about it?"

He asked.

"Sure, but I haven't fasted." I replied.

"Not a problem, we'll schedule you for your labs when we're done." He said as he tossed me a gown and told me to strip down and put the gown on. I complied, noticing that my cock was half hard. I started thinking about things that would take my mind off my cock and before long, I was soft, plump, but soft. Dr. Wasson returned about a half hour later, x-ray films in hand.

"Well, you look as though you've healed. Course, can't officially tell you that until we get the final report but so far so good." He said as he went over the x-rays with me.

"So, let's get the physical part out of the way." He said as he reached underneath the table and pulled up the stirrups.

"OK, please put your feet in the stirrups, lay back and just relax." He said as he donned rubber gloves, pulled out a tube of KY jelly and a plastic looking instrument wrapped in sterile packaging. Sitting on the stool he was eye level with my crotch. I squinted and tensed as he applied the KY jelly to my hole.

"Just relax Craig." He said.

"I am, that shit's cold Doc!" I squealed back as he gently massaged the jelly into my hole. "That's odd," I thought.

"Right, so let's check that prostate." He said as he gently slid a finger inside my rectum, immediately landing on my prostrate. I felt his finger rub and press over my love button and before long, my cock reared up, tenting the fabric of the gown that had been pushed up, giving the doctor access to my hole.

Dr. Wasson continued to massage my prostrate and within a few minutes, I felt another finger gently slide into me. I let out a soft moan as he penetrated me and felt the first drop of pre-cum roll off the tip of my cock and onto my stomach. Dr. Wasson said nothing while he continued to massage my prostate. His other hand soon wrapped around my balls and started gently tugging on them.

"Turn your head to left and cough please." Dr. Wasson said, his voice deepened with sexual lust. I did as I was told and he had me go through this routine a couple of times while his hands massaged my nut sack, his fingers still playing with my hole.

"Pull your gown up please, I need to palpitate your stomach." He said as he let go of my balls and gently slid his fingers out of my ass, my hole twitching, a sudden empty feeling taking the place of his fingers.

He gently pushed down on my stomach, moving his hands over my firm abdomen, prodding, pushing as he felt for the natural movement of my intestines. He asked me if I worked and I replied that I did, although I hadn't done much since I broke my arm and I was looking forward to getting back into the routine again.

"I need to examine your rectum, to do that, I'm going to insert this object into your anus. The rounded ends will spread apart, you might feel some pressure when I do this. Please try to relax." He said as he applied more

KY to the object and inserted it inside me. I groaned as I felt it spread my hole.

"Do you have any problems with your bowel movements? Any bleeding, cramping or sudden bouts of constipation?" He asked as he bent forward, shining a pen light inside my rectum.

"No, I eat healthy enough." I groaned again.

While he looked inside my ass, he reached up, his hand landing on my now erect and throbbing cock. I groaned and he cleared his throat and told me it was perfectly normal for men to get an erection while they got their prostate massaged. He continued to tell me that some men even have an orgasm, as he explained this to me, his glove covered hand roamed over the head of my cock, smearing my cock lube over the head, driving me wild. He soon stopped rubbing my cock, removed the instrument from my ass, stood, removing the rubber gloves and throwing them in the trash and heading to the sink to wash his hands. He told me I appeared to be in good shape but that my rectum appeared to be red and irritated and he asked if I'd been using any objects such as a dildo or a butt plug. I explained that I hadn't but had taken two cocks up my ass a week before and asked if that might be the problem. He nodded his head while he dried his hands.

Dr. Wasson turned to face me and for the first time, I noticed the obvious hard cock that had snaked it's way up the inside of the crotch of his pants. I stared, trying to see if I could figure out how large he was. I grabbed my cock and started slowly stroking it, licking my lips as my eyes traveled up his body and made contact with him.

"I can take care of that if you want." I said, licking my lips.

"I was hoping you would." He replied as he unzipped his fly, pulling the front of his briefs down and pulling his cock out. He was average size in length, about eight inches I'd say, with a thick dark purple mushroom head, a clear string of cock juice hung from the tip of his dick, stretching for the floor. He walked over to where I lay and placed the head of his cock at my lips. I licked the pre-cum from the tip of his cock, he groaned when he felt my tongue make contact with the head of his cock.

"I haven't been laid in two weeks. Hit a dry spell." He panted as I sucked his cock into the back of my throat.

"Oh yeah Craig, suck my fucking cock, yeah, feels good buddy boy." He whispered, his hand removing my hand from my cock and wrapping itself around it. He stroked me a couple of times and then proceeded to remove his shirt and T-shirt. I thought I was going to cum when I looked up from sucking his dick and saw his chest above me. It was covered in thick, curly jet black hair. He had shaved the hair around his nipples and they were both hard, pierced, two small hoops stuck through them. I reached up and ran my hand across his fur, groaning, marveling at how soft the hair was.

"C'mon, let's do this right." He said as he pulled his cock from my mouth and finished undressing while I sat up and removed the gown.

I laid back down on the exam table and he straddled me in a 69. Placing his cock back in my mouth he leaned forward, his ass cheeks parting, giving me a sweet view of his hairy puckered ass. I grunted as I felt his lips wrap around my own pole and he started sucking my cock, grabbing my balls, tugging and twisting on them to the point where it was a mixture of pleasure and pain. We began to devour each other's hard cocks, sucking and slurping, oblivious to the fact that we were in a doctor's office. I reach up and started fingering his ass. He grunted, pushing his ass towards my finger. I removed my hand and put it at his face, letting him suck two of my fingers in, along with my cock, getting them wet so I could penetrate his hole.

I went back to fingering his ass, my fingers now wet with his spit. I slid one finger inside, he groaned, so I slid another finger inside him and started to slowly finger fuck his ass. He pulled off my cock, reared up, back arched and said, "Yeah that's it, work that fucking ass with your hand. C'mon, fuck my ass, get another finger up there."

As I added another finger, he leaned forward and sucked my cock back into his mouth. He bobbed up and down on my cock with a ferocity I hadn't felt in a long time. While his head bobbed on my cock, he started to fuck my face with his cock. Ramming it down my throat, causing me to choke and gag, my fingers sliding deeper and deeper into his ass. He quickly pulled off my cock, jumped off the table, grabbed me and started kissing me, his tongue snaking its way down my throat.

"Want me to fuck you?" He groaned while he continued kissing me.

"Yeah, oh yeah, fuck me with that cock of yours." I said.

"Yeah, fuck your ass, fuck you good. I'll pound your ass hard, fill you up with my cum." He grunted. We continued to kiss, our hands roaming over each others body. He was now on top of me, frotting us, his hard cock sliding up and down the length of mine, our pre-cum providing the natural lube. The head of his cock nudged my balls. The feeling of his wet cock head against the tight skin of my balls triggered my orgasm. I arched my back and grunted as I shot my load between the two us, my cum soaking and matting into the hair on his crotch and lower stomach.

"Yeah, oh yeah, that's it, fucking soak my cock in your cum." He whispered.

He sat up, grabbing my legs he pushed them up and over my head. My feet touched the very edge of the exam table over my head, causing my dripping cock to point right at my face. While the remnants of my cum dripped on my lips, he started eating my ass, his tongue darting in and out of my already lubed hole. He fucked my ass with his tongue while I stuck my own tongue out, the tip just reaching the piss slit in my cock. My cock twitched as I realized I could, quite possibly, lick the head of my cock while he ate my ass.

I don't know if he realized this or if he just naturally pushed down on the back of my legs while he ate my ass. Either way, it was just enough pressure that it lowered my cock to the point where I could lick the head of my own dick. My cock jerked again as the sensation of my tongue on my dick washed over me. I started lapping at the head of my cock like a dog laps at water. I was completely unaware of the fact that he'd quit eating my ass and was now watching me, intently, as I licked at my dick.

"Watch this." He said as he climbed off the table, pushed my legs back down, pulled me up so that my head was over the edge of the table and stood over me so I could lick his balls. While I licked his balls, he started leaning over, slowly, until he'd reached the point where he could suck the head of his cock into his mouth. I groaned as I watched his lips wrap around the head of his cock and he gently and slowly began to bob up and down, sucking his own cock. He groaned while he gave himself a blow-job and

I sucked and licked his nuts. A few minutes later he grunted and I watched as his cock jerked and cum started flowing out of the side of his lips and down the length of his cock. I watched, frantically stroking my cock, as his cum ran down onto his balls. I started licking and sucking his balls again, tasting the sweet load that was still flowing out of his mouth and running the length of his cock.

He pulled off his cock and jerked the rest of his load into my mouth, sticking his dick in my mouth, letting me clean the last of his load off his cock. I sucked and nursed on his now deflating cock, my breathing increasing as my second orgasm began to rise in my balls and up my cock.

Thankfully my mouth was full with his cock, my cries were muffled as I shot another load, he quickly leaned over me, taking my cock into his mouth and swallowing my cum.

We were spent, breathing hard, sweating, nursing each others now soft cocks. He finally pulled off of me and whispered, "We should get cleaned up, someone is going to start wondering what's taking so long." We quickly wiped up and doused our faces with cold water and then dressed.

"Can I see you again?" He asked as we softly kissed one another. "Yes, you still owe me an ass fucking." I said, my hand running down the front of his slacks, playing with his crotch. "I'll come over tonight then." He said, pulling away from me. What time?" I asked. "Around eight. Take care, don't forget to schedule your labs and make an appointment to get that cast off." He said, winking at me as he left the office.

CHAPTER 19

I ran some errands, caught up on my grocery shopping and patiently waited for eight o'clock to roll around. I think my cock stayed hard from the moment I left Dr. Wasson, I couldn't stop thinking about what the evening might hold in store. Once I was home I put the groceries away, started some laundry and began to tidy the place up. The phone rang and I rushed to answer it, hoping it wasn't Dr. Wasson calling to cancel.

"Hello?" I said.

"Craig! What's going on?" Tim slurred into the phone.

"Tim? Have you been drinking?" I asked.

"YUP! And I'm fucking naked, in my backyard and guess what? I just fucking pissed all over my chest! Dude! Check it out, it was fucking hot!" Tim shouted.

"Um, OK, and?" I said, snidely, irritated that he was one, calling me drunk and two, interrupting my schedule.

"Well, fuck buddy, don't gotta be so fucking bitchy about it!" Tim replied back. "I mean, for fuck's sake, I just discovered water-sports and I got a fucking hard cock. Come suck me off!" Tim slurred again.

"Tim, I got plans and I need to run." I said. I'd started to say more when

Tim's groan cut me off.

"Oops! Too late buddy, I just shot my load. Man, I fucking taste good!

No wonder you like drinking my cum!" Tim said again. "OK, gotta run." Tim continued and then hung up.

I finished my house cleaning, made a light dinner and then showered and douched in order to get ready for Dr. Wasson's arrival. The doorbell rang promptly at eight. I practically tripped over my own feet trying to run to the door, anxious to see my new lay. I flung the door open and drooled as

I saw Dr. Wasson standing there. He wore a red polo shirt, unbuttoned and skin tight, accenting his perfectly sculpted hairy chest. I let my eyes drink him in, his shirt was tucked into the waist band of his jeans. 501 button ups, the fabric worn white where his cock rested, his bulge prominent, hinting at a cock and balls that were armed and ready to fire.

"Hi!" I squealed. "Come in Dr. Wasson!" I said as I stood to the side and let him pass.

"Dave, please, my name is Dave. Save the Dr. Wasson for the office." He said as he strode by, his firm ass cheeks flexing in the worn fabric of his jeans.

"Oh GOD! He's so fucking hot!" I screamed to myself in my head.

"I hope you don't mind, I brought an overnight bag with a change of clothing and some, um, fun things for us." He said as he placed the bag in my easy chair and sat down on the couch.

"No not at all, can I get you a beer? Glass of water? Soda?" I asked.

"Beer sounds good!" He said and smiled as I walked over to him to greet him. I sat down next to him and we immediately embraced one another, our mouths quickly connecting. We kissed, rather devoured, one another as though we were two lovers, about to be parted for months. Our hands felt each other's backs as we continued our kissing, our passion rising, along with the heat in the room. His lips and tongue tasted so good to me, sweet, like he'd just eaten cotton candy. The stubble from the day's growth of his beard scraped my chin, making me desire this man even more.

Our breathing increased as my hands quickly found the opened front of his polo shirt and my fingers began to toy and play with the hair that jutted out. Panting, we finally pulled apart.

"About that beer." Dave said. "Yeah, about that beer." I panted back, kissing him again, not wanting to pull away.

A few more minutes of "necking" and I pulled away and headed for the kitchen to get our beers. Returning I handed him his and he took a large gulp from it, inadvertently belching as he set the bottle down on my coffee table.

"Oh excuse me!" He said, his face flushing with embarrassment.

We started talking and before long he was telling me how Dr. Coffey had found him at a job fair his University was holding and had hired him on the spot. He then proceeded to tell me that Dr. Coffey had a huge cock. When

I'd inquired as to how he knew this, he'd told me that he'd checked him out in the staff showers at the hospital they both worked at and that he'd gotten this feeling that Dr. Coffey was not opposed to having male to male sex. I was intrigued to learn more but was more interested in learning more about the hunk that sat in front of me. A few hours later, as well as a few beers, we'd learned all we were going to learn from one another, at least for the moment anyway.

"Come here." Dave said and I quickly slid over to him. Dave reached out for me again, drew me into his arms and started kissing me. My hand went to his crotch, I could feel his rock hard cock though his jeans and I proceeded to trace the outline with my hand, stopping at the base and massaging his balls. Dave groaned in my mouth and I kissed him harder and applied more pressure to his crotch.

"Let's get out of these clothes." I said, panting. We both stood and quickly undressed, admiring each other's bodies. Our hands reached out again, this time, grabbing one another's hard cocks and gently stroking and caressing the soft, velvety skin of our shafts and heads. We sighed and cooed as we took our time feeling one another, our hands roaming from cock to balls to chest to stomach.

"You're so fucking hot Craig." Dave said and quickly sank to his knees, sucking my cock in one fell swoop. His tongue rubbed the underside of the head of my dick as his throat muscles contracted and relaxed, milking the shaft of my cock. I sighed and purred, my hands roaming through the thick hair that rested on the top of his head. Dave started to slowly suck my cock, his tongue playing over the head, piss slit and the sensitive underside. My hips buckled and I thrust my dick further into his mouth.

He gagged and coughed but didn't spit my cock out, instead he relaxed his throat to the point where I could literally fuck his face.

"Oh God Dave, feels good, feels fucking real good." I panted, throwing my head back as I gently moved my cock in and out of his mouth. Dave's fingers had found the crack of my ass and were now gently playing with my backdoor, teasing the lips of my ass with one hand while the fingers of the other twisted and pulled at my nipples. Dave was now still sucking my cock with a slow and steady rhythm, letting his spit run down the underside of my cock and onto my balls. Somehow he was managing to use his free fingers to wipe his slobber up and feed it back to the fingers he had playing with my ass. He'd yet to penetrate me, he was just toying with the lips of my hole while he continued to swallow my rock hard cock. My balls soon began to tingle, indicating that my cum was beginning to rise up, out of my balls and into my cock. I was close to cumming.

"You're going to make me cum Dave." I panted. He continued his slow and deliberate sucking of my cock while his fingers continued their gentle toying with my ass and nipples.

"I'm gonna cum Dave. Fuck, I'm gonna cum!" I shouted as I rammed my cock down his throat and started shooting. He remained motionless as my cock fired, filling his guts with my load. My knees and legs shook with the force of my orgasm and I cried out as my cock continued to pump my pearly cream into his mouth. We said nothing, no words were needed. This man had managed to take me to an orgasmic level few had been able to, except Cappy.

As my cock softened, he licked and sucked the head of it, cleaning the last of my cum from the piss slit. He kept my cock firmly planted in his mouth, his tongue occasionally flicking at my piss slit. I looked down at him and saw the white streaks of his own cum painted across his furry chest.

Dave stood, pulled me to him and we began to kiss again. I could taste the remnants of my cum on his tongue. The wet hair on his chest and stomach from the load he'd shot rubbed into my own chest and stomach. His cock was still rock hard while mine had softened and gone to its natural state. I reached between us and started jacking his cock. He quickly pulled my hand away.

"Not yet, I have a surprise in store for us. Let's go to bed." Dave said.

Curious, I pointed him towards the direction of the bedroom, he grabbed his overnight bag as he left while I turned the lights off and double checked that the doors had been locked. Once that was done, I headed to the bedroom myself. When I got to the bedroom, Dave was laying on the bed, legs pulled up to his chest, his asshole winking at me.

"Look in the bag." He commanded. Following his instructions I quickly unzipped the bag and spied an assortment of dildos along with his clothes.

I grabbed the smallest dildo I could find and quickly scooted between his legs, grabbing the lube from the night stand. Lubing the dildo up, I started to slowly insert it into his ass. Dave closed his eyes and grunted as the head of the fake cock moved past his ass ring. Once I had the head of the dildo past the ring of his ass, his ass quickly sucked in the shaft of the dildo until it was buried completely inside him. Dave moaned and groaned as I did this, his hands toying with his nipples, his cock flaccid.

As I began to move the dildo in and out of him, his cock began to respond, plumping, thickening and hardening as it grew. I increased the tempo in which I was fucking Dave's ass, in response his hands increased their tempo on playing with his nipples while he started fucking himself on the pseudo-cock. Pants and moans were the only sounds that he made, fueling my lust for him, wanting me to take him to another level of pleasure.

"Feel good? You like that in your ass?" I asked.

"Oh yeah, fuck me with that cock, c'mon, fuck me!" Dave cried out. I increased the pace, pushing and pulling the dildo in and out of his with what seemed like lightening force. Dave's hips bucked and ground around the dildo as I did this, his cries of pleasure echoing throughout the room.

I decided to see what else he had in his bag. Dave whimpered as I eased the fake cock out of his ass, my own cock was now rock hard again and leaking. I took a few minutes to play with his ass, inserting my fingers, pulling them out, rubbing the lips of his hole. Dave's cock had hardened again and it now flexed up and down, lifting from his stomach. While I played with his ass with one hand, I went down on his cock again and started sucking him. Letting him fuck my face, his hips bucking up, shoving his cock down my throat.

"Fuck me Craig, c'mon, get that fucking hard cock of yours in my ass and fuck the shit out of me!" Dave cried out. His ass was already well lubed from the dildo play. spitting his cock out, I scooted forward on the bed, placing the head of my cock at the entrance to his ass. I teased his hole with my cock, rubbing the head up and down his hole, not yet entering him.

Dave groaned and panted as I did this.

"Fuck me stud! C'mon, fuck me!" Dave whimpered, "I need that cock of yours in my ass!" he continued. I slowly started sliding into his ass and as I penetrated him Dave arched his back, moaning as he continued to feel the length of my cock slide into him. I buried my cock inside him and laid on top of his, his legs wrapping around my hips and hugging me to him. We started kissing again as I began to slide my cock in and out of him. Dave was so hot our kissing so fierce. He was murmuring and whispering as we kissed but I couldn't tell what he was saying. I felt his hands slide down to my ass cheeks and his fingers begin to toy with the crack of my ass.

"Oh your cock feels so good inside my ass. So good, fuck me, pound my fucking ass!" Dave cried out. I maintained a slow and steady rhythm, not wanting Dave to cum too soon, or myself for that matter. I wanted this to last, it felt too good to rush. I continued my steady assault on Dave's ass while we continued to kiss. Dave suddenly thrust his hips forward, groaned as his cock started shooting cum between the two of us, coating us with his sticky load.

"Remember when I said some men could cum just by having their prostate massaged?" Dave panted once his cock quick erupting. "Keep going, I want you to keep fucking me." he said.

I pulled out of him and before rolling him onto his stomach, licked some of the cum off his chest and sucked the remnants from his cock. I was amazed he was still rock hard as he rolled over. I climbed onto his back and quickly inserted my cock back into his ass. I started to fucking him again, this time a little harder. I wasn't ready for this to end but my cock was now taking the lead and was telling me it was time to cum. Before long I had Dave on all fours and was slamming my cock into his ass. The two of crying out with each thrust.

"Take my fucking cock, c'mon, take it!" I shouted as I increased my pace some more. I reached under him and started jacking his cock, his ass muscles clenching around my cock as I did this.

"Fuck me, yeah that's it, pound that fucking ass. C'mon, pound me, fucking pound me bitch!" Dave screamed. He was matching the speed of my thrusts and I was now close to cumming.

"Roll back over, I want to fucking spray my load on your cock while you jack off!" I screamed, pulling out and letting Dave roll back over and onto his back. Legs up and spread, Dave started jacking his cock, his fist flying over his hard meat while I jacked my own cock.

"Yeah, c'mon boy, c'mon. Give me that load, fucking shoot it, c'mon, fucking shoot that cock all over my cock." Dave cried out. "Get ready bitch, here it comes, here it...AAAAAGGGGGHHHHHH!" I cried out as my cock started firing, painting hand in white with my cum. Dave's fist continued to fly over his cock as he used my cum for lube. As the last few drops of cum dripped from the tip of my spent cock, Dave's cock erupted. I leaned forward, opening my mouth so I could taste some of his cum. He tasted salty and bitter but for a cum slut like me, it still tasted heavenly. I let his cum shower my face, landing on my lips and my chin. Dave quit stroking his cock and just held it up for me to lick and clean. I took my other hand and began wiping the cum from my face, licking it off my fingers.

Satisfied Dave's cock was clean I rolled off of him and laid down next to him. I rolled over on my side, facing him, and started running my hands through the matted hair on his chest and stomach. His eyes were closed and

I watched his chest rise and fall as his breathing returned. I raised my head up, and started licking and sucking his nipple. I moved my hand down to his cock, he was still hard as I toyed with the hair at the base of his cock.

"Fuck Dave. I can't believe you're still hard." I said.

"I told you, I haven't been laid in awhile, I'm still fucking horned up."

Dave said, his hand roaming over my back. "Suck me off, c'mon, it won't take long at all. Please, I gotta fucking cum again." Dave said.

I slid down and sucked his cock into the back of my throat. Dave's hips took over as he started to fuck my face. I played with his balls while I let him slide his cock in and out of my mouth. I let go of his balls and started playing with his hole, letting my fingers slide in and out of his well fucked ass. Dave groaned and bucked his hips as my fingers slid into him. I removed my fingers and went back to playing with his balls, noticing that they'd drawn completely inside him now.

"I'm close, fucking close." Dave panted as the speed in which he was fucking my face increased. My cock had hardened again and I was now rapidly jacking off, I wanted to see if I could time it so we came together.

"Stick your fingers back in my ass." Dave said. I complied and before long was fucking his ass again with my fingers while I jacked my cock with the other hand. I felt the head of Dave's cock begin to swell and knew he was going to cum, at the same time I felt my own balls draw up inside me, signaling I was going to cum again as well. I was groaning and moaning on

Dave's cock, the vibrations sending shock waves of pleasure down the shaft of his cock. Dave suddenly tensed, shoved his cock to the back of my mouth and came again. My own cock started jerking and spasming, a few drops of cum dribbling out of the head. Dave bucked and jerked and shouted as the intensity of his third orgasm over took him. He collapsed back on the bed after he came, his cock immediately softening. I slowly pulled off, letting my tongue dance over his piss slit. He must have had a dry orgasm as I didn't taste anything as I let the head of his cock slip from my lips and land on his stomach with a plop.

"Ummm, man, this was a fucking great night." Dave said.

"Yeah, I will agree with you on that." I said. I scooted back up to him, our lips meeting, we kissed for a few more minutes than pulled apart.

"You don't mind me staying the night do you?" Dave asked.

"Not at all, I'm glad you are." I replied. I grabbed his arm and rolled over on my side so that we were cuddling. His large hand roamed over my chest, and I could feel the head of his cock nudged in the crack of my ass.

I pulled my knees up and scooted back until I felt the head of his cock nudging my hole. I felt his cock begin to stir and harden again, the head snaking into my hole, parting the lips of my ass.

"You want to go again?" I asked.

"No, it's just a natural reaction when a sweet hole like yours nudges the head of my cock. Want to fall asleep with my cock in your ass though?

I've always thought that'd be so hot." David said. I didn't respond, instead I just pushed back until I felt his cock enter me. I moaned and shuddered in pleasure as I felt it snake it's way inside my ass. Before long, Dave has us positioned so that the full length of his cock was inside me. He nibbled on my ear, whispering to me a sweet night as we closed our eyes and drifted off to sleep.

CHAPTER 20

Dave and I didn't move an inch that night. I fell asleep with his hard cock planted in my ass and I woke up in that same position.

I glanced at the alarm clock, the red numbers said it was five in the morning. I knew I didn't have to be up that early but wasn't sure what time Dave needed to be up. I started to ease myself off of his cock but

Dave simply pulled me back to him.

"I don't have to be up just yet." Dave whispered in my ear.

"Good!" I replied back.

Dave moved his hand up my chest and sought out my nipple. He ran his fingers over my nipple, it hardening at his touch, while he gently kissed and nipped on my ear lobe. I closed my eyes and sighed as I started to give myself over to this gorgeous stud. He slowly started moving his hips, his cock beginning to stir inside my ass.

"Uh Dave, I think we should probably pass on the ass fucking thing this morning." I said.

"Yeah? Not fond of muddy sheets?" Dave giggled.

"Uh, no." I replied back as I started to gently ease my ass off of his cock.

"I think we're OK." Dave said as he gripped the base of his cock, keeping it from flopping onto the sheets as a preventative measure.

"Just the same, lets not." I said, rolling over and latching on to one of his nipples with my lips.

"Hold that thought, I'll be right back." Dave said as he got out of bed and headed to the bathroom. I heard the toilet flush and Dave came back to bed.

I was laying on my back, my hard cock flexing up and down off my stomach.

Dave walked climbed back in bed, grabbed my cock, leaned forward and started licking the head of my dick. I sighed in response and then groaned as I felt his tongue dart between my piss lips and taste the inside of my cock.

"Umm, you taste so fucking good Craig." Dave said before he plunged down on my cock and started sucking me.

"Yeah Dave, eat that fucking cock. Swallow it, that's it, swallow my thick cock, take it all down your throat." I grunted as I shoved my cock down Dave's throat.

Dave pulled off of my cock and straddled me. Grabbing the lube from the night stand, he quickly greased up my cock and then his hole. Holding my cock at the entrance of his ass, he ran the head around his ass lips, moaning at the sensation. Dave then gently lowered his ass onto my hard and throbbing cock.

"Oh yeah, your cock feels so good planted up my ass." Dave sighed as he bottomed out on my dick.

"Stay just like that, that big fucking head on your cock is hitting me in just the right spot." Dave said as he began to pant.

Dave's cock was rock hard and throbbing, clear juice was dripping out of his piss slit and running down the underside of his cock and onto his balls. Dave remained motionless, his eyes closed, his breathing labored as he squeezed and relaxed his ass muscles around my cock. Dave grunted once and his cock flexed, a single stream of white cum flowed out and down the underside of his cock.

"Fuck, your cock feels so good in my ass. It's like it was made for my hole, I've never felt a cock like yours before." Dave panted as his cock continued to jerk and throb.

"What just happened?" I asked, somewhat amazed.

"You just milked my prostate." Dave said as he leaned forward and started licking my chest.

I purred and sighed as I felt his tongue bath over my chest and nipples, my cock still buried in his ass, his ass muscles still clenching and relaxing around it. Dave moved up and started nipping at my chin and bottom lip while he slowly started raising his hips, letting my cock slide out to the point where just the head remained in his ass.

Dave then slowly lowered his ass back on my cock. He continued to do this while we made out, our mouths locked with one another, our unshaven faces scraping against each other, adding to the excitement.

"Like this?" Dave asked me.

"Oh fuck yeah Dave. Fuck man, you really know how to work that ass of yours and your so fucking tight." I groaned.

"Yeah, you like your cock in my tight ass don't you? Huh? Yeah? Like it when I ride your big dick?" Dave panted as he slowly began to increase his pace.

"Shit Dave, goddamn, ride my cock boy. Come on, ride that big dick!" I panted back. Dave's tight, and talented, ass was getting me closer to firing. Closer than I normally get with any other guy. I couldn't take it anymore and I rolled us over, pinning him to the mattress while I started to power fuck his ass.

"Fuck yeah Craig! Pound my fucking ass with your cock! Fuck me! Fuck me hard!" Dave yelled as he held his legs back, giving me maximum penetration.

"Unngghh." was all I could respond with as I continued to hammer his ass with my cock.

"Fuck me, yeah, fuck my hole." Dave kept panting, his cock flexing, the head beginning to swell.

I felt the tingle in my balls and increased my thrusting as I worked towards my orgasm. At the same time Dave kept begging me to fuck him, to make him shoot. Dave was close, his hands nowhere near his cock.

"Shit Dave, getting close, getting there buddy. Cum with me!" I cried out.

"I'm close too, just tell me to shoot my fucking load and I'll cum!" Dave said as he continued to hold his legs back.

"Gonna cum, gonna bust my nut in your tight ass. Get ready, get ready!" I cried out.

"Now, fucking shoot your load now!" I screamed as the cum raced out of my balls, up my dick and sprayed into his ass.

Dave cried out as his cock erupted. White cream sprayed out of the tip and covered his hairy chest. I felt as though I was pumping a gallon of cum in his ass and continued to cum while I watched Dave's cock continue to shoot.

I counted five good sprays of cum before the next three slowed to a steady stream. Dave continued to cry and groan and the more he came, the more his ass muscles milked my cock.

"Oh shit, you're fucking cum is spilling out and running down my crack! Fuck!" Dave cried out as his cock flexed again, another small stream of cum poured out and onto his furry belly.

I pulled my cock out of his ass, what seemed like a river of cum poured out and onto the sheets. My cock flexed twice and another shot of cum squirted out, landing on his balls. I rolled over and laid back on the bed, panting, trying to catch my breath.

"Shit! Fuck! Oh God! Oh God!" Dave cried out again as he grabbed his cock and started stroking it.

"Oh fuck, I'm gonna cum again. Oh fuck!" Dave said as he arched his back and screamed. His cock was spent, nothing came out but his orgasm was massive and he literally collapsed back on the bed when he was through.

"God DAMN you're fucking good!" Dave panted.

"Thanks, I think." I sheepishly replied back.

"I have not experienced that since Dr. Coffey fucked me back in Med

School." Dave said, not realizing he'd just outed my doctor.

"He WHAT?" I said. "Dr. Coffey fucked you?" I said again, laughing.

"Oops!" Dave said.

We turned and looked at each other and both of us just cracked up laughing.

I teased him about not being able to keep a secret and that if he'd had any interest in going to work for the CIA, he'd better forget it. I was sure all it would take was a good fucking from the enemy and Dave would be spilling all of our nation's secrets.

"So, is he really hung like you said?" I asked Dave.

"God, is he. Like a fucking horse and dude, he can fuck like no one's business." Dave said.

Dave continued to fill me in on what had transpired between he and my doctor. Dave gave me all of the details and left nothing out, nothing at all. By the time he'd finished telling me about Dr. Coffey, we were both rock hard and ready to go again.

"Know what else Dr. Coffey likes?" Dave asked as he stroked my cock.

"No, what?" I replied while I stroked Dave's cock.

"He's really into water sports. Loves it! Loves to be pissed on and pissed in." Dave said.

"You mean he drinks it?" I asked, somewhat grossed out.

"No, he likes to have his ass pissed in, you know, slide your cock in and let go." Dave said.

"Oh." was all I replied with.

Rather than continue the conversation, I decided instead, to suck on Dave's cock. We soon took up a comfortable 69 position and proceeded to give each other a slow and gentle suck. We would alternate sucking each other's cocks with working on each other's balls. At the same time, I managed to work a couple fingers into Dave's ass.

"Fuck! What time is it?" Dave suddenly said as he pulled off my cock.

"Shit! It's seven, I'm going to be late, sorry Craig, we'll pick this up where we left off?" Dave asked as he jumped out of bed and started throwing his clothes on.

"Uh yeah." I said.

"See ya later." Dave said as he blew me a kiss and headed out of the house.

I laid there, dried cum on my stomach, hard cock in my hand and decided to finish myself off. While I stroked my cock, I used my other hand to pull on my balls and play with my hole. Within a few minutes I was cumming again. As I laid there, panting and coming down from my orgasm, I pictured

Dave and Dr. Coffey together. Dave riding Dr. Coffey's cock and pissing all over the two of them.

"I don't get it. Not sure I understand the whole water sports thing." I said out loud.

I got up, stripped the bed and tossed the sheets in the washer and started a load of wash. I was standing in my kitchen, still naked, making coffee when I heard a knock on my back door.

"Just a minute!" I called out as I raced for the bedroom to grab my bathrobe.

I headed back to the door and opened it to find my hunky neighbor standing there, a look of irritation and sexual excitement on his face.

"Hey buddy, what's up?" I asked.

"Can I come in?" he said.

"Um, sure." I responded as I let him pass, closing the door behind him.

"Look," he started to say, "I don't care how you live your life and I certainly don't care who you fuck." he continued.

"But..." I replied, indicating there was more to follow.

"Well, I could hear you two in my yard! And quite frankly, I found it all." he paused.

I waited for him to finish, after a few minutes of silence I decided to try and help him finish his sentence.

"You found it irritating? Disgusting? Obnoxious?" I offered.

"You know, you should really make sure your windows are closed if you're going to carry on like that. I mean, really, it's all, I just found it all to be very." and he paused again.

I waited for him to finish his statement again, only this time I was not going to help him out. I just stood there, arms crossed, eyebrow raised, waiting to hear what he had to say.

"Well, I found it, oh fuck, here!" He said as he raised his shirt.

I glanced down at the shorts he was wearing. He was obviously sprouting an erection, two large wet spots showed in the fabric where the head of his cock had been, leaking into his shorts.

"I see, so what do you think we should do about this?" I responded, not taking my eyes from his crotch.

Without saying a word, he lowered his shorts and underwear, freeing his extremely hard cock. I watched it sway and bounce and watched as a drop of clear liquid appeared at the head of his cock.

"Um, thought you were married and straight." I said as I reached out and wrapped my hands around his cock.

"Ohh." he moaned, "We're separated, divorce in the, oh man that feels good, works." he finished.

I squatted down and wrapped my lips around the head of his cock. As I did this, he groaned, his legs buckled and he began to shoot his load in my mouth. I pulled off his cock, letting the rest of his load splash on my tongue and lips. He didn't cum much. I figured he'd either been on a marathon jack-off session and was drained or he'd already cum a couple of time that morning. His cum was bitter and it almost made me gag as I swallowed it. Nonetheless, I continued to clean off his cock until it was flaccid again.

I let go of his cock and as I did, he pulled his shorts back up, pushed past me, threw open the door and ran to his house as quickly as he could.

I couldn't help but laugh, it seemed that this was how it always worked anytime a straight married man was in the picture. He gets his first blow job, freaks out, and goes running home to safety.

I barely had enough time to even really check out the equipment, I scoffed at that thought and then decided it was really unfair, unfair that one, he came so fast and two, I didn't even get the chance to really take in his cock. I decided I'd have to fix that and as soon as I felt he could be approached again, I'd make my move.

I was just starting to head for the shower when the phone rang. Dave was on the other end of the line, thanking me profusely for such a great evening and wanting to know if we could do it again some time, maybe even with a three way. I offered up Dr. Coffey and he said he'd see what he could do. We said our goodbyes and I finally got into the shower.

CHAPTER 21

It felt good to finally be back at work. I was halfway through my first week back and as I got myself reacquainted with the men again, I wondered where Cappy had been hiding. I'd been purposely saving my load, hoping my first day would be spent bent over Cappy's desk while he drove his massive cock up my ass and fucked me.

I couldn't hold back anymore and decided to go find Cappy. I checked his office and heard voices coming from his private suite. I decided to go an investigate and stopped just outside his door.

"Get that fucking tongue of yours up my ass probie!" I heard Cappy growl.

"Yeah, just like that probie, c'mon, eat my fucking hairy ass!" I heard Cappy moan.

I quietly pushed open the door to find Cappy, buck ass naked, bent over his small couch while his ass was getting eaten out. The man eating his ass was obviously a new fire fighter. He had jet black hair and strong, broad shoulders that showed off his equally muscular back. Narrow waist that flared out to show two beautifully sculpted ass cheeks. Dark hair formed at the small of the back and fanned down and out over the new fire fighter's ass. I silently groaned as I soaked in the sight before me, reaching down to stroke my hardening cock through my uniform.

"Fuck yeah, that's it probie, get that tongue of yours deep inside my ass." Cappy growled. He was answered by a grunt from the new fire fighter.

"I'm gonna fucking make a man eating fire fighter out of you yet boy! By the time I'm done with your training you'll love cock just as much as you love pussy." Cappy shouted as he arched his back and ground his ass around the young fire fighter's tongue.

I removed my uniform shirt, leaving my T-shirt on and started to quietly step out of my shoes so I could remove my pants and underwear. I was soon nude except for my socks and T-shirt and moved to get closer to the new fire fighter. Neither man heard me enter or strip, they were too wrapped up in their sexcapades to pay any attention to what was transpiring around them.

I had to get closer, had to taste the new fire fighter. I quietly moved until I was standing behind the new fire fighter. He sensed someone was behind him and, pulling his mouth off of Cappy's ass turned his head. His face was just as beautiful as the rest of him and as he started to say something I put my fingers to my lips, indicating he should keep quiet. He nodded and soon dove back down on Cappy's ass.

"Get ready to suck my fucking cock boy!" Cappy panted as he shoved his cock back and through his legs, offering the leaking head to the new fire fighter. He groaned as he sucked Cappy's dripping cock into his mouth and started licking and sucking on the head of his cock.

While he worked on Cappy's cock, I squatted down and moved in behind the new firefighter, wrapping my hands around his chest I felt his broad pecs.

He sculpted the hair on his chest and the hair felt coarse as I ran my hands up and down his rippled stomach and chest, purposely avoiding touching his cock but letting the head of his cock brush against the back of my hand.

I scooted myself forward, allowing the tip of my already wet and leaking cock to brush along the new fire fighter's ass crack. He jumped as my cock made contact with his hole and when he did this, he accidentally bit down on Cappy's cock.

"Ow! Fuck bitch! Don't fucking...what the...!" Cappy cried out as he turned his head to look back at the new fire fighter and saw that I'd now joined their fuck-a-thon.

"Craig! Shit! It's so fucking good, keep sucking my cock probie, to see you! Come to get some of your Cappy's cock?" he growled.

"That or some of this new boy's ass." I panted back as I continued to rub my cock up along the new fire fighter's ass. His legs began to quiver and he began to pant as the sensation of my cock rubbing along his ass while he continued to suck on Cappy's cock began to overtake him.

Cappy eased his cock out of the new fire fighter's mouth and moved us so that he was now standing in the center of make shift living room of Cappy's suite. We positioned ourselves so that we were on either side of the new fire fighter and both Cappy and I began to lick and bite the young man's nipples.

He groaned and threw his head back as the pleasure of having his nipples played with washed over him. I reached down and grabbed the probie's cock.

It was nice, about eight inches long, rock hard, thick and uncut. I ran my hand over the foreskin that kept his cock head enclosed and groaned as I felt the stream of pre-cum pour out of his cock and into the palm of my hand.

I squatted down to get a taste of this man's cock and balls. His balls were already drawn tight within the ball-sack. He jerked as I ran my tongue up the length of his cock starting at the puckered skin around his cock head. Cappy soon joined me and we took turns sucking the man's cock down our throats.

Cappy and soon started kissing each other, momentarily forgetting the young man's cock. "Fuck that's hot." I heard him grown, his voice deep and rich with the hint of an Australian accent.

"Suck it, suck my fucking cock!" he said. "Yeah, fuck yeah, fucking feels better than any chick could do." he continued as we continued taking turns devouring his cock.

Cappy swiped his fingers across the head of his cock, dipping up the clear liquid oozing from the folds of skin. I knew what Cappy was going to do next and as I sucked his cock back down my throat I heard the new fire fighter take a sharp intake of breath as Cappy began fingering his virgin hole.

The new fire fighters hips began thrusting and I let him fuck my face with his beautiful cock while Cappy continued to let his fingers explore his back side. Before long, Cappy had his face planted between the young man's ass cheeks and was soon fucking his tight hole with his wet tongue.

"Unngh, fuck! Oh fuck! Shit!" the new fire fighter cried out. He bucked his hips, shoving his dick down my throat and proceeded to start shooting his load.

"Fuck yeah! Oh FUCK!" he continued to cry out and pant as his shot it's hot load deep into my guts. His cock remained rock hard as he pulled it out of my mouth, the foam of his cum sticking to the folds of his foreskin.

"Time to fuck me boy!" Cappy cried out as he spun the new fire fighter around, grabbing his still hard cock and guiding it to his hole.

"Oh yeah boy, oh yeah!" Cappy sighed as he felt the fire fighters cock slide into his wet hole.

I waited for the probies cock to bottom out in Cappy's ass before I bent him over, exposing his virgin ass to me. The two men remained motionless as I began to eat the young fire fighter's ass, getting it wet and ready for my cock.

The probie started to slowly fuck himself on my tongue, each time pulling his cock in and out of Cappy's ass.

"That's it boy, c'mon, yeah. Slide that cock of yours in and out of your

Captain's ass. Oh fuck, feels good boy, that cock of yours inside my ass feels fucking good!" Cappy groaned.

Satisfied he was wet and open enough, I stood and, holding my cock, began to slowly slide my dick into his ass. The new fire fighter bent back over the Captain, eyes closed shut, he focused on relaxing his ass muscles to allow his first cock enter him.

"Fuck! Stop! Stop! Fuck this hurts!" he cried out.

I stopped, allowing his ass to get used to the feeling of something going inside it. He started to relax and within a few minutes, I felt his ass muscles relax and start sucking my cock inside. As his ass sucked my cock in, I watched his face. His facial expression soon changed from one of uncertainty and pain to a wide eyed, open mouthed expression of pure pleasure. I soon bottomed out in his ass and as I cock made it's final ascent into his ass he cried out.

"Bingo!" I thought, "the point of no return, this tight ass is mine!" I smiled to myself as I started to slowly pump my cock in and out of his ass.

"Good boy, good probie! Now, just relax and let two men take you to the edge and back!" Cappy quietly said to the new fire fighter as he leaned forward, sucking Cappie's tongue into his mouth, moaning as Cappy began to fuck himself on the man's cock and I began to fuck his ass with mine.

His ass was so tight and I hadn't nutted in a week. I was doing my best to keep from cumming and I could tell that the new fire fighter was getting closer and closer to busting his own nut deep into Cappy's ass.

The good thing about all of this was that Cappy had ultimate control over when he could cum. I wished I had that talent. Cappy could fuck you for hours before he'd let himself cum or he could cum simply by feeling your own cock jerk and unload deep in his ass.

The three of us quickly found a rhythm that worked and were soon power fucking. The new fire fighter could only groan and moan as the pleasure of his cock buried deep in Cappy's ass triggered new sensations while at the same time, he was feeling a newer sensation of having a cock up his ass.

The poor man was soon a quivering, sweating writhing mass of male flesh.

Trying to focus on what felt better, his cock buried in a tight ass or a hard cock buried in his ass. It soon became too much for him to try and ascertain and his breathing soon became labored pants of lust.

"I'm gonna cum, fuck! I'm gonna cum!" He shouted as he slammed his cock in and out of Cappy's ass. When he did this, he pulled forward as I was pulling back and my cock plopped out of his ass.

"Put it back in me, put it back in me! I'm gonna cum! Fuck me! Fuck me!"

He cried as he stopped long enough for me slide my cock back inside him.

That was the trigger and as I bottomed out inside his ass again, he stiffened, shouted and started filling Cappy's ass with his load.

"Fuck yeah! Fill me up with your fucking cum!" Cappy shouted as he reached down, grabbed his cock and started shooting his load, painting the floor with his cum.

I pulled back and shoved my cock into the new man's ass and howled as my pent up cum shot out. The young fire fighter moaned as he felt my cum fill his ass. He pulled his cock out of Cappy's ass with a wet plop, a string of cum coming with it and running down the underside of Cappy's balls. He stroked his cock as I continued to fill his ass with my load. "I'm gonna shoot again!" he soon cried out.

He pointed his cock down and ropes of cum soon shot out and hit Cappy's hole. "Fuck yeah! Oh fuck!" he continued to cry as he painted Cappy's fuck hole white with his load.

I eased my spent cock out of his ass and he quickly fell to his knees and started licking his cum off of Cappy's hole. Cappy's cock was rock hard again so I went around the two of them, fell to my knees and began licking the head of Cappy's cock while he stroked himself to another orgasm.

"Fuck yeah! Fuck! Here it comes, here it..." Cappy cried out as his cock head expanded and turned an angry purple. I put my lips around the head of his cock and waited for his load to shoot.

"Unngh! Fuck boy, get ready! Fuck-A-Thon!" Cappy cried out as his orgasm hit him. Cum drizzled out of the tip and into my mouth. I washed my tongue over his cock head as it spasmed and jerked with his massive orgasm.

His load wasn't much but his orgasm was a hard one. He quickly fell to his knees, sweat pouring off the brow of his head and back. Panting, the two of us quickly kissed and then proceeded to clean off the new fire fighter's cock.

The new fire fighter pushed us both off of his cock, saying it was too sensitive and we both joined Cappy on the floor. After a few minutes of kissing one another and lightly stroking each other's chests and backs, our breathing returned to normal and sat back.

"Welcome back Craig! Congratulations probie, you've just been initiated into the team!" Cappy said as he kissed both of us. "Now men, let's get off this floor and get back to work!"

He slapped us both on the ass as we stood and made our way to our clothes and started to get dressed. Cappy was still sitting on the floor when we headed out of his office.

"Fucking hot!" Cappy said as he reached between his legs and started to stroke his hardening cock.

CHAPTER 22

Cappy's cock was still rock hard, even though he'd just shot two loads. He stood, his hand firmly gripping his cock, walked over to his desk and pulled out one his trusted dildos. He walked back over to his couch and sat down on the overstuffed sofa.

Stroking his cock with one hand, he pulled his legs back and used his other hand to tease his wet hole with the head of the rubber dildo. Cappy groaned as he felt the head of the dildo make contact with his wet hole.

"Fuck yeah, feels so good Craig. Take that fucking cock of yours and tease my ass with it." He said quietly as began to rub the head of the dildo around his hole, teasing himself with it, letting the head slip in and out.

Cappy groaned as he felt the young firefighters cum begin to ooze out of his hole and slide down the crack of his ass.

"Oh fuck yeah, got a hot load of cum still inside my ass. Shit! I can't believe how fucking horny I still am." Cappy said as he started to slowly slide the dildo into his ass while he slowly stroked his hard cock.

"Shit yeah boy, slide that cock of yours up my ass, c'mon boy, let me feel your cock." Cappy panted and moaned as the dildo bottomed out in his ass.

Cappy pulled the imitation cock out of his ass and, using the suction cup base stuck it on the tiled floor in his makeshift apartment.

Cappy got off of the sofa and squatted down over the dildo, holding it in place with his hands, he teased himself with it. Letting the now, cum covered dildo rub up and down the crack of his and across his balls.

"Shit, I feel like I could fuck all day now. God I'm so fucking horny for cock. C'mon Craig, feed me that cock of yours. Yeah, just like that boy, you sure know how to fucking satisfy your daddy." Cappy groaned as he lowered himself onto the dildo, sighing as he sank down to the base of the fake cock, squeezing the imitation balls as he ground his hips around the cock.

I'd walked back to his office to ask him a question and stopped, watching him lower himself down on the dildo. My cock hardened again as I listened to his dirty talk, flattered that it was about me, flattered that of all the cocks that Cappy surely had taken up his ass, he liked mine best.

"Let me ride your fucking dick Craig. Fucking feels so good up my ass!

Shit yeah boy, let me ride your fucking cock!" Cappy said, his head thrown back, eyes closed, hand wrapped around his thick cock, stroking it as he got himself off on the dildo. "Fuck I wish I had a cock to suck on right now." Cappy moaned. "I need a cock down my throat while I fucking ride this massive mother fucker!" Cappy continued to pant, his other hand tweaking his nipples while he bounced up and down on the dildo and stroked his cock with the other hand.

I removed my shoes, underwear and pants and quietly walked over to wear

Cappy was. Taking my cock, I rubbed the leaking head of my prick around his lips. Cappy's eyes flew open in surprise.

"What the fuck? How long have you been standing there boy?" He growled at me.

"Long enough Cappy, c'mon, you want a cock to suck, here you go." I responded back.

Cappy leered at me, spitting on the head of my cock. I grabbed my cock and started slapping Cappy's face with it. His tongue darting out, licking the underside of my dick as I continued to abuse him with my cock. Cappy groaned and he increased the speed of which he was fucking himself on the dildo and stroking his cock.

"Fucking let me cum in your face." Cappy growled. I looked down at his cock and could he was getting close, the head of cock was swollen, the lips wet with his pre-cum.

Cappy stood, easing the dildo out of his ass and pushed me to my knees.

"Lick my balls bitch." Cappy growled while he stroked his cock. I shoved my face in between his legs, licking the tight sack that contained his balls, tasting the young probies cum that had leaked out while he rode the dildo.

"Getting close boy, getting close. Get your fucking pretty face up and close your eyes." Cappy shouted.

I did as I was told and, opening my mouth and sticking my tongue out, waited for his load. Cappy groaned and soon, I was rewarded with the warm of his load. For a man who'd just cum twice, he still had a huge load to deposit, the first jet of his cum splashing against my forehead and into my hair. The second jet nailed me right in the left eye and ran down my cheek. His third and final shot found its mark, right on my tongue.

Cappy howled as his orgasm subsided and I quickly sucked his cock back into my mouth. My hands reaching around his waist, my fingers sliding into his still wet and open hole. I nursed and sucked on his deflating cock, trying to get as much of his load out so that he would be completely drained.

I was still stroking my own cock and it soon erupted, a small stream flowing out of the tip and over my hand and onto my balls. I fell back, panting while Cappy towered over me.

"You feel better now Cappy?" I panted as I came down from my orgasm.

"Fuck no! But, we got a new shipment of probies in today and tonight, they're gonna get initiated." Cappy said.

"Yeah?" I responded back.

"Oh yeah. I've already given them their instructions and the boys are getting them good and clean as we speak." Cappy said, his cock beginning to plump again.

"Fuck Cappy! Are you THAT horned up or did you take something?" I asked, amazed that his cock was responding again.

"Both." Cappy said as he slapped on my ass and sent me on the way while he got ready for tonight's events.

I cleaned up, dressed and went about my business. The day dragged on while

I anxiously waited to see what Cappy had in store for the new probies. The dinner bell sounded and I made my way to the kitchen to eat. My chin hit the floor when I saw the probies, serving the firemen in nothing more than their underwear. The bodies these men had were something to behold. We'd received a total of five new fireman and they all looked as though they could've stepped right out of the latest porn magazine. All five of them were built, and judging by the bulges in their underwear, packing some serious meat.

We ate dinner, making the usual light hearted conversation while we ate.

The probies stood around the table, waiting for their turn, hoping for left overs. Once we were done eating, the probies cleared the table for us while the other firefighters began to back the fire trucks out of the station in preparation for tonight's initiation. Once the tables were cleared, the probies were allowed to eat and then escorted to the showers for their final preparation.

I walked into the shower room to take a leak and was greeted by the sight of a handful of men jacking off and cumming in what appeared to some sort of specimen cup. Each one groaned as they shot their loads into the small cup, their cocks remaining hard.

"What the hell?" I said out loud. One of the firemen looked up at me, grinned and said, "Cappy gave us each a special vitamin, guaranteed to keep us hard. Shouldn't you be getting ready too?" he asked me, winking as his eyes traveled the length of my body.

My cock began to stir again and I quickly stripped and jumped in the shower to freshen up as well. I quickly toweled off and as I was stepping out of the shower I noticed the last few firemen leaving, naked, hard cocks bobbing in front them, on their way to the garage. "This is gonna be good." I thought to myself, my cock now at full mast.

I walked into the garage, the men, holding their specimen cups, stood in a line. Padded cushions, like you'd find in a gymnasium, had been placed on the floor. Cappy stood in front of the men and blew two short whistles.

In a matter of minutes the probies were paraded into the garage, blind folded, completely nude as well.

"Gentlemen, we welcome these probies to our team and tonight we initiate them into the brotherhood." Cappy barked. "Probies, on your knees!" he shouted, his voice deep and full of authority.

The probies complied, each of them falling on their knees so that they were now in a half standing position. I surveyed the line of gorgeous men, some who's cocks had already began to puff up. They were truly a sight to see, thick cocks, bulbous heads, some furry from head to toe, others smooth.

Muscled chests, bulging biceps and each sporting the perfect, muscular and round bubble ass. My cock jerked and a drop of clear fluid appeared at the tip of my cock.

"Brothers, POST!" Cappy commanded as the firefighters moved forward and stood in front of each probie. "Probies, you will now open your mouths wide and accept the offering of your brothers." Cappy ordered as each man complied.

With their mouths open, some with tongues hanging out, each firefighter proceeded to pour the contents of specimen cups into the mouths of the waiting probies. Some swallowed right away, while some swallowed and gagged. A few were hesitant to swallow the mysterious liquid that was being fed to them. For those reluctant few, each firefighter held the probies nose closed while also closing their mouths, forcing them to swallow in order to breathe.

I watched to cocks of the firefighters, each still at full mast. All were throbbing, some were leaking streams of clear fluid down the front, onto their balls and dripping onto the mats. The probies cocks were now beginning to respond with want each mans sixth sense must have picked up.

A few of their cocks were at half mast, but most of the mens cocks were not rock hard. My mouth watered as I took in the sight of cock that was displayed before me. I slowly started stroking my own rock hard and leaking cock.

"AttenTION!" Cappy shouted and the probies stood and moved in precision.

"Probies, bend over!" Cappy shouted again as each man bent over, their firm asses fully exposed. Cappy nodded to the firefighters who quickly moved and squatted behind the probies. Another short burst of Cappy's whistle and each firefighter began eating the probies asses, some immediately groaning, others jerking with shock at the sensation of a tongue on their ass.

Cappy's cock was rock hard and as the firefighters ate the probies asses, he walked up and down the line of men, saying something quietly to them, each one opening his mouth in response and licking Cappy's hard cock. I watched, stroking my cock, as Cappy made his up and down the line. It wasn't long before the probies were all moaning and groaning as they worked on Cappy's cock while their asses were eaten and finger fucked. Cappy blew three short bursts on his whistle and I watched again as the firefighters moved the probies and stood in line with them. Another short burst of

Cappies whistle, and the firefighters gently turned the men to their left, the one on the far end of the line was bent over. Cappy walked the line of men, a bottle of lube in hand. He lubed the ass of the first man, the one bent over and then continued to lube the cocks and asses of each man until he reached the last one.

He blew his whistle again and, the first firefighter began to gently slide his cock into the probies ass in front of him. The probie screamed out as his ass fought to accept the thick invader. Once the firefighter had his cock buried up the probies ass, he leaned over the probie. Cappy grabbed the next probies hard cock and guided it to the firefighters ass, the firefighter sighing as the probie slid his cock into his ass. They continued to do this down the line until the only ass left unfilled was the last probie.

I watched as Cappy moved in behind the man, lubed his cock and started to fill his virgin ass with his cock. The probie winced and cried out but continued to let Cappy fill him. Before long he was sighing and cooing his pleasure while Cappy drilled him with his thick long cock. The only sounds in the room were the pants and sighs of men pleasuring men. I walked up and down the line of men, all were lost in the rapture of their joint lust.

Some were biting the backs of the man in front of them, other were lost in awkward kisses, tongues fighting with tongues, teeth nipping at lips, hands roaming chest, pinching hardened nipples.

I squatted down and started sucking the cock of the first firefighter. He was rock hard, long and thick, the head of his cock sliding past my tongue and nudging the entrance to my throat. I was immediately rewarded with the young probies load as he stiffened and came, the sensation of his cock being sucked while his ass was getting fucked was too much. I pulled back and let the rest of his load shoot in my mouth. The clamping of his ass on the firefighters cock that was fucking him set off a chain reaction as each man started shooting their loads deep in the ass they were fucking.

Without a word spoken, the men turned and exchanged positions. Their dripping cocks pulling out of dripping asses only to sink them into the ass of the man that had been fucking them. I was suddenly rewarded with a birds eye view of the young probies ass, his outer lips swollen, wet with traces of cum.

I stood and slid my still rock hard cock into his ass. I heard Cappy cry out as his ass was soon penetrated by one of the probies cocks. The feel of warm cum around my cock sent me over the edge and slammed into the probies tight, wet ass and dumped my load deep inside him. Pulling out I walked the line of men again, all still lost in the rapture of man on man sex. The scene repeated over and over as lips, tongues, hands probed mouths, necks, ears and tweaked nipples.

I reached the end and squatted down in front of Cappy. A string of cum hung down from his rock hard cock. I reached out, wiped my finger across the head of his dick and licked the cum from my hand. Cappy's eyes were closed and he was panting, lost in the feeling of a massive cock buried in his ass. I moved forward and sucked his cock in and began bobbing up and down on his thick cock. Cappy growled, stiffened and fired another load of cum down my throat. As if on cue, the remainder of me began cumming as well, asses that were already full of cum were not filled to overflowing.

Looking between Cappy's legs I watched as ropes of cum slid out of well fucked asses and dropped to be mats below.

The men began to pull out of one another, some slumped over the backs of the man they'd been fucking, each fighting to regain their normal breathing. Their cocks were still rock hard and I had to wonder what exactly it was that Cappy had fed these men. It was then that I got the bright idea to walk the line again and start sucking the men off. My own cock was still throbbing and I knew that being their cum slut would be just the ticket to get me off and good.

I started sucking Cappy's cock and each man, watching, turned so that they were all facing in the same direction. One by one I worked my way down the line of men, sucking their cum covered cocks, licking their balls. I reached the last man and, again, after having sucked his cock into my mouth was immediately rewarded with another load. Satisfied I'd cleaned him off well enough I moved to the next and was quickly rewarded with his load as well. By the time I'd reached Cappy, all I had to do was open my mouth and he came, his load shooting on my tongue.

The men's cocks finally returned to their natural state and as each man had recovered, they headed for the showers to clean off. I walked in the showers to watch, men lathered men up, stroking soft cocks, fingering wet holes. The sexual excitement was still high but their cocks had finally had their fill and while they moaned and groaned, none of them produced erections, to include myself. I moved to the far end of the shower only to be joined by the young probie who's cock I'd first sucked. We washed each other off, dried and dressed.

We all made our way to the dayroom, where each man seemed to collapse on the floor, in chairs, on the sofa, satiated and exhausted. Hands continued to grope crotches and feel chests while they mindlessly watched television.

It wouldn't be long before they'd be sexed up again and I couldn't wait to see what would be next.

CHAPTER 23

I left the men in the dayroom and headed back towards the garage area. My cock was, for the moment, satiated however I still had that tingling in my ass, letting me know that I still wanted had not satisfied my itch.

I opened the door that leads to the garage and walked in, stopping dead in my tracks. I let the door close behind me as I took in the two firefighters, locked in a mutual embrace. Their naked, muscular, sweat glistened bodies bumped up one another and hands roamed over asses and backs. They were locked in a passionate embrace, their lips sealed over each others, tongues licking the inside of their mouths and dueling with one another.

My left hand acted on it's own accord, moving to my right nipple, tracing the outline, making it harden at my touch. The two firefighters were still locked in their embrace, hard cocks butting and rubbing against the other, hands now pulling ass cheeks apart, fingers searching out the wet hole that only a few moments ago was being filled with harden cocks and cum.

I felt a present behind me and before I could turn to see who it was, I felt a mouth tug on my right ear lobe. I groaned, my cock beginning to plump.

"It's a sight to see isn't it? Two gorgeous men, doing what two men thought they would never do, pleasure one another. And pleasure one another in a way that no woman could possible ever aspire to do." Cappy's voice whispered in my ear.

I felt the tip of his cock pressing into the crevice of my ass, touching my sensitive ass lips, making my insides flip and flop in anticipation of feeling his massive cock inside me again. I leaned into him, his arms wrapping around my chest, his hands slowly, lovingly moving up and down my chest, stopping to play with my nipples.

"You enjoy this don't you Cappy?" I whispered back, turning my head, hoping to taste the flesh of the man that I can come to adore and who's cock I'd come to worship and crave. This man had become my drug of choice, I craved him, craved him smell, his taste, his touch. It wasn't love, that I knew, just pure sweet addiction.

Cappy groaned in my ear as he gently pushed his hips towards me, the head of his cock parting the lips of my ass. He held his cock there, poised right at the entrance, teasing the lips of my ass, making me squeeze my cheeks in an attempt to suck the rest of his cock inside me.

Our attention turned back to the two firefighters. They had now moved themselves to the mats on the floor and were locked in a 69. Hands held hard cocks as lips and mouths moved up and down on them. Slowly, deliberately, they took their time. Holding the other's cock as they licked the head and underside, both men groaning with their pleasure. The other hand was busy, rubbing and teasing each others hole, lips swollen with lust as fingers darted in and out the other man's mancunt.

I felt Cappy's cock twitch, a drop of his pre-cum leaking out, wetting the lips of my ass. He pressed forward again, the head of his cock sliding past the lips of my ass. My ass clamped down, welcoming the invader and I shuddered as I felt his cock penetrate me. I sighed, pushing against

Cappy's stocky frame. His left hand had found my cock and was slowly pumping me, timing his strokes to the fire fighters sucking one another's cocks.

Cappy slid the rest of his cock inside me, the head of his cock sliding past my love nut. I cried out as his cock slid over my "G-spot", the two fire fighters momentarily forgetting about the cocks they were sucking on to turn their attention to us. They watched us as Cappy began to slowly and deliberately fuck me, taking his time. Slowly withdrawing his cock, the head pulling out of my ass, rubbing my ass lips before he slowly slid his cock back in.

The two fire fighters motioned for us to join them and Cappy pulled his cock out of my ass and, grabbing my hand, walked us over to where they were now standing. The four of us reached out for one another, our hands running over firm chests, down washboard stomachs to neatly trimmed crotches. We felt one another's cocks and balls and took turns stroking each other.

Cappy squatted down and sucked in the cock of the fire fighter standing next to him, I in turn did the same and the two of us began to suck these two men off. They started kissing again, their hands playing with the others nipples and chests. The fire fighter groaned as Cappy reached around and penetrated his ass with two fingers and started to finger fuck him.

I did the same to the fire fighter I was sucking off and within a few minutes they were bucking their hips, grinding their asses on our fingers, forcing their cocks down our throats. Cappy pulled off the fire fighters cock he was sucking and, grabbing him by the hand, lead him to the center of the mattresses and had him lie down on his back.

Cappy then motioned for me to come over and had me straddle the fire fighter. Holding the fire fighters cock, he guided it to my hole and squatted down over him, sighing as I felt it slide into me. Cappy then gently pushed me forward so that I was now lying on top of the fire fighter, our mouths instantly meeting, kissing one another.

I groaned when I felt the head of Cappy's cock nudging at the entrance to my already stuffed asshole. Slowly Cappy began to slide his cock inside of me, letting me get used to the feeling of having what would soon be two cocks up my ass. My ass lips stretched and I thought for a moment they were going to rip open. The pain began to mount as Cappy continued to slide inside of me, stopping, letting me adjust. I was just about ready to yell out, beg him to stop, it was beginning to hurt like hell, when my ass suddenly relaxed and he slid the rest of his cock deep into my ass.

I did cry out this time, but not from pain, from the pure exquisite pleasure of having two men inside me. The second fire fighter had now come to join us and was offering his cock to Cappy, who gladly sucked it in to the base, momentarily gagging as the head slid down his throat.

We all remained motionless, Cappy using this throat muscles to flex and work the fire fighters cock, moving his head back just enough so he could breathe. Within a few minutes Cappy began twisting his hips, grinding his cock around and around the inside of my ass and over the other fire fighters cock. We both moaned and resumed our kissing while Cappy began to bob up and down on the fire fighters cock.

Cappy started to slowly thrust his hips, pulling his cock in and out of me, running up and down the underside of the other cock that was inside me as well. I pulled off the fire fighters mouth and screamed, "FUCK ME! GOD FUCK ME!"

Cappy took his cue and increased his thrusting. The fire fighter he'd been sucking on cried out, stiffened and shot his load down Cappy's throat. The feeling of two cocks in my ass quickly threw me over the edge. I shuddered, my cock twitched and in a few minutes, I was shooting my own load between myself and the fire fighter I was laying on, coating our stomachs with my sticky white cum.

Cappy knew I'd just dumped my load and he pulled his cock out of me and eased me off of the fire fighter I'd been laying on. He quickly licked up my cum before motioning for the other fire fighter to take my place. He was all too happy to oblige and as he squatted down on the fire fighters cock, his own cock quickly rose back to attention.

He leaned over, his eyes wide with wonder and fear. Looking over his shoulder he waited for Cappy to penetrate him. Cappy did the same with him as he did with me, taking his time, letting his ass get used to the feeling of two cocks inside it. The fire fighter being double dicked cried out in pain, begging Cappy to take his cock out, it hurt too bad. Cappy knew that all he had to do was slide past the ass ring and he'd be golden.

Just as my ass suddenly loosened to accept the two invading cocks, so did his and within a matter of seconds, his cries of pain were replaced by grunts and groans of sexual ecstasy. Cappy wasted no time in getting to business and began grinding and pumping his cock into the fire fighters ass.

I fed my limp and still leaking cock to Cappy, who gladly sucked it in and washed the head and tip of cock clean with his tongue. I let him work on my deflated cock, I knew it was done for the night but also knew that Cappy loved sucking my cock as well, hard or soft. Cappy worked on my cock like an expert, managing to revive some life back into, making it semi hard.

The fire fighter in the middle grunted twice, stiffened and I could tell by the look of pure bliss on this face that he too was painting the two of them with his load. The second fire fighter, the one on the bottom, also stiffened and groaned, his load pumping into the fire fighters ass, coating Cappy's cock with his warm load.

The look on Cappy's face was one of pure bliss. He was sucking cock, double fucking an ass and now he had the feeling of a cock pumping warm cock on him. He pulled off of my cock, threw his head back and howled as he slammed into the fire fighters ass, his cock exploding, cum shooting deep in the man's guts.

Cappy was covered in sweat and I took this moment to move around and squat down to where the three fire fighters were joined. Both men's cocks were still firmly planted inside the fire fighters ass and I watched as cum began to leak out of his hole and slowly slide down the bottom fire fighters balls.

I quickly went to work, licking the small rivulets of cum that were leaking out off of the fire fighters balls. The three men lay there, panting, regaining their composure from the fuck they'd just had. The bottom fire fighters cock had softened to the point where it started to slide out of the mans' ass. The head was slick with cum and it plopped out and fell between his legs. I began to lick the head clean, the fire fighter groaning as I cleaned him off. Cappy's cock was next to slide out, a puddle of cum spilling out with it.

I cleaned all three of them off, all three groaning in pleasure as my lips and tongue went to work. I was hard again and was stroking my cock fast.

I was going to cum soon and knowing how much Cappy loved feeling a cock shoot on his hole, I aimed my cock towards his bulls eye.

"Fuck! I'm gonna cum again, gonna cum all over your fucking hole Cappy!" I shouted. I stiffened, groaned, howled and watched as my cock jerked and spasmed. Nothing came out, I'd finally drained my balls dry, by the orgasm was exquisite. My cock jerked and throbbed, and jerked. My legs shook and I thought for a moment I was going to collapse.

I finally quit cumming and fell to my knees, sweat pouring off my brow and back. "Holy fuck, I panted." The three men came over to me and started wiping me down with towels they'd found. Lord only knew what was on these towels but I didn't care. Cappy picked me up and carried to my bed, laying me down, covering me up I quickly fell asleep.

The men in the dayroom and managed to have one giant orgy while we were out in the garage fucking, one by one, they made their way to their bunks, collapsing on them and also falling fast asleep.

CHAPTER 24

The remainder of the week passed quickly. We'd had a rash of fires that had been deliberately set, fortunately no major injuries. Thursday had arrived and as I ended my shift I headed for the comfort of home.

I arrived to find my block sealed off by several police officers. One of the officers saw my car approaching and started waiving me down. I stopped and he briskly walked up to the driver's side window.

"Are you a resident?" he asked.

"Yes I am." I responded. "What's going on?" I asked.

"Nothing you need to worry about. I need to see your driver's license." He continued.

"Sure" I said as I reached for my wallet and pulled my driver's license out and handed it to him.

"Is the address on this license correct and current?" he asked.

"It is officer. Can I go home, I just got off a grueling week shift and really want to relax and unwind." I complained.

"Not yet, we're still doing some work at the crime scene. It won't be long, they're just about done. So what do you do?" he asked me.

"I'm a paramedic with Ladder Company 49." I responded.

"My brother-in-law just finished his training and is assigned there. I went with him on his first day, met the fire chief. Seems like a good man." the officer said.

"Yeah? We did get a shipment of trainees this week. I haven't gotten the chance to meet all of them yet." I said, wondering if his brother-in-law would say anything about the night they were initiated.

Just then the police officer's radio squawked to life, informing the police officer that he could start letting the resident's return to their homes.

"Well, I guess you heard. You can head for home now. Have a good evening." He said and then proceeded to walk over to two other cars that were sitting, parked, along the side of the street. I watched him in the rear view mirror, my mouth watering at the sight of what appeared to be a gorgeous ass packed in his uniform slacks. As I put the car in drive, I secretly hoped that he would come to the house and give me a thorough patting down, among other things.

As I approached the house I was shocked to see that the commotion had been at my neighbors house. I pulled into the driveway and headed for the house after parking and locking the car. I needed a shower and started stripping my clothes off the minute I walked in the door. By the time I'd made my way to the shower I was totally nude, my cock half hard thinking about the ass the police officer was packing in his uniform.

I'd just started to enter the shower when the door bell rang. I muttered a curse, grabbed my bathrobe and headed back to the front door, ignoring the trail of clothes I'd left behind. I opened the door to find the police officer who'd stopped me at the end of the street standing there.

"Can I come in?" he asked.

"Sure." I said, stepping aside and letting him pass by me.

"Sorry to interrupt you, oh my name is Officer Hanson, Colt Hanson." He said, sticking his had out to shake. I shook his hand, introduced myself to him and led him to the couch.

"I was just getting ready to hit the shower, I'm really dirty, do you mind waiting while I rinse off?" I said.

"Uh, no, no, I um, yeah sure, go ahead. Mind if I get something to drink though? I'm really thirsty." He said.

"Sure, there's soda, tea and bottled water in the fridge. I'll be right back." I said, turning and heading for the shower. Stepping into the hot water, I sighed as I felt the spray wash over my back. I could have stayed in the shower for a very long time, however, remembering I had a guest, I went about washing up and getting out.

"Thanks, sorry, but I really needed to get cleaned off." I said, returning to the living room wearing a T-shirt and a pair of old shorts.

"Did you know your neighbor?" the Colt asked me.

"Naw, I'd only met him once. I don't suppose you can tell me what happened?" I said.

"He was running a male escort business from his house, only it was more than just a male escort business." Colt responded.

"Aren't they all more than just a male escort business?" I asked in response.

Colt laughed and said that for the most part, yes, there were a few honest companies around, but most of them operated a prostitution ring under the guise of an escort business.

"Can I ask you something?" Colt said. "My brother-in-law called me last night and told me some rather odd stuff. Stuff about Ladder Company 49." he continued.

"Yeah? Like what?" I responded back, knowing where this conversation was heading to.

"He said they had an initiation night and some really freaky stuff had occurred." Colt said, looking at me with a questioning expression on his face.

"OK, and?" I responded back.

"Said that the new recruits were lined up, naked, and that there was a bunch of um, you know, stuff that went on." Colt said, adjusting his crotch.

"And?" I said, waiting to hear what he was going to say, my cock beginning to plump and push against the leg band of my shorts.

"Well, I mean, you know, I don't care what people do but I was just thinking about it and all and was wondering." Colt stammered.

"Wondering what? If it was true?" I replied back.

Colt nodded his head yes and then looked down at the bottle of water he was holding. He was nervously bouncing his leg up and down and as I gave his body a good look-see, I could see that the bulge in his trousers and gotten larger. I knew that he must have been doing some thinking about it and obviously was finding it a turn-on.

"Is there a reason you want know what happened, Officer Hanson?" I replied, reaching over and placing my hand on his thigh.

"Uh, I'm just curious." Colt answered back.

"Curious about what?" I replied as I moved my hand further along his thigh.

Colt closed his eyes momentarily and I could swear I heard him moan softly.

"You mind if I take this gun belt off? It's really uncomfortable." He said, standing and removing his gun belt and putting it on the coffee table.

I could see, by the bulge in his slacks, that he was very turned on by the thought of what his brother-in-law had shared with him. He turned to face me and I reached out, rubbing my hand along the front of his slacks, gently squeezing the mound of meat that was stuffed into his crotch. I didn't say a word to him, instead I reached up, unbuckled his belt, unbuttoned his slacks, pulled his zipper down and then pulled his pants down to his knees.

He was wearing cotton briefs and the sizable lump in the crotch told me he was packing some serious meat.

I scooted forward and planted my face right in his crotch. I started licking the head of his cock through his underwear, my hand reaching up and massaging his big bull balls through the fabric. Colt moaned, his hips shuddered as I continued to lick and suck on the head of his cock through his underwear.

While I worked on his cloth covered cock, Colt began removing his shirt and

T-shirt, exposing a beautiful firm chest. His chest was covered in a fine layer of jet black fur, his hard nipples poking out from underneath the curls that surrounded his nipples. He put his hands on the back of my head as I continued to nurse on his underwear encased cock.

"Suck it, please, suck my cock." Colt moaned, pulling me off of his cock.

I pulled his underwear down, his hard cock springing free and practically hitting me in the face with it. He was at least eight inches, his cock root was slender but a thick, meaty mushroom head capped the slender stalk.

I wrapped my hand around his cock and pulled the skin forward, the head of his cock turning purple and a clear drop of fluid appearing at the tip.

I dipped my tongue in and lapped up his sweet juice before I began to slowly suck him. Colt moaned and put his hands back on my head, guiding my head up and down while he slowly started fucking my face.

"Yeah, like that, feels good, feels fucking real good." Colt moaned.

I reached around him and started massaging his ass. His ass cheeks were full and firm and also covered in a light dusting of hair. I kneaded and massaged the globes of his ass, pulling them apart and squeezing them back together. I moved my hands so that they were closer to his crack. Each time I'd pull his cheeks apart, I'd let my middle fingers dip into the crevice of his ass, my finger tips brushing against his hole.

Colt involuntarily jerked the first time I touched his hole and momentarily quit fucking my face as he tried to figure out what I was doing. But the more I touched him, the more it excited him and he was soon fucking my face again with that same slow steady rhythm.

"Feel like trying something?" I asked, pulling myself off of his cock.

Colt looked down at me and said nothing. I took that as my cue and I turned him around and had him lean forward. His gorgeous ass was now right in my face. I pulled his ass cheeks apart and gasped when I was his pink hole winking at my from underneath his black fur. I swiped my tongue up the length of his ass crack and he jumped, banging his head on the coffee table. I swiped my tongue again, this time letting it linger and dance over his hole. Colt moaned but did not jump this time. I did this for several minutes, getting his entire ass crack nice and wet with my saliva.

I decided to take this to another level and so I started playing with his hole, rubbing my fingers around and over it while I continued to lick and eat his sweet cherry.

"Fuck!" Colt moaned and bucked his hips back into my face.

"C'mon, let's head to the bedroom where we have more room and can be more comfortable." I said.

Colt stood and turned around, a long strand of clear cock juice hung from the tip of his beefy cock. I licked the head of his cock, sucking up the clear juice before it dropped on the carpet, then, grabbing his hand, lead to my bed room. I had him climb in the center of the bed and get on all fours. Once he was in position, I went back to eating his ass and playing his with hole.

"Shit that feels good. I've never had anyone play with my hole before."

Colt panted, his head laying on the pillow.

"Feel like trying something else?" I asked. I didn't give him a chance to respond and instead, told him to lie on his back and bring his knees up to his chest.

While he was getting in position, I reached into the night stand drawer, grabbed one of my dildos, a smaller one, and some lube.

"What're you gonna do? You gonna fuck me with that?" Colt asked nervously.

"You'll be fine, I'll go slow. Plus it isn't very thick, so you shouldn't feel any discomfort." I replied as I lubed up his hole and then the dildo.

"I don't know bud, I've never had anything up in me before." He said. "I don't know if I can do this." He continued.

"Just relax and trust me." I said as I placed the head of the dildo at the entrance to his ass. I started to slowly push the head in, reminding Colt to just relax. Slowly I slid the fake cock into his virgin hole. Colt grunted and groaned, his cock flexing up and down off of his stomach, a puddle of clear juice beginning to form.

"You OK?" I asked.

"Yeah, fuck, feels good, nnngggghhhh." Colt moaned. I was watching his cock flexing up and down. The head of his dick was thicker and was now a dark purple. I knew as soon as I slid this thing past his prostate that he'd shoot.

"Oh, fuck, yeah. Are you done, is there more?" Colt asked, looking up at me.

"About half way there." I said and continued to slide the dildo deep inside him.

"Craig, I, oh fuck, I, Craig! Craig, oh GOD! I'm gonna..." Colt's eyes rolled in the back of his head, he arched his back and ropes of pearly white cream jetted out of his cock. Colt started thrashing his head from side to side while he came. His mouth agape, the veins in his neck bulging as his cock continued to jerk and spit. Sweat formed on his forehead and in the center of his chest, matting the hair to it.

I reached over and picked up Colt's cock, just as it fired another long stream of cum. Most his cum had painted his pecs and stomach. There was one dollop of cum though that had landed in his hair.

I moved up so I could clean the cum off of Colt's chest and stomach. His cock was still rock hard so while I licked him clean, I started jerking him off. Once his chest and stomach were clean I went back to sucking on his cock. Colt nudged me, indicating he wanted to try his hand at cock sucking, so I obliged by straddling his head.

My cock was leaking pre-cum as well. Colt took tentative licks on the end of my cock, then deciding he like the taste of it, began to devour me. He sucked my cock like a pro, using just the right amount of suction and, more importantly, no teeth. I started squeezing and playing with his massive bulls while I bobbed up and down on his cock.

His balls began to tighten against his skin, a sure indication that he was getting close to cumming again. My own cock was beginning to tingle and I could feel my balls draw up as well. Colt moaned, realizing I was getting close to shooting my load as well. He increased his speed and suction, fucking his face on my rock hard cock.

I groaned around his cock, stiffened and started shooting my load in his mouth. Colt pulled my cock out, letting my cum shoot on his lips and chin.

He soon groaned and stiffened as well and I was rewarded with another massive load. It began to ooze out of the sides of my mouth, in spite of how fast I was swallowing trying to keep up. Before long, the cum that had leaked out of my mouth was now a whipped up foam.

Colt continued to suck and nurse on my cock and I, in turn, did the same.

We finally pulled off one another, me rolling over and on my back. My spent cock laying against my thigh. Colt reached between my legs and began playing with my hole. I groaned at his touch.

"Colt, man, aren't you done?" I panted. "I fucking came hard dude, I don't know if I can go another round." I continued.

"Naw, I'm done too. Two fucking huge orgasms finished me off also. I just want to see what it feels like to play with another man's ass." Colt said as he continued to finger my hole. My cock plumped up with the sensation of his fingers inside me, but it didn't get rock hard. I lay there, letting Colt finger my ass. At one point he'd gotten between my legs and was licking my hole. I looked over at his cock, it too was only half hard.

"Can I come back sometime and fuck you?" Colt asked, removing his fingers from my ass.

"Hell yeah!" I said. "But there's a catch, you fuck me and I get to fuck your gorgeous ass." I continued.

"Shit, if it feels half as good as the dildo did, you got it!" He replied.

Colt climbed off of the bed, said he should probably get going and we headed back to the living room so he could get dressed. I put on my robe and sat on the couch, watching him put his uniform back on.

"That was fucking great Craig. No wonder my brother-in-law like it so much. We're gonna try it with each other too. Hey, how about the three of us sometime?" Colt asked as he put his gun belt back on.

"Deal!" I said, patting him on his ass as I followed him to the front door.

We say our goodbyes and I picked up my clothes, turned off the lights and headed for bed.

CHAPTER 25

Colt dressed and left, thanking me for a great evening, promising to call me soon. I sat back on the couch, my cock hardening as I replayed our sex over again in my mind.

"This guy is so fucking hot!" I thought to myself as my hand dipped under the waist band of my shorts and grabbed my cock.

"Fuck yeah!" I groaned, deciding to finish this in the bedroom. I stood, made sure the front door was locked and headed to my room. I quickly stripped my shorts off and laid down on the bed, my hand re-attaching to my rock hard cock.

I decided some ass play was needed and so I reached over to the night stand, grabbed my trusty dildo, lubed it up and started teasing the lips of my ass with it. I just ran the tip of it around and around my hole and up and down the crack of my ass. Eyes closed, hand firmly wrapped around my cock, squeezing it, I closed my eyes and began to lose myself in my own self pleasure.

I moaned and arched my back as the tip of the dildo entered my ass. I quickly switched position so that I was in a sitting position and, holding the base of the dildo, I gently lowered my ass onto the imitation cock. I groaned, my body shuddering as I closed my eyes and imagined that I was actually riding a nice hard, warm, thick cock.

"Yeah, fuck me." I groaned as I ground my hips around the base of the dildo, the head rubbing against my love nut, my cock twitching, the lips of my piss slit puffing up, a drop of clear fluid forming at the tip.

"God this feels so good." I groaned again as I slowly slid up until the head of the dildo fell out of my ass and rubbed the lips of my wet hole. I continued my slow and steady ride up and down on the fake cock, my hand sliding along my cock in the same speed. I groaned and sighed as I imagined the array of cocks that I'd had up my ass, imagining they were all here again.

Thin, thick, short, long, my entire sexual past floated past my eyes. I remembered my high school government teacher's long, thin cock as he fucked me. This, of course, only after I'd unzipped his slacks and pulled his, then soft cock, out, begging that I'd do anything for extra credit. He fucked me good that day and when he exploded, he dumped so much cum up my ass that I swear, I shat his cum for days. I thought about the tutor I'd had in college to get through Physics. A nerdy sort of lad, with a nice thick cock. Six inches long and three inches thick. Uncut, his foreskin that hung over the tip of his cock. He'd been trying to teach me one of the many laws of Physics when I accidentally, on purpose, dumped my beer in his lap.

I towel dried his crotch into a full fledged, raging, leaking hard-on. He lost his virginity that night and I aced my Physics exam the following week. I bounced on the dildo harder and harder, faster and faster, dicks with faceless bodies attached flashing before my eyes, all moaning, groaning, pumping my ass. My balls tightened and I felt that tingly feeling in my balls, indicating that my cum would be shooting soon.

My final vision was of my cousin, John. We were sixteen, our families had gone on a camping adventure. We shared a pup tent, away from everyone else. I would learn later in my life that my cousin had planned it that way. It had started as most of these things do, I think anyway. We were in our tent, stripped down to our briefs as it was hot that night. I remembered starting to doze off and rolling over, my hand flopping on his chest.

John then grabbed my hand and slowly moved it down to his crotch. I felt his magnificent hard cock through his underwear. Pretending I was still asleep, I remained motionless. He then pulled his underwear down, the palm of my hand brushing against his thick cock. He positioned my hand so that my fingers were now wrapped around his cock and he started stroking himself off with my hand. The tip of his cock was wet and it made a squishing sound as it traveled over the thick head.

I rolled back over onto my back, my hard cock tenting my own underwear and placed my hand back over his cock. He asked me if I was asleep and I said no. He asked me if I'd suck his cock and I hesitated. I'd never done this before, only dreamt it in my most heated fantasies. I bounced on the dildo even harder, a steady stream of cum running from the tip of my cock now as

I continued remembering the night I lost my virginity and was fucked up the ass for the first time.

Hesitantly, I leaned over, licking the tip of my cousins cock, tasting a cock for the first time and realizing, I liked it. I ran the tip of my tongue over the head of his cock and he begged me to suck it. I then closed my lips around the head of his cock and started bobbing my head up and down on his dick. He moaned and I moaned. This totally new taste and sensation was so overpowering for me, I thought I would cum right then.

I flashed forward in my memory. That's a great thing about memories, you can hit the fast forward button in your mind, or the rewind, as many times as you like. As I continue to ride the dildo and stroke my cock, I stop in my memory at a point where we're locked in a 69. Me bobbing my head up and down on his cock while he lets me fuck his face with mine. His fingers quickly find my hole and he begins to play with it. I moan as I feel his fingers slide into my ass, again I think I'm going to cum but I don't. He plays with my hole, his fingers sliding in and out of my ass with ease.

Another new sensation washing over me. He removes his fingers and I feel his hot breath on my balls and in a matter of minutes, his tongue is now fucking my ass.

I can feel his saliva dripping off of my balls. I flash forward again and now we're laying on top of one another, locked in a passionate embrace, kissing one another, my tongue tasting the inside of another man's mouth for the first time. I'm on the bottom, my legs naturally spread and wrapped around his torso. I can feel the head of his cock, rubbing my hole and I moan again. I can feel the wetness from his cock that is leaking out, providing a natural lubricant and I hunch myself forward, the tip of his cock dipping in my virgin hole.

John pulled his hips back and slowly thrust them towards me again, the head of his cock sliding slowly inside me. I feel the pressure, feel the pain and I whisper to him to stop, it hurts too bad. He starts kissing me again and starts to slowly slide his cock inside me. The pain mounts and I beg him to stop, to take it out of me. I tell him I can't do this, it hurts too bad and then, the head of his cock breaks through and all of that pain is replaced with a sense of pleasure I've never experienced before that night.

He places his hand over my mouth, thinking I'm going to scream out. I'm trying, I'm trying to make a sound, but no sound comes out. I arch my back, my cock jerks, and I start crying. Not from the pain, there is no more pain, only a pure, exquisite pleasure. I go back to kissing him, hard, I bite his lip as he begins to thrust his hips in and out of me. I grab his ass cheeks with my hands and pull on him, trying to get him deeper inside of me. I whisper to him, begging him to fuck me, begging him to dump his load in my ass.

I'm pounding my own ass on the dildo now. My cock is so purple and the head is so swollen that I think it's going to break at any moment now. A small wet stain is now visible on my bed sheets from where I've leaked so much cock juice. I close my eyes and find my place in the memory again.

John is now really fucking my virgin ass. Pulling out and shoving his cock back in, low grunts coming from his mouth as we continue our kissing. He pulls off of my mouth and whispers in my ear how good this feels. How tight my ass is and how he can't wait to cum inside of me. My cock is squished between the two of us and the movement of his hips is causing his stomach to rub over the head of my cock. My cock is on fire with the sensation and I can feel the pre-cum that is leaking out, adding to our body sweat. He's masturbating my cock with his stomach and it feels so good.

My whole body is alive as my cousin continues to fuck me. His thrusting increases and he tells me he's close. I can feel the head of his cock thicken and swell. I reach between us and I feel the base of his cock as it pistons in and out of my ass. I reach further and I feel for his balls, but they aren't there. They're retreated deep inside his body somewhere.

He whispers he's going to cum and he clamps his mouth back over mine as he makes one final shove. He groans in my mouth and his hips begin to quiver as he begins to shoot his cum deep inside my ass.

I arch my back even more and squeeze my ass cheeks, my hole milking his pumping cock. I can feel his hot, scalding cum as it fires out of the tip of his ass and lands deep inside my guts. I start hunching myself, trying to get all of his cum inside of me but also because I'm ready to cum. I rub myself against him until I stiffen, groan and fall back as my cock shoots. Cum coats our stomachs and he's gently pumping my ass now. He kisses me again to keep me from screaming as wave after wave of pure pleasure wash over me.

I slam myself down on the dildo as my cock starts firing. The first shot hits the headboard. I cry out as I continue to stroke my cock, jet after jet of white hot cum shooting out, landing on my pillow, on the sheets.

I'm panting so hard that I think I'm going to pass out and as my cock begins to wilt, I focus on my breathing.

"Holy fuck!" I say out loud as I fall forward onto the bed. I roll over onto my back and gently ease the dildo out of my ass. My cock jerks and

I shoot another rope of cum, this landing on my stomach. I run my fingers through it and lick it off of my fingertips.

"Damn! It's been a long time since I came THAT hard!" I say to the stillness of the house. "I wonder what the fuck John is up to these days."

I say again as I roll off of the bed and begin to strip the sheets to put fresh ones on. Once the bed was made, I headed for the shower to clean up.

I crawled back into bed, closed my eyes and drifted off to sleep, my cousins cock being the last thing I saw before sleep overtook me.

CHAPTER 26

"Fuck me Cappy! C'mon, fuck me hard! Shoot that fucking load in my ass!"

I scream as Cappy pistons his cock, hard, fast, inside me.

"Yeah, fucking love pounding that sweet hole of yours! Gonna fucking shoot my load up your ass! You want it? Huh? Want my sweet cum up that slutty hole of yours?" Cappy shouts back as he continues to nail my ass, holding my legs back and over my head so he can power fuck me.

"Fucking shoot that load in me Cappy! Give it to me, c'mon stud, fucking give me that cum!" I answer back.

I've already shot my load and I rub the sticky cum into the skin on my stomach. Cappy's power fucking my hole like he's never done before. I love it, love the feeling of his thick cock slamming inside of me. The massive head of his cock sliding in and out of my ass. The sheets are soaked with our mutual sweat, the brow of his forehead is dripping and my hands run over the sweat soaked muscles of his broad back.

"Fucking you like the bitch boy you are. You're my bitch aren't you!

Yeah? Your Daddy is fucking his bitch boy, gonna fire my hot cum up that ass of yours." Cappy shouts as he grinds his hips into me, his cock rotating in my ass making me cry out.

There's something raw about him this morning. One, he surprised me by coming over so early and two, there was none of the usual foreplay. He pushed his way into the house after I opened the door, slamming the door shut behind him, while he pounced on me, picking me up and carrying to my bedroom.

I love a good fuck first thing in the morning and Cappy was certainly providing it. Once he had my clothes off, he quickly removed his, hesitating only long enough to give my cock a few sucks before he went to eating my ass and getting me ready for the pounding he was giving me.

"Harder Cappy, fuck me harder! C'mon! Fucking slam that cock of yours into my bitch ass!" I cry out.

"Gonna blow so much cum up that hole of yours. Been thinking and dreaming about this all night. Yeah, that's it boy, fucking work that ass of yours around my cock. Come on! Fucking ride that Daddy cock, make your ass milk my cum out!" Cappy growls back.

Cappy pulls out of me and slides me down to the end of the bed, rolling me over on my back. My feet planted on the floor, bent over the bed, I reach up and grab a pillow and pull it back down to me, biting it as Cappy resumes his fucking.

"Get ready boy! Get ready! Gonna fucking feed that hungry hole of yours, gonna nut, fuck yeah, oh fuck, OH FUCK!" Cappy cries out as he slams into me one last time, remaining still, he grunts and snorts as his cock fires inside my ass. I feel his scalding hot cum shoot out and land deep inside me.

I'm panting as he continues to dump his load inside my ass. He slaps my ass and goes back to thrusting, his orgasm lasting longer than normal. I can feel his hips shaking and quivering as he continues to fight through one of the strongest orgasms I have ever seen him have. He pulls his cock out of my ass, his load beginning to run out and down and over my balls.

He finishes shooting the rest of his load in the crack of my ass, running his still rock hard cock up and down the length of my ass, pushing his cum back into my leaking hole. He's panting and moaning, finally grunting as he milks the last of his cum out of the tip of his cock.

"Get down here, fucking clean up my cock bitch." Cappy orders.

I happily oblige, scrambling to get off of the bed and onto my knees. I kneel before him and start licking the remnants of cum and ass juice from his cock. I'm rock hard again, my fist flying over my own cock, my second orgasm rapidly approaching while I deep throat this man's beautiful cock.

I stiffen, groan and shoot. His cock is now soft and his breathing is returning to normal.

I pull off of his cock and collapse on the bed. I climb up and we snuggle while we come down off our orgasmic high. My hand is lazily tracing circles in the sweat soaked hair on his chest. I look down and see his cock, still thick, still plump, a dollop of cum at the tip. I work my way down and suck his depleted cock back into my mouth, my tongue washing over the piss slit, licking up the last droplets of cum.

"Fuck boy! Shit, that mouth of yours!" Cappy groans as his cock begins to respond, lengthening and hardening in my mouth.

"Fucking suck me off! Dump another load inside you, yeah boy, c'mon, work on the cock of mine." Cappy pants, his hand on the back of my head, holding me down on his cock.

"You know I can cum whenever I want, shit boy, feels good. God Damn!

Gonna get nutted twice this morning! Oh fuck! Fuck yeah, fucking suck my cock!" Cappy groans.

I begin to play with his balls, which are still drawn tight, while I bob up and down on his hard cock. Cappy has pulled me up a little, his fingers now dipping into my wet and leaking hole. He starts to finger fuck my ass, using two fingers, dipping in and out, rubbing the cum that leaks out into my balls.

I let go of his balls and reach between his legs to find his sweat slicked hole. My fingers play with the outside of his ass lips. Cappy groans, spreading his legs wider, giving me more access to his tight hole. I slowly insert two of my fingers up his ass while I continue to work on his cock. Cappy removes his fingers from my ass and I feel him shift and hear the nightstand drawer open.

Cappy grabs the dildo in the nightstand and begins to slid it into my ass.

I arch my back as my cum slicked hole begins to adjust to the fake cock. I quit sucking on Cappy's cock while he slides the dildo in and out of my ass.

"Come here boy!" Cappy growls as he removes the dildo from my ass. "It's good and wet now, fuck me with it while you continue sucking my cock with that hot mouth of yours." he says.

Cappy swings my hips over his head and starts nursing my half hard cock.

We both know I'm not going to cum again but the desire to suck some cock has suddenly hit Cappy. I slide the cum slicked dildo up his ass and resume sucking his cock while he works on mine.

I start fucking Cappy's ass with the dildo while I bob up and down on his thick cock. His balls have disappeared inside of him, I watch the dildo slide in and out of his ass while his cock slides down the back of my throat.

"Mmmpf!" Cappy moans, his mouth full with my cock. I'm now completely hard again, much to my surprise, and working on my third orgasm. Cappy's talented mouth and tongue bobbing and sucking, washing over the head of my cock, his tongue dipping into the tip of my piss slit, licking at the beginning trail of pre-cum.

I pull off of Cappy's cock, pull the dildo out and start licking his stretched hole. Cappy grunts again and sucks my cock into his mouth to the base. I take his rock hard cock and start slapping my face with it, sliding the dildo back into his ass. Cappy groans again and slides two of his own fingers inside my ass.

"Fucking make me cum bitch! Swallow it, swallow that cock so I can shoot down your throat. Your ass is full of my cum, might as well fill your stomach too!" Cappy growls.

I start deep-throating Cappy, fucking my throat with his hot cock. Cappy begins to moan and whimper, the head of his cock thickens and I know he's close. I begin to fuck Cappy's face, my own orgasm getting closer and closer. Cappy's panting and moaning take on a more urgent tone, the pitch increasing.

I stiffen, grunt and start cumming again, shooting what's left of the cum in my balls into Cappy's mouth. He pulls my cock out and lets the last two shots of cum shoot on his face. He then takes my cock and starts rubbing it over his face, his morning growth of stubble scratching at the sensitive head of my cock.

Cappy stiffens, bucks, and I feel his cock pulse and then jerk as he shoots his cum down my throat. I love watching his cock shoot so I pull off of his cock, stroking him, I watch as his piss slit widens and a rope of his cum shoots out and splashes against my cheek. The rest of his cum runs out, down and over my hand.

"God I love watching your cock shoot. Mmmm." I groan as I begin to lick the cum from his cock and my hand. "Fuck Cappy!" I purr. I suck his cock back into my mouth and continue sucking him until he goes soft.

Cappy rolls me over, eases the dildo from his ass and comes and lays down next to me. The bedroom smells of sweat, cum and fucked ass. I curl up into his arms, enjoying the surprise I got on this Saturday morning.

"Craig?" Cappy says.

"Yeah?" I answer back, enjoying his gentle hands running up and down the length of my back. I snuggle closer to him, laying my head on his chest, my tongue darting out and flicking at his hard nipple.

"I'm leaving the station, retiring." Cappy says.

I sit up and look down at him. "What? Why?" I ask him in bewilderment.

"It's time Craig, time for someone else to take the reigns. Been doing this long enough." Cappy responds.

"When?" I ask.

"Now, I put my papers in a couple of months ago. It was effective yesterday." Cappy says.

"WOW! But you didn't say anything, to anyone. What's going to happen come

Monday?" I asked.

"Not my problem anymore." Cappy responded. "Listen Craig, I've been thinking." he continued.

I listened as Cappy told me of his plans. He'd already sold his house and was packed up. Cappy told me how he'd bought some land several years back in Montana. Told me how he always loved Montana and how he was going to have a house built and spend the rest of his life up there. Cappy was a huge sports fisherman and Montana was a good place to go if you loved to fish. Cappy's eyes took on a dreamy distant look as he continued to tell me what he envisioned the rest of his life to be. This is what he'd been working and saving for his entire life. So he could buy land, build a nice home, and spend the rest of his days doing whatever he wanted and not have to worry about money.

"Sounds nice Cappy. Sounds real nice!" I said, trying to mask the sound of hurt in my voice. While I can't say I'd fallen in love with Cappy, I definitely had come to feel something special about this man.

"Got another idea." Cappy said.

"What's that?" I asked.

"You come with me. Craig, I have certainly had my fair share of men. But

I haven't been with anyone that satisfies me like you do, and I don't just mean in bed either."

"Seriously Cappy?" I asked, a smile washing over my face, my heart beating faster.

"Ever fished?" Cappy asked me, pulling me closer to him.

I responded with a no and laid my head back down on his chest. My fingers running through the hair of his stomach, brushing against the tip of his cock. I moved my hand further down and started playing with his cock.

Cappy grabbed my hand and pulled it back up to his chest.

"Not right now boy." Cappy scolded.

"You sure you want me to come along?" I asked.

"You bet Craig. What do you say? Want to do it? Want to come live with me in the wilderness?" Cappy asked.

"Cappy, you're asking a lot of me right now. I mean, this is so sudden, what do I do about my house? My belongings?" I asked.

"Sell the house, bring your shit with you. We'll put it in storage until the house is built. I've already got electricity, plumbing and sewage installed and an RV sitting up there. We live out of that until the house is done." Cappy said.

I remained quiet, thinking about Cappy's proposal. I could spend the rest of my life with this man, that I was sure of, and Lord knows, I'd never grow tired of that hot cock of his or of being with this man.

"Does your hard cock sticking me in the side of my ribs mean yes?" Cappy asked me, kissing me on the mouth. "Let's do it Cappy! Yeah! Yeah! I'll come with you." I said, rolling over on top of Cappy, feeling his now hard cock underneath me.

"C'mon, let's get in the shower. Neither of us is going to cum again, not this soon anyway." Cappy said slapping my ass and pushing me off of him while he got up and got into the shower.

I joined him, the two of us kissing one another while we soaped each other up and got each other clean. Our cocks remained rock hard the entire time and we both resisted the urge to take care of them.

We got dressed and I went to the fire station to submit my resignation.

Over the course of the following months, I put the house on the market and began to go through the things I'd accumulated and started having garage sales. Cappy left for Montana to get the construction of the house going.

The house was on the market for approximately three months when I got an offer. It was lower than I wanted, but it was the first offer I'd gotten and decided to go for it.

Cappy and I talked just about every day. On those days where we were horny, we'd bring each other off over the phone. I couldn't wait to get moved and get settled. A few more months and I was packing my car and heading off to Montana. Cappy had flown down and was driving with me.

Our first night together was spent totally nude, taking our time to get to know one another again, both of us fucking the other. Our cries of passion each time we came caused one of the neighbors in the hotel to call the front desk. We giggled after Cappy got off the phone and made sure that the remainder of our stay we made as much noise as possible.

"Gonna cum!" I screamed, stiffening, shooting my load on Cappy's stomach.

"Me too!" Cappy cried out as he jacked his cock against my ass, painting my hole with his load. We collapsed on top of each other and dozed off.

The next day we checked out of the hotel we were in, ignoring the stern looks we were getting from the night manager and drove off into the sunrise to start our new life.